ACKNOWLEDGEMENTS

For help and encouragement in diverse ways, I would like to thank Fred Oliver of Keystroke Computing; Michelle Lovric; Elsie Browning; and, as always, my family.

'When I hear, when I see, the magical name [Venice] . . . it is not of the great square that I think, with its strange basilica and its high arcades, nor the wide mouth of the Grand Canal, with the stately steps and well-poised dome of the Salute . . . I simply see a narrow canal in the heart of the city – a patch of green water and a surface of pink wall.'

Henry James, *Italian Hours*, 1909

'For so infinite are the allurements of these amorous Calypsoes, that the fame of them hath drawn many to Venice from some of the remotest parts of Christendom, to contemplate their beauties, and enjoy their pleasant dalliances.'

Thomas Coryate, *Coryate's Crudities*, 1611

Venice. Again.

Callie looks across the water for the first glimpse of the approaching city and waits for it to happen. The awe factor, she calls it: the shocked realization that the reality of the city is even more dazzling than one's memory of it. She wonders if, finally, it will be gone.

Venice appears slowly from the sea, like a jewelled siren. A haze hangs over the Doge's Palace, obscuring the top of the campanile and extending out over the water so that the entire basin of San Marco appears opaque, unreal.

The awe factor is still in operation. A shiver goes through Callie as the watery city comes closer, the mist gradually beginning to disperse so that the green outline of trees on the Giardini, the cream and salmon-pink colours of the buildings on the Riva degli Schiavoni, come into focus with a sudden joyous intensity. Venice has not, after all, become mundane.

The crowded *motoscafo* chugs to a stop at the San Marco pier, and tourists of all nationalities disembark. The awe fades somewhat as Callie is jostled and pushed off the motorboat into the early summer crowds. How many times, she wonders as she pulls her case the short distance to the Piazza San Marco, how many times have I done this? Taken the same *motoscafo* from the airport to the city, pulled my suitcase on its sturdy wheels to St Mark's Square for the obligatory cappuccino before heading to the hotel. Ten, twelve times? More, probably.

And how many other cities have there been, she asks herself as she idles up the *piazzetta*, through the granite pillars of the Molo, forgetting that, like many superstitious Venetians, she avoids passing between the columns. It is said to bring bad luck, for it was the site of public executions in the old Venetian Republic.

Too late, Callie glances up at the bronzed winged lion on top of one of the columns and determinedly continues walking; she is *not* superstitious, she tells herself. Nonetheless she wishes she had walked round the columns; it seems a bad omen at the start of a tour to be so careless.

Pulling her suitcase, she walks into the piazza itself, noting with satisfaction that nothing has changed since last year: the square is overflowing with pigeons, with tourists, with the mingled sounds of dozens of languages being shouted and spoken.

Not wanting to go to her hotel just yet, Callie, as she always does, decides to blow a sizeable part of her last tour's wages on a cappuccino in Florian's, sitting at one of the tables outside in the sweet June sunshine and imbibing Venice along with the caffeine. A few days ago she was in Dublin, taking a tour group to see the Book of Kells and around the Guinness factory; at Easter she was in Paris. Mostly, though, she is given the Italian tours to do. She prefers Italy, and her company has recognized the advantage of having an English tour manager who speaks the language of the country fluently. Unfortunately she was given only one Venetian tour this summer, but from here she will go on to Rome, then Florence.

Callie orders the coffee from a spruce young waiter and settles back to enjoy the sights on the piazza. The pianist at the outdoor café is grizzled and sombre, but the Vivaldi he plays is light and jaunty, the two violinists accompanying him saucy and fresh. Turning her head, she faces the Basilica, looks up at its serene

domes and the golden mosaic above its curved doors, and feels oddly at peace.

Home, she says to herself softly. This is the nearest thing I have to a home.

Later, in her hotel, which is tall and thin and narrow, tapering at the top like a candle, Callie unpacks her few belongings: clothes, a couple of English paperback novels and her address book, which she knows will remain unopened for the rest of the season. At the start of each tour she tells herself she will send postcards, stay in touch with friends back home in England, but she never does. There never seems to be time, and because she is abroad so often, the people she has left behind seem shadowy, more like the strangers she constantly meets in her job.

I am a nomad, she thinks, not for the first time. She discovered this about herself when she first left her parents' home in the south-east of England to begin her roaming. Freed from the confines of a family whose rather smug pride in their solid roots felt like dead weights round her young soul, Callie fell in love with the world as other eighteen-year-old girls fell in love with eighteen-year-old boys: wildly, joyously, and not without a fair bit of obsession.

This was not, after all, surprising. An only child, she had been born in the house where her father was born, a house of sturdy bleakness, with ivy-covered brick walls and a cloying feeling of permanence. Callie's parents did not find it cloying; on the contrary, they rarely left the house, let alone the small village where the house was situated. They had their garden, their books and their music – each parent played several instruments – they had each other, two golden labradors and Callie, who was expected to live either at home – the house was certainly large enough – or settle in the village or nearby town and wait for the time when she herself would take over

13

the unwieldy house and sprawling garden.

Callie's parents' self-sufficiency and disinterest in anything outside their home was legendary in the village, and served only to make Callie long for the day when she was old enough to parachute out of the stifling enclosure she had been brought up in, to land in newer, more exciting pastures.

Like *here*, she thinks now as she finishes her unpacking and surveys the room, her home for the next three weeks. It is a small, compact single room with austere parquet floors, nicely polished; a miniature writing desk, made of a decent solid wood, with a chair to match; unobtrusive built-in cupboards; and the bed, of course, narrow but comfortable. There is nothing of Callie in the room: no photographs, no momento of any past life other than the one beginning in this hotel room.

It is what she has chosen. She locks her door, puts her room key in her capacious black leather bag and goes down through the reception area and out into Campo Santo Stefano to let the city seep into her senses.

A mesmerized crowd, standing on the quay, squints down at the water of the Giudecca. The vast canal is deeply still, silky, the colour and texture of a bay leaf. The sun smears the sky with heat; there is no wind, not even a breeze.

A diver, suited up and ready to go into the water, sits at the edge, alert for any sign of difficulty from the other two divers under the water. Another, in jeans and a T-shirt, waits, on call if necessary. An air compressor, motor humming like a tractor engine, hoses going from it into the water, sits on the quay; and on a small work boat moored alongside, a diving supervisor is monitoring instruments, talking to the men below the surface. He speaks Italian, and most of the tourists gaping at the water do not understand it; nonetheless they crane their necks forward eagerly.

Another man, dressed in dark cotton trousers, a blue shirt with the sleeves rolled up and a pale silk tie, is standing on the quay taking notes. He is wearing dark sunglasses and a gold watch. The diving supervisor shouts something to him and the man nods, writes something down.

One of the onlookers, a tiny man with a perky face not unlike a garden gnome, brown head covered with white stubble, grumbles to his wife, 'Wish we knew more Italian. They're investigating something under the water, and that guy over there with the sunglasses must be the engineer. It looks like they're checking on some repair work needed on the quay.' He takes a

step nearer the water, anxious to see more.

His wife looks away, bored, but she would not dream of hurrying him. He was a building engineer, many years ago, before he retired, and he is as drawn to these scenes of engineering activity, whether above or below the water, as she, an ex-primary-school teacher, is drawn to young children.

Callie, who has just left her hotel and crossed over the Accademia bridge, anticipating a pleasant walk after unpacking her bags, is jostled by a German man cutting across the wide walkway of the Fondamenta Zattere to get a better view of the divers. She shakes her head slightly, annoyed. She deliberately headed for the *sestiere* of Dorsoduro, rather than the more touristy area of the Rialto or San Marco, to get away from the crowds.

Nonetheless, intrigued by the diver in his gear sitting on the edge of the quay, Callie stops for a moment, looks at the black hose going into the deep green of the water and tries to see the divers under the surface. At the same time as the man taking notes next to her calls out something to the supervisor in the boat, there is a sudden shout, a huge splash of water. Before the second pair of divers, who are slightly further down the quay, can fathom what has happened, the man with the silk tie drops his notebook, thrusts his sunglasses at Callie and jumps into the water. Within seconds he is pulling out a spluttering, coughing, ancient man with a bald head that looks like a badly shaven chin.

'Oh, Lordy, oh, Pogo!' A woman, obviously the man's wife, crouches next to her wet and dripping husband and bursts into tears. Her face is as crumpled with age as his, but her white hair is thick, abundant. It stands to attention all over her head, as if it, too, is in a state of shock and fright.

'Oh, honey, oh, my sugar,' she croaks before slumping down unconscious next to her sodden husband.

'*Ma è pazzo?*' cries the rescuer to the man, oblivious to his wife. He rants on in Italian: 'What are you, crazy? What are you thinking, standing so near the edge?' He is furious in his huge relief that the man seems to be all right.

Callie, standing next to this tableau of near-drowned man, a fainting wife and a furious Italian, has a sudden weary longing to get away. She has only these few hours to herself in Venice; she will soon be besieged by her own group of tourists. She does not need to get involved with strangers, though she is indeed already involved: she is still clutching the sunglasses the man had put into her hand before he jumped into the water. She looks at the dark glasses and shakes her head in resignation, knowing that, of course, she must help. She is trained to deal with crises and, anyway, her compassion for the shocked old lady has already compelled her to kneel down to try to take her pulse. The woman is reviving, opening her eyes in stunned bewilderment. Callie lifts her gently to a sitting position and soothes her husband, who is now panicking about his wife. Above them hovers the man's rescuer, who seems to have forgotten them, more concerned with remembering what he did with his sunglasses than worrying about the elderly couple.

Callie, feeling dumped upon, mutters with exasperation, '*I've* got them, you vain sod.' She speaks in English so that he will not understand her, an ironic smile on her face as she holds out the sunglasses and mutters, 'So typically Italian, making sure your hair is beautiful and your designer shades are safe before you make your heroic rescue leap into the lagoon.'

The man, who has taken off his wet shirt and tie, exposing a naked brown chest, shakes his head to dry his longish hair, and the drops splatter over Callie. Reaching his hand out for his sunglasses he says, in perfect English, 'Thank you for taking such care of my Armani shades.' Using his fingers in an exaggerated

combing of his hair he adds, again in English, 'They're, beautiful, no? Though I'm afraid the murky water of the Giudecca is not the best of hair shampoos, eh?' He grins cheekily at her and taps her cheek in admonishment. 'I'm sorry to disappoint such a beautiful English tourist, but these are not Armani shades. They are prescription lenses. Boring, it is true, but without them I can barely see you.' He grins again. 'Which would be a pity,' he adds, looking at her appreciatively.

Callie feels her face grow hot with embarrassment. 'I'm sorry. I thought you were Italian. I didn't think you'd understand me.'

'I *am* Italian. You are too quick to jump to the conclusions.'

The diver underwater has surfaced to see what is going on. The man in sunglasses talks to him, seemingly forgetting Callie and the woman cradled in her arms, the wet near-drowned man holding tightly on to his wife and croaking endearments in an American accent with a thick Southern tinge.

The woman says to her husband, 'I'm just fine, honey, don't fuss. You just gave me such a scare, fallin' in the water like that.'

'You two should both get checked by a doctor,' Callie says, wondering how in the hell she got into this. She sees her precious hours slipping away; her group arrives early this evening. As a tour manager she is constantly plagued by emergencies in foreign cities; she doesn't need this one which has nothing to do with the Comet Trail Travel company. The couple must be at least eighty, probably more. A shock like this wouldn't do either of them any good.

The man with the sunglasses leaves his divers and kindly says to the couple, 'How are you, eh? Still shaky? I'll go with you to your hotel; we will call a doctor from there.'

The two turn in unison towards him, thanking him profusely. 'You saved my life,' the old man cries, and

his wife adds, 'If you hadn't jumped in real fast like you did, Pogo would've been a goner. Why, you didn't even stop to think!'

'Except to take off my designer shades,' the Italian says for Callie's benefit.

Callie feels herself flushing, and turns to the woman, who is now asking the engineer for his address, the address of his company, *anyone's* address so that she can write and thank people properly.

'*È niente*, it's nothing, forget it. I'm in charge of this job, and now I'm responsible for you, no? Since you decided to jump in the water on my site,' the man says with a grin.

'My fault, got too near the edge, though the crowd didn't help. Too many people pushing to get a closer look at the diver.'

'Let's get you to your hotel. You're getting chilled even though it is hot; you must get out of those wet clothes.' The Italian seems to be oblivious to his own wet trousers, now beginning to dry in the blazing sun.

'Oh, but we don't have a hotel. Uh, what did you say your name was, honey? I'm Lavender, and this is my husband Pogo. That's short for Pogoccelli – his dad was from Naples. We're on our way there to trace Pogo's family before we kick the bucket. And your name?'

'Tommaso Venturi. Look, I must do something about you two.' He stands helplessly shaking his head.

Callie, trying to slink away, is clutched again by Lavender. 'And we didn't thank *you* either. Golly, didn't we both make fools of ourselves, Pogo falling in the canal like that—'

'I was just trying to get a glimpse of the divers, sweetie pie,' Pogo protests.

'And me falling in a swoon right in the arms of a stranger! I don't even know your name either, honey.'

'Callie Miller.'

'Well I'm mighty pleased to meet you, Callie, and

you, too, Tom,' Lavender says, shaking their hands graciously, as if this were a social occasion.

Tommaso says, 'So, if you haven't a hotel, where are you staying? I'll take you to your lodgings, yes?'

Pogo says chummily, 'We're in a caravan site, Tom, in Mestre, outside the city, a real basic joint of a place but handy, y'know? A short train ride and you're in Venice.'

'We're not in any hurry getting to Naples,' Lavender carries on. 'We've gotten enough cash saved to spend the winter there, in our fancy camper van thing we bought over in England. It wasn't cheap, but boy are we saving the dollars now. No hotel rooms to pay, not that you'd be able to get one in Venice at this time of year anyway.'

Tommaso turns to Callie and rolls his eyes behind his prescription sunglasses. The couple look set to remain on the water's edge for ever, oblivious to the fact that Pogo is wet and beginning to shiver as the sultry air is sliced by a sudden capricious breeze, and that Lavender still looks frail and weak after her fright and her faint. Their faces hold the kind politeness of true American Southern hospitality, ignoring their own discomfort as they try to make Callie and Tommaso feel at ease, as if they were sitting on the veranda of their own gracious home in South Carolina.

Callie, knowing she shouldn't get involved, knowing she has twenty of her own clamouring group members arriving shortly, says, 'Why don't you come to my hotel? It's not very far, just over in Campo Santo Stefano across the Accademia bridge. The owners are very kind; they can give you hot tea, towels, call the doctor—'

'Oh, we don't need a doctor.' Both Pogo and Lavender are adamant about that, and will not be shaken.

Tommaso, looking at Callie with huge relief, says, '*D'accordo*, a good idea; we will take them somewhere

near by to dry themselves. But my place is even closer, right here in Dorsoduro, just before the bridge.' He turns to the other two. 'We can go to my house and you can rest, dry yourselves, before you head back to the campsite.'

Pogo begins to protest that it is all too much trouble, but Lavender, seeing the trembling that is now beginning to grip him as the breeze from the lagoon turns into a sharp wind, says, 'Maybe that's a good idea, Tom. As long as we're not causing you and this nice English lady here any inconvenience.'

Tommaso assures them they are not as Callie says, 'I'll be off then. You won't need me now.' She tries to scurry away but is delayed by all three. 'But we haven't thanked you properly!' Pogo and Lavender both say at the same time as Tommaso pleads, 'Come along with us, please.' He adds, in a whisper so that the older couple can't hear, 'I'd be happier if you stayed. The woman looks more shaken than the man, and she might need another woman . . .' He trails off, looking uncertain behind his dark glasses.

Callie cannot say no. Lavender does look exceedingly pale, and has now taken Callie's arm and is clinging to her, trembling slightly. 'All right,' Callie sighs. 'Lead on, Tommaso.'

Later, Callie will remember her first impression of Tommaso's courtyard. Cool, dark, after the searing sunlight outside, a sudden sanctuary, both forbidden and compelling behind great black wooden double doors. Old marble pillars and arches hold a beamed roof on either end, but in the centre it's open to the sky, where a japonica tree waves green arms towards the hidden sun. The tree's roots go deep and are beginning to crumble the stone slabs around it. Standing nonchalantly under the arches are several lifesize marble statues, some cracked, others with arms or noses missing, stoically looking straight ahead. The courtyard

21

ends at the Grand Canal itself, with four or five stone steps, now nearly covered with a high tide, leading straight into the water.

'Wow! This is neat,' Pogo says. Tommaso opens a second door on the canal end of the courtyard, next to a statue of an imposing bearded patrician with an ear chipped off. They enter into a cool inviting hallway with wide marble steps leading upstairs. Callie can see a small neat kitchen opposite the door and an open window leading to a garden ebullient with red roses, lavender, pale-pink oleander, blue hydrangea and a deeper, purple-red hollyhock. Callie smiles slightly, and Tommaso, noticing, stops himself from commenting upon the beauty of her smile (this is not, he decides, the right moment) and says instead, 'You like my garden?'

'Oh yes. But I was smiling at the hollyhock. It's so English somehow. My parents have masses of them in their garden at home. How ironic, all that running away, only to come face to face with what you are running away from.'

Tommaso looks from the flower to Callie's face, which is lightly tanned and still has traces of a contemplative amusement. He notes the wide mouth, the round grey eyes, the thick brown hair, cropped short and spiky, the heavy fringe, almost long enough to hide the black eyelashes. '*Molto bella*,' he murmurs.

Callie looks at him sharply. 'The *malvone*,' he says, pointing innocently to the hollyhock. 'It's very beautiful, no?'

There is a fragile flowery scent coming from the garden through the open window, mingling with the faint, not unpleasant smell of wet stone and canal water: unmistakably Venice.

Lavender, who has been looking at everything with great interest, cries, 'But, Tom, your kitchen is all on stilts!'

'Only the cooker and the washing machine and

22

electrical equipment. Sometimes the courtyard floods, and the canal water creeps into the hallway and kitchen during the *acqua alta*, the high tides. Luckily we live mostly upstairs.'

He leads Pogo and Lavender up the steps to the next floor. Before following, Callie goes into the kitchen to take another look out of the window. Right outside is a squat gardenia bush, heavy with white flowers, and next to the rose garden is a pergola covered with jasmine. Callie stares appreciatively. Gardens are hard to find in Venice, and those that exist are hidden away, glimpsed through iron fences, behind high stone walls, a tangle of green, a jangle of colour, tantalizingly out of reach, out of sight.

'So, here is the bathroom, and here are towels,' Tommaso is saying as Callie joins them upstairs. 'There is all the hot water you'll need. I think you must have a hot bath to warm up, while I make you both a drink. A brandy, yes? Or tea, or coffee?'

'I hate for you to go to all this trouble,' Lavender says, but Tommaso repeats, 'Brandy? I know, what about an espresso with brandy in it. Just what you need to get over the shock.' Without waiting for an answer he disappears into another room off the top landing, while Pogo and Lavender go together into the spacious bathroom.

'I'm just changing my wet trousers,' Tommaso calls out from what Callie assumes is the bedroom. 'Go on into the living room, it's straight ahead.'

Callie goes into a large room with massive oak beams on the ceiling, a polished wooden floor, a window overlooking the garden and two tall double windows looking out over the Grand Canal. The room is sparsely but pleasantly furnished, with two pale cream sofas at either end, a rosewood desk with a matching armchair, and against the long white wall between the windows, an applewood cabinet with a large mirror reflecting a bowl of fresh lilies. The sweet, heavy perfume of the

lilies tinges the air like dew, mingling with the fragile garden scents, the briny canal, the ubiquitous smell of damp brick and marble. For a moment it makes Callie slightly light-headed.

'What a super place,' she says as Tommaso comes back into the room in a clean white shirt and a pair of jeans. 'Have you lived here long?'

'I stay here when I'm in Venice. The apartment belongs to the family.'

'Not the whole *palazzo*?' Callie smiles.

'Ah no, we are not so grand as to own such a large and magnificent building. Palazzo Valier – that's the name, though everyone calls it Casa Valier, or Ca'Valier – was divided up in the nineteenth century, when the ancient nephew of one of the old doges lost his fortune. My parents bought this apartment some years ago, when they came to Venice from Milan. It was their dream to die here.'

'That's a rather sad dream to have,' Callie says. 'And did they? I hope not yet.'

'So many people come to Venice to die,' Tommaso says. 'Was it Thomas Mann who wrote how the gondolas resemble coffins? Black boxes gliding through mist on the dark waters of death, that sort of thing, yes?' His smile is ironic. 'Robert Browning died here, so did Wagner. It's very literary, you know, and my parents were great readers. They died over a year ago, within months of each other.'

'I'm sorry.'

'They were very much in love; they would have wanted it that way. They were also old; they met late, married late, had their children late. They were ready to die. Or so they told us, anyway.'

Callie cannot think of a reply to this. She is disconcerted as her initial impression of Tommaso – the insouciant, flirtatious Italian worker on a repair job on one of the city's waterways – is superseded by this slightly sardonic, more sophisticated man who is

talking to her now. She wonders where he learned English, for it is perfect, with only the slightest accent. She is about to ask, when Lavender comes into the room, carrying a plastic bucket with Pogo's wet clothes. 'He's soaking in a steamy tub,' she explains. 'Can I hang his clothes out there in the garden for a little while? With this hot sun they'll be dry in two shakes of a lamb's tail, as my ma used to say.'

Tommaso takes the bucket, says, 'I'll throw these in the washing machine, they will reek of the canal. I'll find something for your husband to change into.' Heedless of her protests, he disappears again into the bedroom, thrusts some clothes into her hand, and says, 'I'll make the drinks now. Give these to him; they will be large, but they are clean. If you give me the address of the campsite, I'll post your own clothes back to you when they are clean and dry, or you can pick them up here, or at the worksite, whenever you like.'

Lavender begins to protest again, but Tommaso has already gone downstairs to the kitchen. 'Such a nice guy,' she says, overwhelmed with admiration and gratitude as she disappears into the bathroom again.

Left alone, Callie goes to the window at the far end of the room to look over the canal. As she pulls aside the thin white curtains, she realizes that it's not a window, but a double door leading to a balcony terrace over the water. Unable to resist, she opens the two doors and goes outside. The balcony is tiled with tiny white marble slabs, and the waist-high balustrade round it is also of the same stone, but a rougher, darker kind. There is a plain garden table with four chairs, and a ceramic pot with a hibiscus plant boasting two expansive red flowers.

Skirting round the table and chairs, Callie goes over to the marble balustrade. Right in front of her is the Grand Canal, lively with its summertime hustle and bustle. As she watches, a water bus – a Number One *vaporetto* – chugs indolently by, crowded with tourists

standing squashed in its centre area. Four or five gondolas, meandering in the opposite direction, idly give way for the *vaporetto* and for the faster speedboat of the *carabiniere* whizzing by, and a couple of water taxis coming from the airport with Japanese tourists. A small barge carrying large white sacks of laundry from one of the hotels is chuntering past, the driver calling out a greeting to one of the gondoliers. The scene is paradoxically both dreamy and tranquil, and vibrant, active. Boats of all shapes and sizes seem to be meandering in every direction, without purpose or reason, yet there is an efficient overlying order to the scene.

Callie has done many Venetian tours, has thought herself impervious to the city's charms. Yet she cannot pull herself away from the outdoor terrace. Looking to her left, she sees the wooden bridge of the Accademia, energized with people purposefully walking over it, or lingering at the top to take photos of the view. To her right is the mouth of the Grand Canal, where it meets the Giudecca to open up into St Mark's Basin. Carving stately niches in the deep blue sky are the great domes of Santa Maria della Salute, the Baroque church built to give thanks, in 1630, for the end of the plague.

Tommaso, appearing carrying a tray laden with four cups, a bottle of brandy and some almond biscuits, says, 'Good, you've found the best spot to have our coffee. Or would you rather go into the garden? It's not ours, which is just as well because no-one lives in this apartment permanently. But the Venetians who live at the front of the *palazzo* also own the garden, and let us use it.'

Callie is tempted: she sees much more of the Grand Canal than the gardens of Venice when she is working here. But the canal is hypnotic. The water today is still, with a sheen of silk, its colour an opaque green that is both pale but rich. There is a sudden lull in the boat traffic, as sometimes happens, and there is no noise but

the sound of water lapping at the stone of the steps and the building. 'You can see why Venice is called *La Serenissima*, the serene one, at moments like this,' Callie says. '*È perfetto, Tommaso. Mille grazie.*'

Tommaso puts down the tray and looks up at her. '*Parla italiano?*'

'I get by. I'm not a tourist, you know. I've worked a great deal in Italy, and I'm working here now.'

Tommaso laughs. 'Ah, I see, it upsets you that I called you a tourist. But then we are even. You said we Italian men are vain and think of nothing but the designer sunglasses.'

Callie smiles. 'OK, we're quits. Do you never take them off, by the way?' She is finding herself wondering what colour his eyes are.

'I wasn't joking when I say I can't see without them. I do have a plain non-tinted pair.'

'But you're too vain to wear them,' Callie says mischievously and then giggles.

'Touché.' He smiles. He finds himself wanting her to laugh again; it is a good laugh, deep, spontaneous.

Pogo and Lavender join them, both looking much healthier and stronger than they did earlier. They each accept a little brandy in their coffee, drink it quickly and say they must be off, they have imposed enough. 'What is the firm you work for?' Pogo asks Tommaso. 'You speak real good English, but you sure didn't learn it in the good ole US of A, that Brit accent.'

'My home is England; I have lived there for nearly twenty years,' Tommaso replies. 'The company I work for is based in Bristol.'

Pogo pumps him for more information, and is intrigued to find out that Tommaso is a site engineer for an international marine engineering firm. 'I was an engineer myself,' Pogo says. 'Mostly superhighways, nothing as glamorous as the canals of Venice.'

'Not exactly glamorous,' Tommaso says. 'I get sent to Italy often though, being Italian.'

27

'So you don't live here, you're just passing through,' Callie says. 'Like most of us in Venice.'

'Are you here for a holiday, honey?' Lavender asks Callie.

'I'm here on a job.' She goes on to explain about Comet Trail Travel.

'There must be easier ways of seeing the world,' Tommaso says with a grimace.

Callie laughs again, which delights him – she has such a sweet laugh, and it makes her attractive face quite special – and says, 'You are so right. But when you're not rich, getting paid to travel all year round is better than staying home and getting away for the odd two weeks once or twice a year.'

The Pogoccellis say again that it's time for them to leave. 'Please, can we take your pictures?' Lavender asks. 'To show the grandchildren? The man who saved Pogo's life! And you, too, honey, come on into the picture. You kinda saved mine, I was scared silly.'

They try to protest, but Lavender is insistent. Embarrassed, Tommaso and Callie agree to be photographed, first with Pogo, then with his wife.

'And now one of you two, on your own!' Lavender cries. 'Go on, stand closer, look a bit friendlier.'

Tommaso, putting his arm carelessly round Callie's shoulder, says, 'Hope my wife doesn't see this.'

Callie, who has been wondering what colour eyes Tommaso has under the dark glasses, and how long he's going to be in Venice, and whether she should be bold and ask if he'd like to come out for a drink with her one evening, says to herself, Shit, another married man. Wearily, she disentangles herself from his arm, tells him and the others that it's been nice meeting them all, and tries to get away.

Tommaso says, 'Look, are you free for a drink tonight? Or tomorrow, or whenever you have the night off? I know a quiet place, not many tourists, good wine.'

Callie refuses politely and makes her escape. Bloody Italians, or rather, bloody married men, she thinks as she leaves the *palazzo*, waving cheerily at the door to the Pogoccellis, who are shaking Tommaso's hand and thanking him yet again. Always the same when out on their own. Working away from home, they forget they *have* a home, forget they have a poor sod of a wife waiting for them, worrying about them, keeping things together.

Callie heads for the Accademia, crosses over the bridge, which is still packed with tourists, and walks across it and through to Campo Santo Stefano, where her hotel, the Isabella, is situated, squashed on the *campo* between a dilapidated *palazzo* and a cheery, busy café with tables overflowing into the square. Disappointed with Tommaso, she tells herself smugly that at least *she* didn't make the mistake that he did, trying to juggle a spouse at home and commitments abroad. It never works, getting married or trying to have a permanent relationship when you're in a job that turns you into a perpetual nomad. At least, after over sixteen years in the travel business, she's wise enough to know this.

She didn't always. When she finally escaped from the snare of her parents' heavy roots, she went to college as far away as she could, in the north of England; where she got a degree in Modern History, thinking that if she were going to explore the world, it would be useful to know something about it. Her first serious relationship was with a young man on the same course; when they fell in love he assumed they would be married in due time and settle down and have children. Callie didn't know what frightened her the most, the settling down bit or the children. She wanted neither.

From college she went to London, to a job in an upmarket travel agency where she soon worked her way up to a managerial position. Though the work

entailed short trips to many of the exotic locations offered to eager holiday makers, mostly it meant long hours in the office, dealing with faxes, phone calls, correspondence and a large staff that seemed to do much more travelling than she did. After a few years, Callie began to feel the familiar suffocation of the surroundings in which she had resided too long. Her office began to seem very like her family home; her boss, avuncularly, was beginning to fuss over her like a parent. Remembering how her mother and father refused to budge from their tiny patch, she panicked and found a job as a tour manager, where she could do the travelling herself, rather than organize trips for others.

Now, in her hotel room in this unique watery city, which is not unlike the hundreds of other hotel rooms Callie has stayed in, she pulls out the sheaf of Comet Trail Travel forms and begins to look over them, studying details of her new group who are arriving shortly from London at the Marco Polo airport. As she reads, Callie allows herself a twinge of regret as she thinks of Tommaso one last time. She had liked the kindness with which he had treated the older couple, once his flash of temper had subsided after Pogo had nearly drowned himself. She liked his sense of humour, the way he was able to laugh at himself and not take offence when she poked fun at him.

'And I'll never know the colour of his eyes,' she says aloud. Talking to herself is something she seems to be doing more of lately. It's the price one pays for all this freedom, all this wandering about with no roots, she supposes: having conversations with yourself, since there is so rarely someone in your room to talk to.

She shakes off an uncharacteristic melancholy, not quite sure where it's coming from, and begins to read through her papers to see what tour member is on special drugs, or has specific dietary needs, or may have a health problem. As usual, she becomes

absorbed in her group, in their similarities and their differences, even before they arrive. Group dynamics have always intrigued her, the way disparate individuals with nothing in common forge links, bonds, begin to become a whole.

Tommaso Venturi and the colour of his eyes are almost, but not quite, forgotten as Callie prepares for the tour ahead.

3

The omens as the tour begins are not propitious. Callie meets her group members at Marco Polo airport and finds twenty-four instead of the twenty that Comet Trail has listed. She spends over an hour on the phone to London trying to find someone at head office who knows something about this, to make sure that the extra four are not booked for an entirely different holiday. This done, she has to arrange boat transport to take her group to the hotel, since they have missed the large *motoscafo* that had been waiting when they arrived. This entails more hanging around, and it has become quite hot; the group is understandably prickly.

Finally, they arrive at the Hotel Isabella, tumbling into its long, narrow reception room with its red patterned carpet and heavy, solid furniture. Signor Alberti, the proprietor, who looks like Pavarotti and has been known to sing arias from Verdi while helping his waiters serve in the dining room, wrings his hands and gesticulates in the most operatic of fashions, pretending he neither knows nor understands English, which is entirely untrue. Callie, if she didn't know him better after years of lodging in his hotel, and didn't know he was a dedicated performer, enamoured with his audience of English tourists, would have sworn he was about to burst into tears.

'*Ti sei bevuto il cervello?*' he accuses himself soundly.

'What's he saying?' asks one of the group members, eyeing the *signore* suspiciously.

'He's asking himself if he has swallowed his brains,' Callie explains. She does not add that it is because he has taken on another Comet Trail group. The company has not booked the four extra travellers into the hotel, and the *signore* is not pleased.

His wife, Signora Alberti, tall and thin with a strong Venetian face, appears in reception and quietly asks, *'C'e qualcosa che non va?'*

'And what is *she* saying?'

'She's asking us if there is a problem.' Callie smiles at herself as she says this, for with two couples roomless, the others milling about crossly after the delay at the airport, any fool can see there most certainly is a huge problem.

But Callie knows that the *signora* can work miracles: somehow rooms will be found – there is always something in reserve for emergencies of this kind – the customers placated. Nonetheless Callie is cross with Head Office. This is not a good beginning to the tour.

After some grumpy bickering between the group members – unusual, so early in a tour, Callie thinks with a growing sense of unease – over room allocations, they are finally settled for a late dinner in the dining room, which is roomy and entirely pleasant. Fresh flowers sit in small coloured glass vases that match the lampshades covering the many light fixtures. Signor Alberti and his assistants serve the food, which is quite good, and, although there is some muttering about the slowness of the service, instigated by a sullen, smartly dressed woman who seems unduly impatient, there are no further problems. With relief, Callie is at last able to leave her charges and escape to the privacy of her room.

The next morning, after breakfast, she begins to put names to faces as she takes her group on a short preliminary tour round St Mark's Square. There are dozens of groups like Callie's, of every nationality. Most tour leaders now have small microphones that

they carry round, but Callie, able to put on a deep, booming voice when necessary, does without.

'Well, here we are, Piazza San Marco,' she begins heartily, her group gathered around her like knots on a string necklace. 'As many of you know, piazza is the word for square in Italy, but here in Venice, when we talk of the piazza, we mean only one: St Mark's. The rest of the squares are called *campi*, that's the plural of *campo*, which actually means field, or ground. Venice was built as a cluster of buildings round an open space, open ground, each with their own church, drinking establishment and inn, just like a small village. These have evolved into the *campi* of today, like our own Campo Santo Stefano, where the Hotel Isabella is located.'

One of her group protests. 'It says here on the map, that it's called Campo Francesco Morosini. I am completely confused.' He says it belligerently, challenging. Next to him his wife is perusing their guidebook, as if looking for other facts with which to contradict Callie.

'You are right,' Callie says placatingly. 'Campo Francesco Morosini is its official name. But no-one calls it that. It's always referred to as Campo Santo Stefano, after the Gothic church at the end of the square.'

A small, bemused, elderly woman says, 'Oh dear. How will we ever figure out what is what if nothing is as it's supposed to be?'

Callie replies lightly, 'That's one of the enticements of Venice, one of her mysteries.' The woman looks terrified by this, so Callie goes on reassuringly, 'You'll soon figure things out.' The woman shakes her head doubtfully.

Her group members listen with varying degrees of attention as Callie points out the relevant landmarks of the piazza: the Basilica, the Doge's Palace, the Campanile or bell tower, the clock tower. The sun is, at mid-morning, prodigiously strong, and the English

34

tourists look understandably pale after weeks of May and June rain back home. Noise and colour swoop over them with the same nonchalant arrogance as the pigeons that claim the piazza for their own, out-numbering even the visitors themselves.

Callie, surrounded by her group members, finishes her brief talk by telling them, 'I've pointed out the landmarks, shown you how to get to the piazza from our hotel by foot. You can also come here by the *vaporetti*, the water buses. The closest stop to us is the Accademia, right beside the bridge. To get there from the hotel, you turn right as you come out, go across the *campo* and then through another tiny square, San Vidal, to the bridge. Cross over to the *vaporetto* landing stage. You all have your map of Venice, compliments of Comet Trail Travel.'

After a bombardment of questions, Callie finally says, 'I'll leave you now to wander about, get the feel of the city. Remember you are on your own for lunch, but I'll meet you at the hotel at three thirty to take you on a leisurely walking tour of some of the places of interest. Then at five there is the optional gondola ride. Those who want to go, meet me here.'

The older woman who had seemed bewildered earlier is full of fretful queries, though her travelling companion, a neat woman with sandy-grey hair and a resigned, faded face, keeps telling her to stop worrying. The fretful one whinges, 'But, Ellen, I want to ask Carolyn if it is safe, walking on our own.'

Ellen says that since the two are together, she is hardly on her own. Callie says would they please call her Callie, and yes, it is entirely safe in Venice to walk on one's own.

'There, you see, Candice?'

'Yes, but we are *women*, Ellen. And we have all heard about Italian men.'

Ellen replies that since in all of St Mark's Square she hasn't heard Italian spoken except by the street

vendors, then perhaps Candice is unduly worrying. 'Besides,' she finishes finally, 'in my limited experience, it seems as if young Italian men, like young men anywhere, are more interested in young women than in old-age pensioners such as us.'

Italian men taken care of, Ellen sweeps Candice away, saying, '*Do* stop pestering Callie; we're quite capable of wandering about on our own. And we're wasting precious time standing about here; there's so much to see!'

Callie is alone at last, and hurriedly leaves the piazza. She is hungry, for she missed breakfast to sort out some problems, and tired as well. She didn't have a break between her Irish tour and this one. Her precious free hours yesterday she spent with strangers, the two odd, old Americans and the Italian with the sunglasses. How much of my life is crammed with strangers, she thinks as she walks across the piazza. Like Venice herself, full of people passing through, becoming intimate and familiar for a few days, or weeks, even longer, but always moving on again into their own lives.

She had been restless last night, couldn't sleep, but that's not unusual on the first night of a tour. What is unusual is her restlessness now, the way she is aimlessly wandering round the piazza like a bewildered tourist herself, instead of doing something positive in her few hours off before meeting the group again.

' I need a good lunch, a glass of decent Veneto wine,' she says aloud. This talking to herself has got to stop. Perhaps she needs a cat; she adores cats. But how could she have a pet when she's never home? She can't even keep pot plants. The last time she did, they all died when she went on tour, even with a neighbour coming inside to water them occasionally. Even pot plants need love, need to be cherished, paid attention to, she thinks as she walks down past the Doge's Palace along the *piazzetta*. Like friends, they cannot be

neglected, as I neglect mine through necessity, through the distance there always is between them and me.

Once again Callie feels unsettled, slightly wistful, which unnerves her. She has chosen her lifestyle, chosen, joyfully, the life of a wanderer. What is up with her that she is mooning about cats and pot plants? She is here in her favourite city; she has just completed a successful Irish tour; in the autumn she is to take her first groups to Prague and Budapest, and to Kiev and Kraków. She thinks of her parents, who most likely have gone no further this summer than from the bleak brick house and overwhelming garden to the village shop and post office.

Callie takes the *vaporetto* to the Accademia and decides to walk to San Trovaso, to her favourite *enoteca*, a unique combination of wine shop and bar. The place is small; its wooden shelves are crammed with assorted dusty bottles of wine and spirits of all kinds, and a long rough wooden counter defines the bar area. There are no tables or chairs, only a few stools at the counter; most people stand crammed in lively groups, holding a glass of wine or an *aperitivo*. Finger foods are sold at the local *enoteca*: bits of cheese, olives, tomatoes on a slice of bread. Callie orders her white wine and a selection of antipasti: salt cod on fresh bread, a hunk of mozzarella, a couple of slices of prosciutto, anchovies on olive bread. Callie is pleased to see that everyone at the *enoteca* is Italian. Perhaps the bar looks too rough for most tourists, she thinks with private relief. Although her livelihood depends on them, she is glad to be free of them for an hour or so.

The sun tempts Callie to take her plateful of food and a glass of prosecco outside. A narrow canal, its water paper-smooth, runs along beside the *enoteca*, a stone bridge going over it. She sits on the steps of the bridge, where she can be in the sunshine and glimpse the milky-green water. She is just settling her food on

the step and taking her first sip of the slightly sparkling white wine when a voice says, '*Salute*. Do you mind if I join you?'

Callie looks up and sees Tommaso standing in front of her, holding a small bottle of cold beer and a plate of fresh tuna on a slice of bread, with tomatoes and olives. 'Please do,' she says. He's still wearing his shades, but then so is she. The sun's reflection on the canal dazzles.

He sits on the step above Callie, taking a swallow of his beer. He looks preoccupied, and Callie remembers that she first saw him not very far from here, at the quay, and asks, 'Any more near-drownings today?'

'Nothing that exciting.'

'What exactly are you doing?'

'Checking the extent of the damage to one of the stone quays.' He looks away from her, thinking of work. Although the job is similar to others he has done countless times before, he is a perfectionist and needs to oversee his team in every detail. The quay is made of masonry blocks, and the cracks running through the mortar between the stones on top of the quay probably mean that the foundations underwater are eroded or cracked, damaged by chemicals and other pollutants, and also by the impact of waves, propeller wash and docking boats.

Callie says, 'And how long does all that take?' She is wondering how long he will be in Venice.

'We should finish our survey by the end of today and know exactly what the damage is.'

'Oh.' He'll be leaving, then, going on to his next job, wherever it is. She watches him as he eats an olive, then a tomato. She doesn't know if his skin is tanned or naturally that clear, golden-brown colour; and she still doesn't know what his eyes look like. She sees that his hair, which was wet yesterday when they met so dramatically, is thick and straight when dry, with splashes of grey haphazardly streaking the black. He

has a gold tooth, on the top row towards the back, which she catches a glimpse of when he smiles widely. She decides she likes the tooth; it somehow suits him. She says, 'Where are you off to next, then?'

Tommaso shrugs. 'I was supposed to be going home, back to England, for a couple of weeks break, but I've been asked to supervise the work here. We start the actual repairs as soon as the survey is done. It'll take two, three weeks. I don't really mind. I hear it's raining back in Bristol.' He grins and looks up at the hazy blue sky, the bold bright sun. 'Well,' he says, looking back at Callie, '*Salute,* once again.' He clinks the beer bottle against her wine glass, lightly. 'Here's to Venice. And us.' He takes a long swig from the bottle.

Callie looks out at the canal. The church of San Trovaso on the other side gleams benignly back at her. A young couple are sitting on the patch of dry grass, so rare in Venice, passionately embracing in front of the church. Callie, turning her eyes away from the couple, says steadily, 'I don't go out with married men.'

Tommaso doesn't seem surprised at her bluntness, though she has surprised herself. She tells herself that, from her experience of Italian men, they need things of a sexual nature to be made perfectly clear from the beginning.

'I wondered why you wouldn't come out for a drink last night,' he says easily. He pauses as a very old woman slowly crosses over the bridge from the other side, stopping in front of the *enoteca.* From the open door comes the sound of laughter, loud voices, the clinking of glasses, but the woman seems oblivious. Callie sees that she is crossing herself in front of the rather sad, neglected statue of the Madonna, encased in an iron-barred shrine embedded in the outside wall of the bar. As they watch, the woman, dressed in a long brown skirt with a housewife's blue plaid pinafore on top, puts a coin in the box underneath the Madonna, mumbles a silent prayer and goes on.

Tommaso says, after a moment, 'Does that mean you don't sleep with married men? Since we are being blunt. Or do you mean that you never have them as friends?'

Though Callie began this conversation, it suddenly seems strange, surreal, sitting on this bridge drinking wine and discussing adultery, the Madonna in her niche juxtaposed to the wide-open door of the wine shop. She thinks of the huge chasm between herself and the woman crossing herself at the religious shrine, thinks how, often though she may come to Venice, she does not belong here, like the woman does. Yet she knows Venice better than she does Kent, knows the Hotel Isabella better than the small house she bought in Whitstable several years ago. There are boxes in that house she has still not unpacked: books, the hand-painted dinner plates she brought back from one of her Italian tours. Her work keeps her away most of the year now; there are tours both summer and winter, as well as speciality holidays for Christmas, Easter, and just about every event on the calendar. Her house has certainly not become a home, but then, she has never wanted it to be. The thought of a world confined by brick walls and prickly hedgerows has always terrified her.

Callie again looks out over the water, not immediately answering Tommaso's question. She is feeling floaty, a bit dizzy, as she often does in Venice. Sometimes, in her hotel room, or in one of the many churches or museums she visits with her group, she can feel the ground swaying slightly beneath her. She wonders if it is just a touch of vertigo, brought on by being constantly on water or surrounded by it, or if it really is the Serenissima herself, gaudy, flamboyant, a trifle seedy, rocking gently on her ancient lagoon.

Callie shakes her head, tries to focus. She says, 'I have several married male friends. We don't sleep with each other, nor do we fancy each other. That is the only

40

way it can work.' As she says this, Callie feels calmer: more grounded and in control of the situation. She begins to eat her food, which she has so far left untouched, with gusto.

Tommaso is watching a sleek motorboat manoeuvring down the small canal and going under their bridge. When the boat is out of sight he says, 'I, too, have women friends who are married. I'm afraid I have slept with some of them in the past.' He looks surprised as he says this, as if he has not intended to.

A troop of American college students, complete with rucksacks, baseball hats and a harassed teacher leading them, mill over the bridge, having lost their way to the Accademia gallery. Tommaso is glad of this diversion. As he listens to Callie give the Americans directions, he wonders what possessed him to say what he just did; he knows she must be thinking him both arrogant and promiscuous. It's her bluntness, he decides, it must be contagious. He is usually extremely secretive about his extra-marital affairs, out of respect, and affection, for his wife. He believes it would be unspeakably cruel to talk about them to anyone.

'Sorry about what I just said, it was tasteless, crude,' Tommaso says as the Americans march out of sight, having glanced into the *enoteca* and glanced away without much interest. 'I'm afraid your honest approach is catching.'

He sounds so regretful when he says this that Callie laughs, and once again Tommaso surprises himself by wanting, suddenly, to catch that laughter, have access to it, much more than he wants to go to bed with her. He doubts now that she would believe him if he told her that. After what he has just said, he wouldn't blame her.

Tommaso works long weeks away from home, and has accepted the occasional affair as part of the perks – or price – of working hard hours away from the comforts of wife and children. The women have not been

many; there have been two or three, and none were complicated by love, neither on his part nor on the woman's. All were married, and wished to remain so, as did he. His English wife, Sandra, never asks about other women, and indeed, if she did, he would protect her by lying. Sometimes he wonders if she cares, or rather merely accepts the fact that, since he is away from home so often, he is bound to become involved, if fleetingly, with other women. She never asks, though, never hints that the thought crosses her mind. When he returns from one of his jobs abroad, she greets him cheerfully, with absent-minded enthusiasm, and asks only about the work itself, never of the things he does to alleviate his solitary life away from the family. She doesn't seem resentful of his work; indeed, she seems often to see him off with a barely concealed sense of relief, so eager is she to return to the full life she has created for herself, in which he is superfluous. She has her children, her friends, her job as a sports teacher at a local college. She is a keen tennis player and plays in tournaments throughout the southwest. Tommaso thinks that even if she did have occasional suspicions about his casual forays into extra-marital sex, she would be far too busy to care.

Certainly, Sandra does not seem to care about sex all that much, never has, especially since the children arrived. She and Tommaso had married young, far too young, after meeting in Tuscany on a summer holiday. Tommaso had followed her to England, married her not that long afterwards, bringing her back to Italy so that he could finish college.

There were problems from the beginning. Tommaso was too young, impetuous, to settle easily into married life, while Sandra was more mature, ambitious. A keen sportswoman, she had already come to terms with the fact that she would never be a professional tennis player, but she was determined to make the most of both her game and her life. As soon as Tommaso had

42

his engineering degree, she persuaded him to move to England, where she qualified as a sports teacher.

Though already their lives were slowly angling in different directions, they had one thing very much in common: both intensely wanted children. Sitting here in the sunlight with this stranger, another English-woman, Tommaso remembers the first eleven years of his marriage, when no children came, when Sandra, becoming more and more desperate, launched herself into one tennis competition after another, determined to become a winner in this one field at least, to assuage her bitterness as she felt herself losing in the mother-hood race.

Eleven years later, when both had given up hope, their first son, Antonio, was born, and a year later, the second one, Marco, came. Sandra, joyous, now had neither time nor energy for any passion other than that of motherhood, and as a result, both her tennis and her marriage suffered. As the children grew and began school, she was able to bring her tennis up to full marks again; unfortunately, this didn't happen to the marriage.

Tommaso admires his wife. He has great respect for her abilities as a mother, for the way she handles her students at the college where she works. He appreci-ates her slim sturdy body, likes, occasionally, to watch her play tennis, admiring the fierceness and concen-tration she brings to her game. And yet more and more he finds that, although the bonds of affection that bind them, through the children, seem as strong as ever, he sees Sandra as a woman in a film: he can admire what he sees, but sometimes fails to understand what it has to do with him.

Callie isn't saying anything, but is insouciantly eat-ing her food as if they had been talking about the weather. Tommaso is surprised at how easy it is to be with her, how lacking in awkwardness, despite the bizarre nature of their conversation. Even the silence

between them does not seem strained, but gentle, serene, like the slow gliding movement of the gondola now going down the canal. Tommaso watches the black, sleek craft with genuine appreciation. As a marine engineer, he has never lost his admiration for the skilful construction of a boat so perfectly adapted to the narrow, shallow canals. Without taking his eyes off the boat he says, 'So we are being honest, eh? *D'accordo.* If I'm honest, I must say to you that I never go out with single women, they are far too complicated for a married man. I try not to hurt people, if possible.'

'And what about your wife? You think she is beyond hurt?'

Tommaso, who has been about to eat the anchovy Callie had indicated she could not finish, stops and stares at the near-empty plate. 'My wife probably knows more than you would think, and accepts it perhaps. She is happy with our life, with our sons; she is deeply involved with the home, with her life, which is very full. Just as I am deeply involved in my own work.' He stands up abruptly. 'Will you have another glass of wine? I'm having another beer.' He doesn't want to talk about Sandra and his sons any longer.

Callie, suddenly not wanting to hear about this man's beloved family either, says, 'Yes, I would, thank you.' Though she usually never allows herself more than one glass at lunch when she has an afternoon session with her group.

When Tommaso returns they talk of other things. 'Do you know that the Pogoccellis stopped by my apartment before I left for work this morning, to return my clothes? They had been washed and dried and even ironed,' he says.

They talk about their work, and he tells her a bit about his company. 'They've expanded so much in the twelve years I've been with them,' he says. 'I was with another English firm, but they didn't work in Europe. I like being able to return. I miss Italy, but Sandra prefers

living in England. So this is a good compromise.'

The sun glinting on her face and on the smooth green of the canal, the soporific sound of water lapping, the pleasant languor of the Italian language coming out of the *enoteca*, are hypnotic. Callie doesn't want to move, doesn't want to look at her watch, to see if it is nearing the time she must return to the hotel.

Tommaso asks more about her work, and she tells him about past tours, making him laugh. He finds himself wanting to make *her* laugh more, thinking how rare it is for a person to have a laugh you can lose yourself in, like you'd lose yourself in music or drink or sex.

When Callie at last does look at her watch she is horrified to see that it is well after two thirty. She had intended to have a nap before meeting her group at three thirty; she cannot believe she has lingered so long.

'The lunch hour *should* be long,' Tommaso tells her as they get up and take their glasses and plates back inside. 'But I must get back to work myself.' He wants to ask her to meet him again for a drink, dinner, anything. But she has told him her feelings about married men; he knows she would refuse.

'Well, *ciao*,' he says, standing over her, but reluctant to move. Callie says goodbye, too, and there is another silence, awkward this time. He wishes she would help him out; she must know he doesn't want to leave her without the assurance of seeing her again.

But Callie is silent. Finally accepting this, Tommaso says, 'Well, it's been fun meeting you, Calypso.'

Callie looks up. 'Calypso? What do you mean?'

'Isn't that where your name – Callie – comes from?'

'No, not so interesting, I'm afraid. It's short for Carolyn.'

Tommaso shakes his head. 'I think it's Calypso. And your island is in the middle of a *laguna*, and you are bewitching me to stay here.'

Callie picks up his bold, bantering tone and replies, 'I know my classical mythology too. Odysseus the wanderer, far from home. Lost, lonely—'

'Like me—'

'Shipwrecked on the island where Calypso reigns. Poor Odysseus. Unable, or perhaps unwilling, to get away; stranded for years on this strange island.'

Tommaso grins. 'Lucky Odysseus. Such a beautiful island, in the middle of all that strange sea. And such a beautiful siren, enticing him to stay. He hadn't a chance, poor man.'

Callie looks at him steadily. 'But Odysseus went home, in the end, breaking Calypso's heart. He went home to Penelope.' She looks at him and reflects his smile. 'His wife,' she adds unnecessarily.

Now Tommaso laughs out loud. 'Ah, Callie, but think what fun they had before he did.'

She has to laugh,too, and Tommaso feels a prickle of regret. He cannot remember ever having felt regret before. Sorrow, grief, yes, but regret, never. Callie says, softly, 'I'm not Calypso. She was a myth. Like Venice.'

'Venice is real.'

'Only for some people, those who were born here perhaps, who live and work here permanently. For the rest of us she's no more than a symbol.'

'A symbol of what, Calypso?' Tommaso's voice is teasing. 'Of our dreams? Our fantasies?'

'Of whatever we want, Tommaso. Whatever we want her to be.'

They are standing outside, in front of the Madonna, who seems to be watching them sadly. The sun is sprinkling the water of the canal with fragments of beams, like reflected glass. Tommaso doesn't speak, nor does he go. Finally, Callie looks at him and says, 'I'm not Venice. I'm not a fantasy, I'm real. I'm ordinary and often bad-tempered and I get hurt easily, and I'm old enough now to steer clear of tricky, painful situations.'

She smiles, and makes her voice as light as his was earlier. 'Now, Tommaso, it was lovely meeting you, and I enjoyed our lunch together very much, but you'd better go. Your job is real, but will probably vanish if you hang around outside bars all day hankering after fantasies.'

Tommaso laughs out loud, and Callie can see the gold in his back tooth. A man driving a boatload of olive oil in great wicker-covered bottles looks up and waves.

'*Ciao*, Calypso,' Tommaso says. Then he is gone.

Callie knows she should get back to the hotel, get herself together before meeting her group again, but instead she stares thoughtfully into the water, not wanting to move. What an extraordinary conversation, she thinks, and what an extraordinary man. As it did with Tommaso, regret pricks her skin like a hundred irritating gnats.

A plump white finger suddenly prods her arm, and a pale face, washed with sweat, like a vanilla *gelato* dripping in the sun, blocks the empty space newly vacated by Tommaso. 'Calypso, eh?' The face has lips the colour and texture of a sugared cone. 'Who's she when she's at home?'

The body attached to the face plops itself down next to Callie. It is as white and flabby as the face, and draped in a Union Jack T-shirt, khaki army shorts and sturdy sandals with white socks.

She forces herself to be professionally polite. 'Hello, Sylvester. Calypso? She was a siren in classical mythology.'

Sylvester's sweaty white body spasms, which Callie knows by sad experience signifies laughter. 'That bloke you were with don't know much about Greek whatsit then. You, a siren?' His body twitches in another bout of mirth, not unlike a fish dying on a dry shore.

Callie resists the impulse to boot him into the canal. Instead, she reminds herself that it is her job to be

polite to the customers and goes inside the bar with Sylvester, at his request, to help him order a beer and some food. She says mildly, 'This is your third Venetian tour, Sylvester, not to mention the trips to other parts of Italy. Wouldn't it be helpful to learn at least a word or two of the language?'

He ignores her and says distrustfully, 'What are these things on my plate? Is that what I ordered? This isn't real food, it's poofter's food, nibbles. What kind of a restaurant's this?'

Callie gently steers him outside, smiling apologetically at the owner behind the bar, for Sylvester's complaining whinges are easily understood in any language. She decides that it's not worth explaining to him what an *enoteca* is, and begins to make excuses to leave him by the canal with his beer and food and head back to the hotel.

A chattering contingent of English tourists suddenly rolls like a pastel wave down the *fondamenta*, the slim walkway alongside the canal. The wave knocks Callie back down onto the steps of the bridge with loud shrieks of pleasure at finding her. 'Ooh, look at this little glass gondola Dexter bought me,' cries a young woman in a short ponytail and pristine white shorts. She kisses her husband coyly on the lips. Dexter, pleased with himself, says, 'Anything for you, Minnie,' and glances down at his reflection in the canal with a satisfied smirk.

'Oh, you two,' says a middle-aged woman. 'Newly-weds, aren't they sweet?'

'Just too, too sweet.' Irony oozes from the scarlet lips of a tall blonde woman with blood-red fingernails of dangerous length. She picks up the glass gondola and runs her fingers over it sensuously, looking at Dexter while she does so, managing somehow to convey that this is how she would like to run her fingers over *him*.

Oh God, Callie thinks, the Vamp from Hell.

The vamp's daughter, a pleasant, plain young

woman, says to her mother, 'Angela, do you want a drink?'

Angela, who is wearing high strappy sandals and a low-cut sleeveless dress, pouts seductively at Dexter. 'What do you think, Dexter darling, should we all have a glass of wine to start off this tour the way we mean to continue?' She lets her eyes linger on his face.

Callie groans to herself, then looks to see how Minnie is taking all this. But the young bride has other things on her mind and starts to harangue Callie about the towels in the hotel. Sylvester echoes the complaints like a Greek chorus, while the Vamp from Hell, slick and predatory, claws her way into Dexter's consciousness as she stares at him over the rim of her wineglass.

Candice, the older woman, has been listening to Minnie's complaints with a worried look on her face. 'Oh dear,' she cries, 'do you think Minnie is right, Ellen? Do you think we should demand thicker towels, as she says? What do you think Rodney and Ralph would do?'

'Don't be ridiculous, Candice, our husbands would not give a toss. They would have found the golf course on the Lido and left everything else to us,' Ellen retorts. 'Our towels are perfectly adequate.' She looks defiantly at Minnie, who stares back at her rudely.

Callie listens to all this with a sinking heart. She has been a tour manager long enough to recognize a group that is not going to gel, no matter how hard she tries to make it so.

'Are you all right?' Callie looks up to see who is speaking to her. She cannot remember being asked by a tour member if *she* were all right. Deirdre, the Vamp's daughter, is gazing at her with a concerned look on her face. 'You seem a bit hassled,' Deirdre goes on.

The others are now talking amongst themselves, comparing notes on what they've seen and done in the past two or three hours. Deirdre looks so kind, so

genuinely caring about how Callie feels, that she allows herself a real smile, not the professional one she has been using with the others. For a moment she would like to be herself, not the tour manager; she would like to say, Actually I am not all right. I have met a man I am overwhelmingly attracted to, the first one for ages, and he is married and I shall never see him again. I am filled with regret about this, and it has triggered off other, deeper regrets, feelings that I never knew I had until now. Regrets that people such as you, and Tommaso, and even that sweet American couple yesterday, touch my life briefly and then, because it's the nature of my job, you all disappear and I never see any of you again.

'I'm fine,' she says to Deirdre, because there is no way she can dump all this on a customer no matter how kind, how sympathetic. 'Absolutely fine.' She smiles brightly, professionally.

Sylvester, pushing his way between them, is muttering disparagingly about the plateful of antipasti he has just eaten. Callie says, 'Deirdre, this is Sylvester Avery. You probably didn't meet him last night, he didn't fly in with the rest of the group. He's joined us from another tour. Where was it this time, Sylvester? The Dolomites, or was it the Rome tour?'

'You obviously enjoy your holidays,' Deirdre says politely.

'This is my third trip with Callie here.' Sylvester pokes her playfully but sharply in the ribcage. 'I could run one of these tours, I reckon, with me eyes closed.'

'Try,' Callie says cryptically, forcing herself to smile.

'I'm a lab technician, see, at a local college back in Chelmsford, so I have long holidays. I'm not one for sitting home, see, like I tell me mates. I'm single, free and easy, now's the time to see the world.'

From a Comet Trail Travel holiday coach, Callie thinks cynically. God help us.

She extricates herself from her group as soon as she

can. Suddenly, the tour ahead – a special one of three weeks – seems grim. Callie, unused to feeling like this, wonders what is wrong with her. For the first time ever, her unloved and neglected house in Whitstable, which she has used merely as a stopover between tours, beckons to her temptingly. She had bought it purely for practical reasons: to store the many items she had accumulated on her travels, to avoid paying rent on flats she inhabited only for a few weeks of each year. And to avoid, of course, going back to her parents' home between trips. She is fond of them, sees them briefly once or twice a year, but is happy to stay away the rest of the time. She has a strong suspicion that they feel the same about her.

I'm getting old, she thinks, and I'm not even forty yet. Can I really be longing for my little house when I am here in Venice? She tells her group she must return to the hotel to prepare for the afternoon excursion, and quickly walks away from them. Instead of going straight to the Accademia bridge, the quickest way back to the Isabella, she plunges into the side alleys, walking aimlessly. After the idyllic lunch by the canal with Tommaso, she finds the narrow *calli*, the alleyways, dark and shabby, unhelped by a sudden whiff of decaying food mixed with putrid water. A tired coating of flotsam – plastic coke bottles, paper, other debris – in the corner of another snaky, murky canal depresses her further, as does a forlorn, near-derelict house which must once have been splendidly beautiful as it stood looking out across the water.

Callie finally crosses over the Accademia bridge and walks into the tiny Campo San Vidal and through it to Campo Santo Stefano and the Hotel Isabella. But somehow she cannot bring herself to go into the hotel, so she walks past it and through the square towards the Rialto market, stopping at the Campo Manin to bestow a sympathetic smile at the rather pathetic winged lion, sea-green with age, in the middle of the square. On the

stone steps round the lion several bronzed and fit Americans are consulting guidebooks. One of the women says, 'Someone fill me in on the art in Venice.'

A young man in shorts replies, 'Titian's the only big guy here; there's really no-one else important. There's nothing major, like the Mona Lisa or something.'

Callie groans, resisting the impulse to shake the man and shout, 'Carpaccio, Tintoretto, Bellini, Veronese,' and on and on until she has pummelled him with her voice. But it isn't just the Americans who come out with remarks like these; she's heard worse from members of her own group.

'Yahoo, Callie, smile!' The shrill voice of Minnie rattles through the crowd looking over the Rialto bridge, where Callie has ended up during her pointless ramble. 'Isn't this a coincidence, we meet again!' Minnie dribbles on. Dexter snaps her photograph. 'Please, take one of us,' Minnie trills. She poses with him on the bridge. 'I can't wait until our gondola ride.' She clutches her husband's hand possessively. 'So romantic.'

'What time did you say we were meeting the others?' Dexter asks.

'At three thirty, but the gondola trip is scheduled for five. But only if you want it. Optional extra. If you'd prefer to go off on your own . . .'

They look at her as if she were slightly unhinged. 'Oh no,' Minnie squeals. 'It's much more fun in a crowd.' Dexter nods his head in agreement.

Callie says, 'See you soon, then.' The couple watch, seemingly at a loss, as she snakes away from them. Then they spot some of the other group members, and, relieved at being rescued from an afternoon on their own in Venice, rush to join them.

Callie walks on past a canal which is being dredged. Shuddering at the smell and the noise of the dredging machines, she gives up on Venice and walks as fast as

she can back to the hotel to get ready to meet her group.

'Callie, there you are! I knew you'd be in the piazza somewhere. I'd recognize that red scarf anywhere.'

A stout, solid woman, holding up a black-and-yellow striped umbrella, is greeting Callie amongst the pigeons and tourists in the Piazza San Marco.

'Patsy, when did you arrive? I thought you were due into Venice later this evening.'

'We got an early start this morning from Lake Garda. Good to see you, how's the group?'

Callie looks around surreptitiously to make sure her group members aren't hovering about listening. 'Early days yet, but they don't seem to be blending into one harmonious whole, not yet anyway.' She rolls her eyes. 'What about yours?'

'The group is fine, but Lake Garda was hell. Rained the whole week. I hope Venice is better.'

'This is your last week, right?'

Patsy juggles her umbrella, and grateful sightseers spot her and cluster round. 'The last week on this tour,' she says. 'But another group is arriving immediately; I'm meeting them here. Another major balls-up from Comet Trail; I was the only tour manager available. I don't even get a couple of days' break.'

While they've been talking, Callie has been holding up her scarf so that her own group can find her in the throng. Sylvester, sidling up to Callie, says, 'I don't know why you don't carry an umbrella like Patsy, or a proper banner on a stick. It's much more professional than just waving a scarf.'

'You found me,' Callie says sweetly, smiling with lips tightly closed.

'Callie, there y'all are!' Two figures in identical green tracksuits and white trainers leech onto her like pigeons onto popcorn. 'We've been looking for you and your nice young man. He wasn't at his work site and he

wasn't at his apartment. We've been telling everyone at the campsite how he saved Pogo's life.'

Behind Callie, Dexter makes a snide, witless comment – meant to be funny – about the American couple to Minnie, who laughs and clings appreciatively to his arm. Dexter decides that this marriage thing is hugely OK. Free sex at any time of the day and night, and someone who smiles adoringly at all his jokes. He can't wait to tell the lads back home, the ones who warned him against being tied down.

'Nice young man, Callie?' Sylvester mimics and goes into another silent spasm of laughter.

'He's not my young man,' Callie says distractedly. 'And he's not particularly young.'

'Nor are you,' Sylvester reminds her unhelpfully.

'What's this?' Patsy wants to know. She has known Callie for years; they have worked on many Comet Trail holidays in the same countries, the same cities. 'What young man? Or old one?'

'Neither,' Callie mutters impatiently. 'Neither young nor old, in between. Like we all are, Patsy dear. And not my man, whatever age. He's lovely but he's married.'

'Lot of them about,' Patsy says then she bellows in a loud voice for her group to pull in closer in preparation for charging the Basilica. 'See you later, Callie,' she calls as she marches off, like a formidable general with her sandalled army following along behind.

Callie begins to move forward as well, down the *piazzetta* towards the Riva degli Schiavoni and the gondola piers. It's not easy getting through the crowds of tourists, and a babble of French, German, Japanese, Spanish and Polish assails her as she leads her group along. And not only her group: Lavender and Pogo seem to be clinging to her like snails to a vine, chattering away about Pogo's near-drowning, about Tommaso's rescue, about her own part in this major drama in their lives.

54

Angela, the Vamp from Hell, mincing like one of the pigeons in her high, thin heels, says loudly to Deirdre, 'God knows why I'm doing this. I remember when one of my admirers took me to the Cipriani in a gondola. Christ, he was in love with me. We drank Bellinis all night, first at Harry's Bar and then at the hotel. What that must have cost.' She sighs noisily, looks round her distastefully. 'That it's come to *this*,' she says scornfully. 'A bloody package tour of Venice.'

'You didn't have to book it,' Deirdre says softly.

'Darling, we had no choice. I cannot go a season without Italy, and unfortunately this is all I could afford. Hopefully it will be a laugh, if nothing else.'

Deirdre doesn't answer, but walks on stoically. Despite her loose shorts and shirt, she can feel sweat pouring down between her breasts and under her arms. The day is close and humid, but Angela looks cool and poised even though she has changed into a black trouser suit, gold chains dripping down her white silk shirt. Dexter stares at her admiringly. Minnie, sensibly clothed in culottes, canvas shoes and a loose blouse, looks at Angela disapprovingly. 'Aren't you hot?' she asks.

'I'm just right,' Angela says, and indeed, to the annoyance of the other woman, she *looks* just right, too.

Candice and Ellen, following behind, are also sensibly clad in knee-length skirts and flat, sturdy leather walking sandals. 'Ellen, I do hope we don't lose our tour guide. Can you see her red scarf? Oh dear, there seem to be so many banners and things flying about, how do we know which is Carolyn? I dread to think what would happen if we lost her. Venice is such a maze, all those tiny alleyways, and the canals suddenly crossing one's path in a totally unexpected manner.'

'I believe our tour leader wants us to call her Callie. And though I agree that she is a splendid guide, I'm

sure we would stumble our way round the city eventually on our own.'

Candice cries, 'Oh, Ellen, do you really think so? You've made me feel more confident already. Ralph was right, saying I must leave everything to you, that you would make certain everything went smoothly.'

He would, Ellen thinks as she plods along with the rest of the group. Just as I have made certain that his life has run smoothly, from the day we married almost fifty years ago now.

She takes a deep breath, suddenly tired, as she often is when she thinks of her husband. Dear Ralph, kind but absent-minded, willing but inept. Very early on in her marriage, Ellen realized that she would have to be the strong one, and took up the role reluctantly. I have worn my mask well, she thinks, not without irony. Not only Ralph, but our grown children, our friends, look to me to take charge, to guide them, even lead them. How very exhausting it is, when it is not your natural role.

Callie, leading her group, is also weary, a bad sign at the beginning of a tour. She blames it on the weather; she feels stifled, unable to breathe in the muggy air. Lavender and Pogo claw at her, trying to get her attention, as do several other members of her own group. Sylvester is causing dissent by loudly telling horrific tales of the last time he was in a gondola, when the stench of the rotting canals was so bad he had to puke over the side, thus nearly capsizing the whole boat into the polluted waters.

'I notice you're still queuing up with the others for another go,' Callie says. She tries not to sound waspish.

Angela has lost an earring and is looking thundery beneath her black straw hat. 'Christ, Deirdre, why didn't you notice it was gone?' she shouts. 'I definitely had both on at lunch, so one must have dropped off

afterwards. If only you had *noticed*, Deirdre. Christ, they cost a mint.'

Deirdre listens, stone-faced. Callie thinks, Why does she take it? Why doesn't she just walk away?

Pogo and Lavender are still at her side, nodding with pleasure. 'Isn't Venice just wonderful? We don't want to leave, but that's the nice thing about living in a trailer. We can take off whenever we want, or stay as long as we want.'

Callie nods distractedly. She's having enough trouble with her own group, and sweet though Lavender and Pogo are, she doesn't need two more tourists following her about, especially two octogenarians. She turns her attention to her own travellers, checking that they are all following her. She notes that one of them, Archie, a man in his seventies on his own, has fallen behind, and slows down to wait for him.

'So sorry,' Archie says. 'I have a bad hip, I'm afraid. Sorry to be a nuisance.'

Suddenly there are shouts of recognition, hearty handshakes, exclamations of, 'Well I don't believe it!' and, 'Archie, is it really, really *you*?'

'Do you three know each other?' Callie asks, rather superfluously, for Archie and Pogo and Lavender are shaking hands, slapping each other congenially on the back.

'Pogo and I met Archie three years ago, on an over-sixties holiday in Mexico. One of those cultural trips. Poor Archie here had recently lost his wife, and we kinda befriended him.'

More than that, Archie thinks with great affection. I was in despair, and you both made me smile, even laugh again.

Callie resigns herself to finding room for the American couple in one of the gondolas with her own group. They are so keen, so buoyant, so delighted to be in Venice, delighted to be reunited with Archie. She hasn't the heart to turn them away.

'Have a good ride,' she calls to the first gondola that sets off. In it are Archie and the Americans, Minnie and Dexter. Sylvester, annoyed that he was not in the first boat to push off – he sees himself as tour leader – says, 'Fifteen quid each, that's a lot of dosh for group rates, for being crammed in with five others. I got on one for a tenner when we came to Venice on a day-trip, on that Lake Garda tour with Patsy.'

'That was several years ago,' Callie snaps, her patience with him suddenly frayed. 'These are the going rates, take it or leave it.' She nudges him crossly into the gondola. I must watch it, she mutters to herself, I'm losing it.

Angela digs her nails suggestively in the gondolier's arm as she enters the second boat. He is a young man with a brash smile. '*You* can row me to the Cipriani Hotel anytime, darling,' Angela murmurs. The gondolier, who understands English, looks at her appraisingly. Callie, who has been watching this, says, 'How is your wife, Guido? Your baby?'

Guido forgets Angela. 'My son, he is now not a baby, is big boy. He has the ten months. I show him to you one day.' His pride in his son beams from his face like a searchlight, scanning the crowd for others with whom he can share the light.

'Guido has a lovely family,' Callie explains to some of the others as they climb into the gondola after Angela and Deirdre. They are not interested, do not even look at the gondolier.

The first gondola is heading out into the canal. 'Oh,' Minnie squeals, 'photo, photo, Dexter, please! Here, I'll move over to the other side, and maybe Archie here can take one of both of us.' She jumps up and the gondola tips precariously, nearly flipping over. The gondolier in this boat, an older man in traditional black trousers, striped red-and-white shirt and a straw hat, swears at them in Italian. 'I don't think you're supposed to move round in a gondola,' Archie says mildly.

'It's very precariously balanced. Quite an art, you know, steering one.'

Callie, watching the near mishap, holds her breath as the gondolier regains the balance of his craft and they head off under the Bridge of Sighs. Angela, in the second craft, has taken the best seat and is posed seductively against its crimson velvet upholstery. Dexter, in the first gondola, watches her across the water as she opens another button on her silk shirt, complaining of the heat while she openly stares at Guido. Sylvester, in Angela's boat, says crudely, 'Why don't you take off the whole thing and be done with it?' He is miffed because the vamp is taking no notice of him.

Callie gets the rest of her group into the waiting gondolas and waves them off with great relief. She is free of them until dinner at seven o'clock, and decides to go back to the Hotel Isabella, have a short nap, a shower and try to sort out names and faces in her head before meeting the group again.

The *vaporetto* takes her to the Accademia landing stage. She gets off and crosses over the bridge. There is a slight breeze at the top of the steps and this, she tells herself, is what makes her stop, lean over the rail, and look out at the Grand Canal.

The sky has become murky with heat, the air sticky. The water is the colour and texture of a rich pea soup. The cupolas of the church of the Salute undulate like snow-covered hills in the near distance, and closer, the *palazzi* line the canal like tarnished jewels. Callie's eyes go from one peeling, faded building to the next, finally picking out the Palazzo Valier, or Ca'Valier, as Tommaso called it. From where she stands on the bridge, she can see the opening of the courtyard, where she stood with Pogo and Lavender admiring the canal, while Tommaso unlocked the door of his apartment. The tide, high then, is low now, and several mossy stone steps can be seen leading straight from the

courtyard to the water. A wobbly wooden pier juts out beside the steps, wide enough for one or two people to step off from a gondola or speedboat. There's a single *palina*, or wooden mooring post, at the end of the pier.

Callie raises her eyes to the terrace balcony of Ca'Valier. It is empty, though she can see a flash of bright red through the balustrade: the hibiscus flowers on the plant she had noticed on her one and only visit.

Unhurried, she looks at the *palazzo* for a long time, as if either implanting it indelibly in her memory, or exorcizing it once and for all.

4

'So tell me about him.' Patsy takes off her Comet Trail Travel navy jacket, throws it on the coach rack and flops next to Callie on the seat behind the driver. It's two days later and they're on their way to Verona, having combined their two groups for the optional excursion.

'Tell you about who?'

'This not young, but not old either, married man who seems to have preoccupied you far more than he should. You were very quiet last night when we met for a quick drink at your hotel. And you're not exactly bubbling today.'

Callie looks out of the coach window at the waters of the lagoon as they drive over the causeway. The air outside looks slightly opaque, not quite clean. The day is already hot.

'Well?' Patsy says.

Callie takes comfort from her phlegmatic bulk, from the way Patsy waits calmly for a reply, not pressing, but at the same time honestly interested. Callie begins, 'Well, his name is Tommaso.' She pauses, not quite knowing what exactly to say about him. 'He's so unlike my usual type of man that I am quite surprised at myself. He's too self-assured, too confident, for my liking.'

'Italian?'

'Yes, but he's lived in England for years. His wife's English.' She looks troubled.

Patsy says warningly, 'Callie, you're not seeing him again, I hope.'

'No, of course not, I have no intention of seeing him again, and he knows it.' She sounds so disgruntled as she says this that Patsy has to laugh. 'It's all right for you,' Callie goes on. 'You can sit there all smug and secure, you've got a husband sitting at home waiting for you. What do I have? A dusty, empty house with not a living thing in it, not even a pot plant.'

'I thought that's what you wanted. Travelling, meeting lots of people —'

'I did,' Callie interrupts impatiently, then wonders why she used the past tense. 'Or rather I *do*.' She looks out of the window contemplatively. 'Maybe,' she says slowly, 'maybe I didn't quite realize that not having roots, being a nomad, is more than just seeing new things, meeting new people, having unique experiences. Oh, it's that, all right, and I love that part of it. But then—' She breaks off to look at Patsy. 'Sometimes, don't you ever get tired of all these goodbyes? Oh, I know, mostly we're delighted to see the backs of the people we meet, but sometimes, if you're not careful, you get close to someone. And then it's still *arrivederci*, or *au revoir*, *adiós*, whatever, and promising to write, maybe visit each other, but it never happens. Distance, all that.'

Patsy ponders this. 'Maybe it doesn't bother me so much because of Stuart.' Stuart is her husband. 'Though everything else in my life is temporary, or rather most of the people that go through it are, he is permanent. That and the job. Nothing else really matters to me.'

'I envy you, you know. Every time I tell myself it can't be done, juggling a marriage with a travelling job, I meet up with you again. You've been doing it for years.'

'Fourteen. We've been married almost twenty.' Patsy looks startled, as if the years have accumulated suddenly, unexpectedly. 'Stuart's got his own career, his

own life. I suppose if we'd had children it would have been a lot different.'

They talk of other things, mostly about their groups, their last tours. Finally they withdraw into a companionable silence. Callie tries to read her paperback, but cannot concentrate. She ends up staring out of the window, not seeing much. As they approach Verona, the coach slows in a traffic jam. Callie watches a handsome Italian in a black leather jacket and the ubiquitous sunglasses weave dangerously in and out on a flashy motorbike, oblivious to the hoots of car horns and the imprecations of those he cuts in front of. Such insouciance, Callie thinks. She had a lover like him once; rode a Honda, though he was blond and half-German, not Italian. He lived in London and worked at the same travel agency as Callie; he moved into her flat in West Kensington for nearly a year. They had an easy, comfortable time together, sharing a mutual passion for obscure foreign films and Thai restaurants, but when Callie changed her job and began the travelling with Comet Trail, the relationship became moribund and finally died, without any fuss or heartbreak on either side.

Thinking of him now, Callie wonders whether she really loved him, though she'd thought she did at the time. But during her year with him, she was already thinking of leaving her job in London, breaking away from the routine of a nine-to-five job, only occasionally disrupted by a short trip abroad. As their life together settled into a routine, she began to find comparisons with her own parents' lives: the Sunday newspapers over coffee, the domestic trivia that seemed to occupy a great deal of their conversations. She probably did not love him: she was too relieved when he went for it to have been love.

Callie contemplates the motorcyclist, now himself stuck in the morass of traffic, and looking surly. Her parents had been wary of her blond half-German lover,

believing him to be as flighty, as unchartered, as she was. Callie frowns, wondering why her parents' lives were such anathema to her. They were blameless after all; they were happy in their own way. She decides that it was because they tried too hard to impinge their way on her. An only child, she was encouraged to stay at home, find fulfilment in the roots of the past, as they did. But she was already curious about the world outside their brick house, and the more her parents seemed uninterested in it, the more she longed to experience it.

Callie stirs in her seat, thinking of that period in London, of the friends she had there whom she has mostly lost touch with. It was fun, but she'd been glad to move on, glad to begin her exploration of Europe. She rarely goes to London now, though it's easily accessible from her house in Kent; she doesn't miss it. She hardly goes anywhere when she's at home between tours; there doesn't seem to be that much time once she has unpacked and sorted out her clothes, done the mundane things like visiting the dentist and stocking up on new clothes or paperbacks for the next trip.

The coach has finally wound through the traffic and come to a stop. Patsy hoists herself out of her seat and stands up, taking the microphone from the driver.

'Well now, welcome to Comet Trail's first optional excursion here in the Veneto. For those of you in Callie's group, let me introduce myself.' She proceeds to do so, then tells them something of the history of Verona. 'Callie and I will first show you the Roman Arena, the best preserved amphitheatre in Italy. You can go inside for a small fee, but before that we'll show you a few other places you may like to explore later at your own leisure: the Piazza dei Signori with its twelfth-century buildings, the Piazza Brà, which is full of wonderful cafés where you can sit and drink coffee and watch the world go by. We'll finish at Juliet's

house, made famous by Shakespeare's play, then leave you to have lunch, do some shopping, visit the arena if you like, and meet us back at the coach at four.'

A buzz of questions drones round Callie's head; she's glad Patsy has taken over today. She feels stale, lethargic, without the usual buoyancy she has at the beginning of a tour. She tries to recapture floundering enthusiasm and helps her group members down the steps with a pleasant word for all of them, trying to remember their names and where they're from. She answers all questions, even the most repetitive, the most ridiculous, with good grace, and listens to the inevitable complaints about the coach journey and the heat with sympathy.

The Roman Arena looms over them as they skirt round it. As Patsy gives them a brief history: 'Built in the first century AD to hold twenty thousand people—', Angela interrupts loudly, 'I came here for a few days' shoot, in the amphitheatre. We stayed at that four-star hotel over there on the piazza, all of us, models, photographers. Cost the magazine a mint, but we needed a new angle.' She doesn't add that the new angle didn't work, that the magazine went downhill even faster that month than in the previous months since she had taken over as editor. She turns to Dexter, the only interesting man – or woman, for that matter – on this tour, and says, 'You should have seen the tourists, gaping at us as we set up the shoot. It was better than the opera.'

Before he can reply to this, Minnie grabs his arm and says, 'Oh, Dexter, can you imagine what it was like, all those gladiators? Just like the ones on telly!'

Dexter smoothes back his hair, which is wavy and richly auburn and of which he is very proud, and winks at Angela, poking Minnie playfully. 'Can you imagine the pong? All that blood in this heat. Talk of heat, I'm parched, could do with an ice-cold lager.'

'This heat's nothing,' Sylvester says. 'The last time I

was in Verona on a Comet Trail tour, it reached a hundred, and the air-conditioning on the coach packed up.'

'It is indeed hot today,' Ellen says. She wishes she'd abandoned her tights and gone bare legged, but Candice had reminded her of her veiny thighs and calves. And I succumbed to the pressures of vanity, she thinks now, and I am suffering for it. The sweat pours like rain down her legs.

Candice says, 'I suppose we must go into the arena.' She looks extremely doubtful. 'Rodney and Ralph will be expecting photographs. It's frightfully formidable.'

'It's a bloody rip-off,' Sylvester says. 'Nothing but stone steps, steep ones at that, you gotta watch that you don't trip and break your neck. On my last tour this bloke fell and broke his leg, and we hung round for hours in the heat waiting for an ambulance.'

'We're off, Sylvester, are you coming or not?' Callie rallies her group and, along with Patsy's, they march purposefully along the crowded streets. Finally they end up at a small courtyard to gape at Juliet's balcony, along with hundreds of other tourists. The packed square defeats Callie, who points her group inside, reminds them the time and place of their regrouping later, and pulls Patsy aside to say, 'We've done our bit. Let's find a quiet place, get some food.'

As they walk along to the market square further down from Juliet's house, Patsy says, 'I forgot to tell you, we're meeting someone for lunch. That nice Italian man, Giovanni, I met here on my tour last spring. I told him you'd be with us.'

'Patsy!' Callie stops walking to stare at her. Patsy blithely walks on, square and solid in her Comet Trail navy skirt and white blouse with a comet blazing across her breast. Even her sandy hair looks box-shaped; it is pulled up squarely in a bun on top of her head. Callie has to run to keep up with her, and exclaims again, 'Patsy! What other secrets are you

keeping from me? I knew you were friendly with some student in Venice, but not *this* friendly. Lunch dates, eh? You married women never miss a trick.'

'Give over, Callie. He's a mature student, in fact I'd say he was pushing forty. He's doing research for a book he's writing. Actually, he's not exactly a student, though I thought he was at first. He's a lecturer at the university in Milan, but he spends his summers in Venice. And he's also off to the States in the autumn to do a year's lecturing there.'

Patsy leads Callie through the market street, past the food stalls selling fruit and vegetables, hot slices of pizza, fresh ripe cheeses and olives. 'I'm weak with hunger,' Callie says. 'Where are we meeting this scholar of yours?'

'Here.' Patsy steers her into a restaurant in the next street. They sit outside at a table overlooking a cobbled square with an antique fountain. 'Giovanni said he might be late. He had a meeting with someone this morning.'

Patsy asks Callie to order wine. 'Anything, so long as it's white and cold.'

'Something from the Veneto?'

'Whatever. You know I'm usually a beer drinker, but I fancy some wine with lunch. And let's have a bottle of mineral water, the sparkling stuff.'

Callie orders a bottle of Soave and savours it appreciatively when it appears. Patsy gulps hers like beer, enjoying every mouthful, washing it down with the fizzy water. After they have eaten all the bread sticks, Callie says, 'So where is your friend?'

'He'll be here.' Patsy is complacent.

'I must say, you have a nerve. Warning me about Italian men, especially married ones, and you here, married yourself, arranging lunches in this seductive city with handsome Italian scholars.' Callie takes another sip of her wine and begins to relax. Though the square is milling with people, there are none of

her group members about. In fact many of the people clustering round the fountain are Italian: two or three children playing with the water, an old woman in black carrying a bag of groceries, sitting for a rest on the low wall circling the fountain.

Patsy rolls her eyes at Callie. 'Really, I think all these Venetian tours are making your head go soft. You're assuming he's handsome, married, and that I'm madly in love with him. As a matter of fact he's gay. He's also shy and rather awkward, as if he doesn't quite fit into his own space. I think he's lonely in Venice, that's why he's attached himself to me. And here he is!' She stands up and greets a thin man with black and silver hair, brown-rimmed glasses, and a face that is homely and vulnerable, as if it is missing a layer of skin. 'Callie, this is Giovanni.'

He greets them in Italian, though he speaks fluent English, and they change to that language quite quickly, as Patsy's knowledge of Italian is slight despite her many tours in the country. There is a flurry of small talk until the waiter comes and lunch is decided upon.

When the waiter leaves, Giovanni says, 'I hope you don't mind, but my brother will be joining us. I will be ordering for him also. He had some sudden business in Verona this morning and drove in with me from Venice.'

'How did you and Patsy meet?' Callie asks.

'It was our mutual friend Signor Goldoni who introduced us,' Giovanni says. 'In his very own house.'

'I'm afraid I don't know a Signor Goldoni,' Callie says politely. 'A descendant of the playwright?'

Giovanni laughs. 'It's our little joke, Patsy's and mine,' he says, and something stirs, ever so slightly, in Callie's consciousness. 'I mean the great Venetian playwright Carlo Goldoni himself, who, of course, died in 1793. I met Patsy in the house where he was born, which is now a museum in his honour.'

Patsy takes up the story. 'Do you remember that pedantic tour member I had last spring, the artsy one who used to quote obscure Venetian plays and operas to me, and make sarky comments when I didn't get the reference? He dragged me and some of the others to this tiny museum, but we couldn't get in.'

'It was, like so many things in Venice, *in restauro*, being restored,' Giovanni explains. 'And therefore closed to the public, *sai com'è*, you know how it is.'

'Well, this bloke in my group had a fit, ranted and raved as if it were done deliberately to thwart him. He even blamed me for not knowing that it was closed. As if you could ever know in Venice when something is suddenly being closed for *restauro*. Luckily, Giovanni came along at that point and saved the day.'

'I know the proprietor, you see, and after I had a little chat with him, the group was allowed inside.'

Patsy nods her head with satisfaction. 'The bloke was meek as a lamb for the rest of the tour, delighted to be let into Goldoni's house when it was closed to everyone else. You're a star, Giovanni.'

He looks both pleased and embarrassed, and goes on hurriedly, 'Afterwards, Patsy very kindly took me to a café for a Campari to say thank you, and we have become friends. I want to have her to my house for a feast; I love to cook, you see, but always she is too busy with her group. Perhaps you will convince her to come? With you, too, Callie.'

Callie thinks this is a good idea, and says so emphatically. All too often it is difficult to meet the residents of the cities and towns she travels in, and for weeks at a time she's surrounded by nothing but English tourists. Remembering that she got into this business in the first place not just to see foreign countries, but also to meet the people, she insists on making a definite date. When Giovanni mentions tomorrow, Callie says, 'Yes, let's, Patsy, please. I know we have to be with our group for dinner at seven, but we have a

free evening after that. We don't have to eat at our hotels, we can nibble on the antipasti and eat at Giovanni's later.'

Giovanni is delighted, and they make a date for a late dinner at his apartment at nine. As Callie is about to ask for the address, she hears a shout of greeting, a torrent of Italian and a burst of laughter, a laughter that is already familiar to her. And without looking up, she knows why the timbre of Giovanni's voice echoed in her ears so reminiscently. It is uncannily like Tommaso's.

'This is my brother, Tommaso,' Giovanni says.

'Nice to meet you, I'm Patsy.' She shakes his hand.

Callie says, 'We've already met.'

'So we have.' Tommaso kisses her like an old comrade. 'I had no idea that my brother's English friend was you.'

'It isn't. I just met your Giovanni half an hour ago. Through his friend Patsy, who is also my colleague.'

Patsy, listening to all this, opens her eyes in sudden realization. 'Oh, uh, Tommaso? *Tommaso?*' She looks at Callie, her face a large question mark.

As the two brothers exchange a few words in Italian, Callie hisses to Patsy, 'Yes, he's the one. Just remember that if I become completely undone, it is all your doing.'

Their risotto arrives, and the conversation centres on food until Giovanni says, 'Tommaso, how is the work in Verona going?'

Callie says, 'I thought you were beginning the job in Venice. On the Zattere, where you were doing the survey.'

'The divers start that tomorrow. In the meantime, we have some repair work on a mooring on the river here in Verona. Just a small job, but there was a slight problem and I was asked to take a look. And you, Giovanni? Was your morning successful?'

Giovanni looks mournful. 'Such a disappointment. I

70

had a meeting with this man who said he had original letters from one of Goldoni's many mistresses, but they were no such thing. They were clearly fakes.'

'My brother is a great Goldoni biographer and scholar. I believe he has dedicated his life to the playwright, the way saints dedicate their lives to God.' Tommaso looks fondly at his brother.

Callie looks from one to the other, trying to find some resemblance. There is none except for the resonance of their voices, and the fact that they both need to wear glasses. Giovanni's glasses are small and round and scholarly, while Tommaso is still wearing his prescription sunglasses. Disconcerted, Callie wonders if she will ever know the colour of his eyes.

The brothers are only a year apart in age, but Giovanni, though younger, looks much older. Both are tall, but where Tommaso is lean, Giovanni is gaunt. Despite his frequent laughter, Giovanni is more pensive. Occasionally he seems to drift away from the conversation and look out towards the fountain and the children playing round it with a slightly wistful air, as if he did not quite belong here.

'Are you still brooding over Goldoni, Giovanni?' Tommaso asks at one point.

Giovanni turns, looks slightly surprised, as if he has forgotten where he is. 'Ah, Tommaso, what a find those letters would have been, had they existed.'

The risotto is tasty, filling, and when they finish, they order espresso but no dessert. Patsy begins asking Giovanni some questions about his latest bit of research on the Venetian playwright, and he launches into what sounds like the continuation of a previously explained theory. Tommaso takes advantage of this to begin his own conversation with Callie. 'Isn't this extraordinary, Calypso. You've bewitched me again, enticed me here to Verona.'

'Bullshit,' Callie retorts. But she answers his smile with her own wide one.

'Fate,' Tommaso goes on unperturbed. 'And I was sure that I would never see you again.' His tone is light, and it would spoil the moment to say how disturbed this thought made him yesterday as he tried to work. There was a great deal to do, as there always is at the start of a job: dealing with the contract, ordering boats, divers, equipment. His mind was not on it, which is not usual for him.

His hand brushes Callie's arm and remains there for a moment. She has noticed how he touches everyone: his brother, Patsy, herself, have all been the recipient of a pat on the arm, a brief pressing of the shoulder. It's an unselfconscious gesture, and it makes Callie suddenly realize how long it has been since someone has reached for her with fondness. Her last serious lover was the divorced man living in the house next to hers in Whitstable, but looking back, Callie realizes that that relationship was born out of mutual loneliness, a need to be number one in *somebody's* life. That, too, ended fairly painlessly, when the man grew bored during Callie's long and frequent absences and found solace with a local schoolteacher, who could be counted on to remain where she was, at least during term time. Callie found that she was not as anguished as she thought she would be. She had been feeling guilty over how little she thought, while she was away, of the kind, gentle man who was always there when she came home from a tour, welcoming her back from his house next door with a hot meal and genuine affection. But though she had enjoyed his attentions, she felt guilty about him, too, about the times he was left alone. When he found someone else, the relief that she no longer had to feel guilty soothed the sadness she felt, and she found that it didn't take long to forget him.

But somehow, watching Tommaso, Callie finds that what she misses is not a lover, but something else: a hug from a friend, an embrace from a relative, the touches of affection, of warmth.

Tommaso notes the saddening of her expression, and is moved to leave his hand where it is, on top of her hand, rather than taking it off as he usually does after he has made a point. There is a moment of silence as they both look down at their hands, as if they were two alien creatures unnaturally joined together in a strange mating rite.

'Tommaso,' Callie says carefully, 'this just isn't on, OK?'

He understands what she's saying and wonders why it bothers him so much. The woman is pretty enough, but beauty is not uncommon in Italy. Her short spiky hair is badly cut, and though that huge smile and those smoky-grey eyes deserve more than just a second glance, her slight, boyish figure is certainly quite ordinary. There is a woman in Venice – and one in Verona, too, if truth be told – right now, both of whom are much more attractive than Callie, and who have hinted outrageously that they would like him in their beds.

She is looking at him now with kindness in her eyes, and with something more: honest affection, mingled with open regret. Perhaps this is what he finds so appealing, the kindness, the honesty. The bluntness, too; he likes that. The women he knows are never blunt but subtle, existing on hints and innuendoes. Even Sandra, his wife, tries to hide things, like the fact that she much prefers the children to him and that being a wife is much inferior to being a mother.

A burst of laughter from the other two distracts them from their preoccupation with each other. Callie says, as she removes her hand and places it in her lap, 'What an odd friendship. Patsy is so grounded, so pragmatic, and your brother seems so . . .' She gropes for the right word. 'So cerebral,' she finishes.

'Giovanni lives in his head, *è vero*, it is true. This playwright that lived over two hundred years ago is his

life, his reason for living. He's translating all of Goldoni's plays into modern Italian, for a new anthology. The man wrote over two hundred, so it's a major undertaking. Then there is this biography he's working on, which promises to uncover new facts about the playwright's life.'

Callie shakes her head. 'But what has Patsy to do with all this? I don't think she's been to see a play in her entire life, let alone one by an eighteenth-century Venetian.'

Tommaso glances at the couple. Both seem to be oblivious of the others. Giovanni is now doing most of the talking, waving his arms and raising his voice in his enthusiasm for his subject. Patsy looks comfortably solid as though enjoying her role as listener.

Tommaso says, 'For my brother, it is relaxing to have the friendship of a non-academic, someone who will listen without criticizing, without barbed comments. It also helps his English, to explain Goldoni in your language. Not that he needs to practise his English, as you see, but he's nervous about this year's lecturing in the States. He's not very confident, despite being at the university in Rome, then in Milan, and even for a year in Paris. His French is excellent, too.'

'Another wanderer,' Callie says. 'What a nomadic lot we are.'

A roar of laughter from Patsy, at something Giovanni has said, drowns her out. Giovanni looks modestly pleased, as if he's surprised to have told a joke well. Tommaso says, 'I confess, I don't know what Patsy gets out of my brother.'

'Oh, I can. He must be so soothing for her. In our job we are constantly explaining things, solving problems, giving advice, dealing with hotel staff and coach drivers and the customers themselves, God help us. It's very pleasant just to listen to someone else's problems and know you're not going to be asked to deal with them.'

'I doubt if Giovanni expects Patsy to sort out Goldoni for him.' Tommaso smiles.

'Exactly. She doesn't get all the trivia from him, like why dinner is at seven instead of seven-thirty, or why breakfast cannot be served in the bedroom.'

'Only eighteenth-century trivia. But I wouldn't let Giovanni hear me call it that.' Tommaso looks affectionately at his brother.

Patsy has glanced at her watch and is standing up, saying they must settle the bill; they have lingered all afternoon and it is time to meet the two groups again. Giovanni reminds them that they are to come to his place the next evening, and says, 'Tommaso, Patsy and her friend have agreed to dinner at Ca'Valier tomorrow. You will be home? You haven't any other plans? I will cook, of course.'

'Certainly,' Tommaso replies. 'I will provide wine. It will be an enchanting evening.' Callie swears his eyes are twinkling behind the dark glasses.

She knows she should refuse, and wonders how she will manage this, having eagerly accepted earlier. As Giovanni and Patsy peck each other's cheeks and murmur, *Arrivederci, ciao*, goodbye, Tommaso takes Callie aside and says, 'Please come, don't back out. Giovanni would be so disappointed.' And I would be distraught, he thinks, but is too wise to say so.

She looks troubled. 'Tommaso, I really meant what I said. About married men.'

Once again his hand is on her arm. His face instantly becomes serious, the eyes sombre behind the black shades. 'You said you have married men who are good friends. Can I not be one of them, now that we have been properly introduced? Not just by your friend Patsy, but also by my brother.'

'I also said that I don't go to bed with my married friends.' Callie looks up at him, her face now as earnest as his.

'It's better than nothing, the friendship,' Tommaso

says solemnly, but his eyes are merry behind the shades. 'We'll be friends, like Giovanni and Patsy.'

She nods at him with such relief that he promises himself he will indeed keep strictly within the bounds of friendship. Suddenly it seems important to him not to transcend these. Somehow he knows that if he did he would lose more of himself than he is prepared to part with.

A few of the more timid group members are already waiting in front of the arena when Patsy and Callie arrive, twenty minutes before the agreed time. 'Oh, there you are, Carolyn!' Candice, hovering in the shadow of Ellen, cries out in relief. 'We were so terrified we wouldn't find our way back to the coach that we got here half an hour early.'

'*You* were terrified, Candice,' Ellen retorts. Though she's travelled before with Candice, her old and dear friend, she has found her company somewhat stifling on this trip. Ellen blames it on Venice, on the flamboyant melancholy of the city. It disturbs the order she has had to impose on her married life, plays havoc with the control she has had over herself for years. She feels she would like to be as gaudy as Venice herself, flaunting her peeling, decayed *palazzi*, her silted canals, her past grandeur. Yet Ellen knows she is trapped in who she is: she cannot even abandon her tights, flaunt her varicose veins, revel, like Venice, in her own history.

Sylvester ambles up to the group, eating a *gelato* on a dark crusty cone. 'Wanna lick?' he says to Callie, holding out the cone. Chocolate melts down his chin and onto his Union Jack T-shirt, staining the already grubby white background.

'Look what you've done,' Callie says, refusing the lick with a grimace. 'You'll have to wash that T-shirt as soon as you get back, so it doesn't stain.'

'About time, too,' Patsy hisses softly, so that Sylvester cannot hear. 'It pongs. And it's vile, all that

76

fluorescent blue and red on our dear old flag.'

'I didn't know you were so patriotic,' Callie says as Sylvester wanders over to annoy Ellen and Candice.

'I'm not in the slightest. I just hate blatant bad taste, especially on sweaty, smelly beer bellies. A stained cloth covering a loathsome body.' Patsy shakes her head distastefully.

'My, you *are* lyrical today.' Callie grins. 'It must be all that Goldoni over lunch.'

'No, I've just had Sylvester on too many tours myself. He brings out the worst in me.'

Patsy's group is assembled and she leads them off to the coach, holding her umbrella up high. Callie and her charges wait for Angela and Deirdre, who are late.

'Maybe Angela fell down the steps of the amphitheatre and broke a leg or something,' Sylvester says unhelpfully. 'Those fuck-me heels she always wears, wouldn't surprise me.'

Minnie frowns at his language, but agrees with his sentiments. 'It's very bad manners to keep us waiting,' she says. 'Especially in this heat. I don't like her anyway, do you, Dexter?'

Dexter, taken by surprise, hesitates. He rather fancies Angela, though she's old enough to be his mother. She's got a nice tight little bum and he can just imagine those long, scarlet-painted nails lightly clawing his chest, and those thick black eyelashes gently swishing over his belly.

Dexter stops himself abruptly. He knows, as a married man, he must give up these thoughts. Still, he wishes Minnie would tart herself up a bit more and wear thin high heels and dresses with plunging necklines, like Angela does. She used to before they were married, he remembers. Maybe it's just the heat that's making her wear those shapeless shorts and baggy tops she seems to live in since they got to Italy.

'Dexter, did you hear me? Do you like that peculiar woman?'

77

Dexter takes a deep breath and tells the first lie of his marriage. 'No, Minnie, not much.'

As Callie walks the group back to the coach, she falls back with Archie, who, with his bad hip, cannot quite keep up a normal pace. 'I'm terribly sorry,' he says. 'I do feel such a burden on you. I know I'm dreadfully slow.'

'Not at all. We're in no great hurry. It's too hot to walk fast anyway. Did you enjoy Verona?'

Archie's broad, pleasant face expands like a flower. It's remarkably unlined for a man of his age, though the creases round his eyes are deep, reminiscent of old wounds. 'Verona is delightful. Of course, with my hip I couldn't do much sightseeing, but I walked a short distance and I had a leisurely lunch in one of the restaurants on that street where the market is. It's better than a cinema, watching people. It's almost as delightful as looking at a Carpaccio painting.'

Ellen has also fallen behind the rest of the group to wait for Candice, who is complaining of sore feet. Ellen turns to Archie and says, 'Carpaccio? You like his work? I've already been to the Correr Museum on my own, to see his painting, *The Courtesans*. Have you seen it?' She looks at Archie with new eyes.

'Why, yes. *The Courtesans* was a great favourite of John Ruskin's.'

'I'm afraid I don't know Ruskin's writing very well, but I know the painter. I did an Art History course in adult education not that long ago.'

Archie says, 'You must read what Ruskin wrote about Carpaccio. I have his writings, you shall see for yourself. You must read Ruskin in Venice.'

He says this so firmly that Ellen is taken by surprise. No-one has spoken firmly to her in years, told her what she must do. Everyone else *asks*. She is so weary of it all.

'And then, when you have read Ruskin, you must go to the Schiavoni, the *scuola*, and see Carpaccio's

St George and St Jerome cycles.'

Candice asks what a *scuola* is, and shakes her head doubtfully when Ellen explains that they were Venetian institutions, mostly founded in the thirteenth century. 'So muddling, all these strange names and places,' she says.

By this time they have arrived at the coach. Patsy and Callie count their groups, make sure everyone is there and settle down for the return trip to Venice.

'Well, well,' Patsy says. 'What an extraordinary co-incidence. My friend Giovanni is your married Tommaso's brother.'

'It's unreal, isn't it.' Callie shakes her head. 'Do you think it's Fate? Destiny?' She opens her eyes wide in mock awe.

'Bull. You know what they say about Venice. It's really just a small town; sooner or later everyone meets.'

'For a moment, Patsy, that's all. We meet, touch, pass through. Like everyone in this maddening city.'

Patsy pats her hand kindly. 'Now don't get morbid. Venice does that to people. All this myth and melancholy writers go on about. Venice is what you make of it.'

'Or what it makes of you,' Callie retorts. 'Do you think it's turned me into Calypso? A siren, one that male wanderers cannot resist? Do you see me as a siren, Patsy?' She flutters her eyelashes in exaggerated seductiveness.

'There's no way anyone in their right mind would call you a siren. Sorry about that. Now keep quiet and let me sleep. Verona has exhausted me, and we've got a bloody Vivaldi concert to take the punters to tonight.'

Callie turns away from Patsy and looks out of the window, but all she can see is her own reflection in the gleaming glass. 'Calypso?' she murmurs.

Sighing, she closes her eyes. 'On the whole, I'd much rather be Penelope.' Then she, too, falls asleep.

The coach pulls into the Piazzale Roma. The area is heavy with diesel and petrol fumes, with hundreds of coaches parked to expel passengers on day trips to the city. Some tourists are on their way back to their coaches now, laden with souvenirs: Murano glass, straw gondoliers' hats, elaborate masks. Out of bags and rucksacks and pockets hang guidebooks and maps, round most shoulders a camera is slung.

'This place gets worse every year,' Patsy says as they emerge from the coach. 'Fumes, heat, exhaust smoke – it's vile.'

'At least it stops here. Just think if cars and coaches were able to get into the city.'

Candice is getting out of the coach, helped by Ellen. She looks pale, shaky. 'Candice suffers from travel sickness,' Ellen explains.

As Deirdre, who is walking by with Angela, shakes her head sympathetically, the Vamp from Hell snorts loudly to the two older women, 'Imagine coming on a coach trip when you suffer from car sickness. How profoundly stupid.'

Deirdre flushes with embarrassment. Ellen says, 'And how profoundly rude,' and walks on with Candice.

Patsy scowls as she stares at Angela. 'Nasty sort,' she murmurs to Callie. 'Do you think all that elaborate blond stuff piled on top of her head is real?'

'That's what you call big hair, Patsy. Looks stiff as a corpse, too. I think she must use a lot of mousse.'

'And gallons of bleach. Does she have a husband?'

Callie shrugs. 'Several, I should imagine. None on this trip, thank God. Just that poor daughter.'

Patsy and Callie have gathered their group and are leading them to the water's edge to catch their boat into the city. Angela is flirting outrageously with one of the sailors on a smaller vessel moored near by.

'Her Italian is appalling,' Patsy mutters. 'I know mine is, too, but I don't flaunt it. What does the woman do, anyway? Run a brothel?'

'She was an editor on some glossy fashion magazine that lasted a couple of years, then went bust. Unfortunately for Angela, it folded when she had been hired to push up circulation. According to Deirdre, she couldn't find another job anywhere, and now does freelance stuff.'

'So that's why she's reduced to a Comet Trail tour.'

'Can't afford anything else.'

Patsy stares at Angela, who has become bored with the sailor and has gone back to whinging to Deirdre about the heat. 'Pity about the daughter,' Patsy says. 'She seems OK.'

'Yes.' Callie looks thoughtfully at mother and daughter. The vamp is going on at great length about the humid air and her sticky clothes, and is managing somehow to insinuate that it is all Deirdre's fault. 'I don't quite know why her daughter sticks it,' Callie says. 'Angela is quite vicious with her at times, and embarrassing at others.'

The *vaporetto* landing stage is filled with hot, harrassed tourists. The platform, on a pontoon in the water, is swaying slightly; a breeze has whipped into the city with its usual Venetian suddenness. Patsy embarks on a Number Eighty-two *vaporetto* with her group, and Callie and the others board a *Numero Uno*. It is crowded, and as she stands pressed against the others, waiting for the *vaporetto* staff to untie the rope, close the railing and begin to move, Minnie cries to the

others, 'I didn't think much of Verona. Not much there.'

Angela shudders. 'You must go round with your eyes closed, darling. Verona is one of the most charming cities in Italy, bursting with art and architecture. Surely even you must have noticed *something* of this.'

Callie, though agreeing with Angela, is appalled again by her rude manner. She says, somewhat curtly, 'We were only there a few hours, Angela. It's hard to absorb Verona's charm in so little time.' As she says this, she knows she has got the tone wrong, knows she should have been placating instead of snappish. Now both Minnie and Angela are irritated. Callie is annoyed at herself; she has often dealt with difficult group members, and usually knows exactly the right way to handle them. She has been short with Sylvester more than once, and, though he has deserved it, it's her job not to let her own irritation show through when dealing with the customers.

As the *vaporetto* chunters down the canal, the breeze is more noticeable, refreshing. The light on the water is pale, iridescent. The old decaying buildings, the peeling *palazzi* that line the canal, reflect the light like a glass chandelier in a candlelit ballroom. In the water, a second shimmering city is reflected, so clear it's hard to tell where reality ends and illusion begins.

As they approach the Rialto bridge, the light changes and becomes a deep yellow, then a pearl-grey. 'It's going to rain,' Sylvester says. 'We'll never make it back to the hotel.'

The sky is indeed darkening with thick cloud. By the time the boat steams through *la volta*, the bend in the Grand Canal where it backs onto itself, streaks of lightning slice the clouds and thunder growls over the noise of the water and the boats. Callie tells her group, 'We'll get off here, at San Samuele, and make a run for the hotel. If we go one more stop to the Accademia,

there's a good chance it'll be pouring with rain.'

They make it back to the hotel just in time. 'Told you it would rain,' Sylvester says smugly. 'Some of the others who lingered on the way back from the *vaporetto* stop are going to get soaked.' He says this with such satisfaction that Callie has to bite her tongue not to make a sharp retort. I mustn't be waspish with the customers, Callie tells herself, and wonders why her tolerance for their rudeness and bad behaviour seems to be at an all-time low this tour. For the first time, an uneasy feeling that perhaps she has been doing this job for too long creeps into her consciousness.

Shaking this thought out of her head, she decides that her strange mood is due to the fact that she has been with real people, rather than customers she is obligated to be polite to, no matter how rude they are themselves. She smiles to herself as she thinks of the contrast between the easy, relaxing lunch with Patsy, Giovanni and Tommaso, and the snide hectoring of her group members during the rest of the Verona excursion.

Tommaso. Now that she is free of her group, she can think of him. How extraordinary it was, meeting him a third time, and through Patsy. She would like to succumb to the idea of fate, of destiny, but remembers too well the uniqueness of Venice, city without cars, where people still walk, meet in the streets and in the squares. If you stay long enough, sooner or later paths cross, people intertwine.

Callie hesitates, suddenly loath to go back to her room, nor does she particularly want to talk to Signor Alberti, who is having some kind of a crisis in the back office. The desk clerk rolls his eyes while the *signore*'s voice competes with the thunder as he rants, soothed by the calmer, more resigned, tones of his wife. Callie rolls her eyes back at the clerk, and runs outside into the rain. She has an umbrella in her bag and puts it up against the sodden sky, and without

thinking she walks quickly across the Campo Santo Stefano, passing the dripping statue of Nicolò Tommaseo, scholar and rebel of the 1800s. 'Poor *Cacalibre*,' she says, using the Venetian's nickname for the statue: bookshitter, for under poor Nicolò's frock coat there are indeed a pile of books that look as if they had been expelled from his backside.

She goes through the Campo San Vidal, over the bridge, which the downfall has washed clean of tourists, and turns right, then left, to find she is passing the *enoteca* where she and Tommaso ate antipasti in the sunshine on the small bridge over the canal. The open doors of the tiny wine bar reveal a packed room, people standing in close proximity with drinks in their hand, chatting easily to friends, colleagues. By the side of the door, the statue of the Madonna behind her iron grille looks watery, tearful.

Callie, under her dripping umbrella, hesitates, then slowly turns away from the *enoteca* and crosses the bridge to the other side. The church of San Trovaso is still open, and Callie goes inside and sits on a pew in the front. It's a dark church, even in the best of daylight, and she can barely see the two Tintorettos on either side of the choir. Sitting in the gloom, water running from her closed umbrella and trickling at her feet, she tries to recapture the serenity that this dark church, and other favourite churches, *scuole* and galleries give her when she is in Venice.

But it will not come. There is a restlessness inside her that cannot be appeased by her job, which, until this tour, has given her much satisfaction; nor by the Serenissima herself, where Callie has in the past felt more at home than anywhere else.

She sits in the empty dark for a long time, as if waiting for an omen, but none appears. She only begins to stir when a dark-robed priest materializes at her side and tells her gently that it is seven o'clock and time to shut the church.

Callie goes downstairs to breakfast the next morning to find Signor Alberti waiting to pounce. Before she can get to the dining room he waylays her in his office, raging in Venetian dialect. Callie knows he can speak and understand English perfectly well when he chooses, but that often he chooses not to, to make a point.

After a few minutes the dialect turns into Italian, and Callie knows he is finally calming down. Callie can understand him now; he is raging over something her group members have said, demanding that Comet Trail Travel do something with them before he goes completely crazy.

'Signor Alberti, *per favore, mi ascolti*, listen to me,' Callie says, when she can finally get a word in. 'We have a problem, in that I cannot do anything for you until I know exactly what my group members have been saying.'

'*Madonna, madre di Dio*, you do not know? This is the last time, *veramente*, that I have one of your tour groups here. I would rather starve, you understand? Starve!'

'*Capisco*, I understand. Now please, tell me what this is all about.'

'Before breakfast, they attack me. *Cos'e quell'-odore?* they want to know. Odour? In my hotel? Never!'

'*Signore*,' Callie says gently, 'they were telling the truth. There was definitely an odour in the hotel last night; I myself smelled it.'

Signor Alberti draws himself up with great dignity. 'Does not the great city of London smell occasionally, in hot weather? Do not all cities smell? It is the nature of a city after all. What do these English tourists want? Venice should smell like lilies at all times? They are dredging the canal down the *calle*; there is always an odour when a canal is dredged. Do you want the canals

in Venice to silt up completely, just to please your English tourists?'

He raves on in this manner for several more minutes, until Signora Alberti appears. Callie tells her what has happened. 'It is the drains,' the *signora* says enigmatically, nodding her head sagely. It is always the drains in Venice, Callie thinks wearily. But the *signora* ensures her that the trouble is gone now, and indeed the rain of last night has washed the air clean; from the open door of the hotel it smells fresh, flowery.

Later, on the walkway of the Fondamente Nuove, Callie muses, more to herself than to Patsy, 'Smell the air. Lovely, after the rain. Interesting how no-one comments on *that*.'

Patsy is looking round impatiently. They are waiting for their groups to assemble, to catch a boat to the island of Murano. Once again Angela and Deirdre are late. Sylvester, yawning, says, 'I thought you told us to meet here at ten. It's now ten fifteen. I could've had another cuppa back at the hotel, not that the tea's anything to write home about, bloody awful muck they call tea here. Coffee's not much better, lukewarm and muddy.' He beams with satisfaction, having found and passed on the first complaint of the day. Several of the other members of the group, who hadn't noticed anything wrong with their own breakfast drinks, begin to feel a glimmer of discontent: perhaps they have missed something; perhaps the breakfast was not, after all, as adequate as it had seemed.

'What *is* he wearing?' Patsy says when Sylvester is out of earshot. 'Those trousers are the colour of puppy-dog shit, and he's got a T-shirt the same colour. Does he dress like this at the college he works at? What do lab technicians do, exactly?'

'Cut up rats, I suppose.'

'Takes one to know one. Does he really?'

'He did when he was in the science department,

86

prepared poor dead things for dissection by the students. He's been transferred to the art department now, he says, in charge of all the equipment, video recorders and cameras and things.'

'Lucky he left the science lab before someone dissected *him*. It would have been a natural mistake.'

Patsy looks at her watch. 'This is ridiculous, they are now twenty minutes late. I'm going to have to get my group on the next boat, it's not fair making them wait round any longer. I'll see you in Murano.'

'We'll come with you if they're not here by then. It's not fair to my group either.'

Cries of greetings, of relief that they have not gone yet, interrupt them. It is not, however, Angela and Deirdre, but Archie, limping along between Pogo and Lavender. The Americans are again wearing identical clothing, but this time yellow, knee-length shorts, yellow T-shirts and the same white trainers. Pogo's legs look like the legs of tiny white birds, while Lavender's are heavy but surprisingly firm and solid. Archie, in his light summer suit and a shirt with no tie, looks old-fashioned and formal next to them.

'We found him in the Campo dei Miracoli, sitting all by himself,' Lavender cries, clutching Archie's arm as if he were about to make a run for it.

'Resting my hip, my dear,' Archie says with dignity. 'And looking at the Miracoli, my favourite church in Venice. All that exquisite marble. Ruskin says—'

'Yes, yes,' Pogo interrupts excitedly. 'It's our favourite, too, but you had intended to go to Murano.'

'He was real keen last night, when we had a drink together,' Lavender volunteers to whoever will listen. 'He wanted to see the glass workshops and the museum.'

'Did you change your mind, Archie?' Callie asks gently. 'Your name wasn't on the list this morning.'

'My hip was causing me some discomfort, so I felt I'd be a handicap to you and the group.'

Lavender and Pogo both begin protesting at once, saying that how could Archie *ever* consider himself a handicap to anyone, and that *of course* he was going to Murano with the group, and that they, personally, would come along as well, to keep him company if he lagged behind. 'We'll keep an eye on ol' Archie here,' Pogo cries as Lavender nods her white head vigorously in agreement.

Patsy and Callie exchange looks and try not to smile. 'The blind leading the blind,' Patsy mutters, and indeed, Pogo and Lavender look fully ten or twelve years older than Archie.

The *motonave* is at the quay, and as they are about to board, Callie sees Deirdre and Angela hurrying along the Fondamente Nuove. Deirdre is full of apologies, and the vamp is complaining loudly about the early hour.

It's a large boat, and fairly empty. Everyone troops to the deck upstairs to get a better view of the lagoon. As the *motonave* pulls away from the Fondamente Nuove, there is a shout from Ellen. 'Oh stop, stop! We've left Candice.'

'What? But I counted the right number getting into the boat. Nineteen signed up to go to the island.'

'You must have counted me,' Dexter says. 'I had a spot of tummy trouble, so I didn't sign up, but at the last minute felt better, and here I am!'

Callie looks at him with open-mouthed frustration.

'I thought Candice was right behind me,' Ellen says, adding drily, 'she usually is.'

'Well, we can't turn the boat round. She'll have to wait for the next one. It won't be long.'

'She will be distraught. Venice terrifies her. So do most things, but that's another story. She'll be waiting on the Fondamente Nuove frozen with fear, until someone comes to collect her. It will have to be me, I suppose.'

Ellen sounds so regretful that Callie says, 'No, you

stay and look round the island and I'll go back for her. We were going to visit the glass museum first, so if I tell you where it is, the group can go ahead and I will meet you there. I was just going to let everyone wander about the museum on their own anyway; it's all self-explanatory.'

Ellen feels that she should go back herself, that Candice is her responsibility, like her husband Ralph, like her family, like the endless people who have always relied on her. She is about to say so, but then glances at Archie, sitting with Pogo and Lavender near the open sides of the boat. Archie catches her eye and motions for her to join them. Something turns inside Ellen: a worm, perhaps? she thinks with a wry smile. Turning back to Callie she says warmly, 'Thank you, I would so love to stay in Murano and not rush back for Candice.'

Feeling slightly disoriented, as if she has just shed a second skin, along with the tights she abandoned this morning, Ellen joins the other three. Pogo, who has been facing the water, suddenly turns to her, and she jumps, shrieks slightly. 'Oh gosh, didn't mean to scare you,' he says, voice muffled behind a papier-mâché mask. It is one of the typical Venetian masks sold in countless tiny shops, a carnival mask, the Plague Doctor with his sinister white face and his long beak. 'Do you like it?' he asks, still behind the mask, and Ellen finds that his voice, usually so amiable and good-humoured, has altered, taken on the eerie quality of the mask.

'Spooky,' she says frankly.

Pogo chuckles, takes off the mask and is himself again. 'Lavender and I bought it for one of our grand-sons, just before we found Archie.' He puts the mask away in its plastic bag.

'I have to say,' Lavender laughs, 'I like you lots better without it, honey.' She snuggles up to him and he pats her hand.

Archie says to Ellen, 'Are you returning for your friend when we get to Murano?'

'No, I'm being wickedly irresponsible.' Ellen grins widely, feeling suddenly relaxed, happy.

Archie says, without thinking, 'How different you look when you smile.'

How different we all are when we take off the masks, Ellen would like to say, but contents herself with another smile. Archie, at whom it is aimed, is dazzled. After four years of living alone after the death of his wife, of solitary days and nights, of lonely package holidays, there is suddenly this: two long-lost friends who appear to enjoy his company, and an attractive woman who has smiled at him twice in the past five minutes.

He looks out into the waters of the lagoon, quivering and translucent, like a bowl of green jelly. They are passing the cemetery island of San Michele, the dark cypresses and high terracotta walls are clear and sharp, as is the air after last night's rain. It is pleasantly warm today, the sky a hearty clean blue. 'There now,' Lavender cries. 'Archie, aren't you glad we dragged you along?'

'Oh indeed, yes, oh yes. I cannot tell you how pleased I am to be here.' He looks fondly at the three of them, and foolishly, without warning, his eyes fill with grateful tears. Turning away abruptly, so that no-one will see, he keeps his eyes fixed on the open water.

Callie finds Candice exactly where Ellen said, waiting piteously on the Fondamente Nuove. 'But where's Ellen?' she cries.

'There was no need for us both to fetch you,' Callie says, trying to hide her irritation. Why Candice couldn't have taken the next boat to Murano on her own was beyond her. The thought had apparently never even occurred to Candice, as Ellen knew it would not.

'Oh Callie, I've been so upset! I was feeling

somewhat queasy, so I sat down on the bench to shut my eyes for a moment. I never dreamed Ellen would leave me.'

They get on the next *motonave*, and Candice, with a rush of confidence in her relief that she has been rescued, says, 'I am really quite surprised that Ellen did not come back with you to find me. My Rodney would be upset about that; perhaps I ought not tell him. He only let me go to Venice because Ellen was going. "She is completely reliable, completely responsible," he said before I left. I was rather nervous, you see.'

'About what?'

Candice looks at Callie as if she were slightly simple. 'About Italy, of course. One hears so much.' She presses her lips firmly together, as if she has said enough.

The short journey back to Murano seems endless for Callie, but they finally arrive. Trying to hustle Candice along, she goes into the tiny glass museum, to the cool and slightly scruffy courtyard where she has arranged to meet her group. Four or five cats, of all sizes, colours and shapes, recline on a stone wall, beneath some overgrown wisteria. Great pots with unidentifiable plants are placed haphazardly round the cracked stone pavement. The cats stretch, yawn and look completely at home. Callie cannot resist stroking the glossy black female before facing her group in the courtyard.

She is later than she had intended, and they have finished in the museum and are all waiting for her. She does a hurried count and says, 'Where is Angela?'

Deirdre, who has been sitting on the massive stone well-head in the courtyard, along with Pogo and Lavender, says, 'She decided not to come to the museum. Said she needed a drink.'

Something in her voice is not quite right. Lavender catches Callie's eye and shakes her head warningly. Archie and Ellen are sitting together on the opposite

wall, watching Deirdre sombrely. Candice joins them, but Ellen doesn't look particularly grateful to be reunited with her friend.

Deirdre has been crying, Callie is sure of it. The other group members are looking at her with odd expressions on their faces, some with sympathy, others with disapproval. Callie asks quietly, 'What's wrong?'

To her consternation, Deirdre begins to cry again. Pogo and Lavender start to fuss over her, but Callie leads her away from the others and sits her down next to the cats. Sylvester, his face avid with curiosity, appoaches them, but Callie says, 'I think I'd better talk to Deirdre alone.' The cats look up lazily, and the ginger one begins washing himself. Callie feels a great longing to curl up in the middle of them to be stroked and petted and fussed over.

'What's happened?' she says to Deirdre.

'Sorry, I'm being stupid, it's nothing really; I'm afraid I'm over-reacting. It's just Angela. She made a dreadful scene, so embarrassing. I don't know what I'd have done without Pogo and Lavender; they somehow rescued me, pulled me away from her.'

'What do you mean? How did it start?'

'So stupid, all of it. She wanted to skip the museum and go for a drink. I happen to be very fond of anything made of glass and wanted to see some of the older work. I mean, imagine coming to the most famous glass-blowing island in the world and not seeing any samples of antique glass.'

'Did you tell Angela that?'

'Of course, but she couldn't see it.'

'Why did she need you? Couldn't she get a coffee or whatever on her own?'

'She hates being alone. Needs people round her constantly. She made a scene. Right in the foyer here, as we were trooping in and Ellen was buying the tickets for the group with the money you gave her. Angela can't cope with not getting her own way and she . . .

well, she was very unpleasant, shouted and swore; some dreadful language, I'm afraid. In the end the museum guard asked her to leave.'

'Good Lord, it must have pretty bad. Where is she now?'

'God knows.'

Callie gets up. She doesn't need this, not now, not with the rest of the group looking restless and unhappy. She's desperately sorry for Deirdre, but she cannot get involved in the dynamics of the young woman's relationship with her mother. She has an equal responsibility to all of them.

'Well, Angela will get over it; she'll have to, won't she,' Callie says firmly. 'I'm sorry she took it out on you in such a dreadful way. But hopefully you had a good look at the glass?' She goes over to the cats and strokes the black one again. 'I wish I could have a cat,' she says sadly, talking to herself again, for Deirdre has rejoined Lavender and Pogo. 'Even more than a pot plant.'

She goes to her group and does another count. 'Who's missing, besides Angela?'

Minnie, sour-faced, says, 'Dexter. I don't know why he isn't back yet. When Angela stormed out of here in a snit, he noticed she'd dropped her guidebook and ran off after her to return it. We can't leave until he gets back, or he won't know where we are. I can't think what has happened; he's been gone at least an hour. I went all over the museum without him, and he has our camera, too. I suppose he's got lost, looking for that woman. Dexter is just too kind for his own good.'

Callie listens to this tirade in dismay. Before she decides what to do, the glass doors leading into the courtyard open and both Dexter and Angela appear. Angela looks smug, Dexter sheepish and rather flushed. 'Here we are!' Angela cries. 'Dexter was so sweet, catching up with me to return my Dorling

Kindersley; such a marvellous guidebook, I'd have been lost without it. I insisted on buying him a cappuccino to thank him.'

Dexter slinks over to Minnie, whose mouth is unappealingly slack, so great is her surprise. Angela breezes over to Deirdre and talks to her as if nothing has happened. Callie says wearily, 'Shall we be off, then?'

The rest of the morning is not a success. Angela is ebullient with goodwill, which only makes the other group members sulky and suspicious. Deirdre is silent, stoic. Callie takes them to a glass-blowing workshop, but by now everyone feels rushed, hungry, disgruntled. Callie leaves them in the shop adjacent to the workshop; here the collective spirit of the group picks up slightly when confronted with garishly coloured glass objects: bright-blue dolphins on stands, gaudy parrots, flamboyant chandeliers as multi-coloured as Joseph's coat. 'There are many more shops, some with lovely beads, jewellery, glassware,' Callie tells them, but though some listen and take down the names of the glass manufacturers she recommends, most in this particular group are content with the kitsch.

She leaves them to find their own, rather late, lunch and arranges to meet them in a couple of hours. She hasn't seen Patsy's group, nor did she have time to arrange with Patsy whether or not they would be meeting for lunch, so she goes into a small food shop she knows just over the bridge in front of the glass factory. Here there is a comforting smell of warm bread, melted cheese and coffee being made in the back kitchen. '*Buongiorno*,' she says to the woman who owns the shop, a big woman with a white apron and slippers on her swollen feet.

'Ah, *buongiorno, come va*?' The woman smiles in recognition, for Callie has been coming into her shop since her first tour to Murano, years ago now.

'*Molto bene, grazie*,' Callie replies, thinking, I know

this woman, this stranger, better than I know the shop-keepers in my own town. I know about her arthritic feet, her husband who is a fisherman, her neighbour, who is often in here for a chat.

They exchange pleasantries, and Callie buys a mas-sive slice of cold pizza and two small bottles of chilled beer, feeling the need for something slightly alcoholic after her unrelaxing morning. She takes this down a narrow side alley, away from the tourists and the countless shops selling Murano glass, and within a few minutes she's in a tree-shaded square full of cherry-red benches overflowing with island residents: Italian housewives, stopping with their laden shopping carts for a gossip; children riding tricycles; old men gravely talking politics. She finds a free bench in the shade of an elm tree, and has just taken her pizza slice out of the brown-paper bag when Deirdre, full of apologies, comes up and sits beside her.

'Look, I know it's your lunch hour, I know you need to be away from us sometimes, but I had to talk to you. I want to apologize for my mother.'

Callie, munching pizza, says, 'It's all right, forget it. It's finished. And it wasn't you that made the trouble anyway.'

'It was in a way. I should have gone with her.'

'Why? You wanted to see the glass. Look, have some of this pizza, I can't eat it all.'

'She pays me. That's why.' The bitterness in her voice makes Callie stop eating to look at her. 'She pays me to be her personal assistant, as she calls it. And I need the money.'

Callie starts to say something, but Deirdre interrupts with, 'Look, I don't want to talk about it. I just want to say sorry, and warn you that she has a volatile temper, but gets over it just as quickly. I'll try to keep her lid on anyway. And if there are any problems, see me first, and I'll try to sort her out. It's my job.'

'Where is Angela now?'

'Oh, shopping, of course. Her favourite pastime in Italy. Well, anywhere. It's the only time she likes to be on her own.' She gets up. 'Look, sorry to hassle you during your lunch break. I'll go now.'

Callie, mourning her free time, knows she cannot let Deirdre go like this. 'Look, sit down again. Here, I've torn off half this pizza; this slice is so huge I can't finish it. And have a beer. I bought two bottles, must have known I'd have company for lunch. Unless, of course, you want to go somewhere proper and eat. Doesn't Angela have lunch?'

'She's too busy shopping. And she's dieting, as usual.' Deirdre, with huge relief, collapses gratefully onto the bench, takes a bit of pizza and a beer, and looks round her. 'Pleasant, this.'

'Yes, it's my favourite square in Murano. I love to sit and watch the people.'

A bent, white-haired man is standing in front of them, watching a young boy, his grandson or even great-grandson, precariously trying to ride a brand-new bicycle. The man helps him on when he falls, and shouts words of encouragement each time he tries again. Others gather round, give advice and bolster his confidence. When the boy finally gets the hang of it and belts proudly round the square, there is a burst of applause and shouts of 'bravo' from the men and women scattered round on the four benches.

Deirdre smiles as the boy rides jauntily about the *campo*, passing them with a grin. When she smiles her thin face lights up, curves attractively. She needs some roundness, Callie thinks, the lines of her face, her body, are pencil straight. Her hair is fine, shoulder-length, with not a wave in it, her pale fringe cut as if with a ruler right across her forehead. Her body too is angular, and her clothes are cut straight, severely. She can only be in her mid to late twenties, Callie thinks, but looks older.

Deirdre catches her scrutiny and says, to deflect her,

'Is your name really short for Calypso? That's such a lovely name.'

Startled, Callie says, 'Now where did you hear that?'

Deirdre looks embarrassed. 'I heard that man in the wine bar call you Calypso. Or rather outside, on the tiny bridge over the canal. I didn't mean to eavesdrop, only Angela and I were standing behind Sylvester, trying to find the church of San Trovaso. I suppose you didn't notice us behind our map.'

'No, I didn't.'

Callie is silent for a moment. This reminder of her complete lack of privacy on a tour rankles, and she knows it shouldn't. It's my job, she tells herself. On a tour I no longer belong to myself, but to my group.

'Angela certainly noticed *him*. She thought he was dishy.' Deirdre takes another long swig of beer.

Callie has to laugh. 'He is, I suppose. He's also married, and Italian – though he lives in England – and no, my name is *not* Calypso, it's Carolyn. I suspect he called me that because he's a wanderer, and wanderers sometimes need reasons not to return home.'

Deirdre is looking perplexed, but interested. 'They need sirens, you see,' Callie explains. 'They need a Calypso to keep them from returning to their faithful wives, their Penelopes waiting at home. But Calypso never wins. They go back in the end.'

Deirdre says perceptively, 'You sound very fond of this Italian.'

The empathy in her voice is soothing, tempting, like the siren's song, but Callie has already said too much. 'I hardly know him,' she says quietly, and Deirdre knows the subject is closed.

Callie throws a bit of pizza crust to the pigeons, and the birds quickly flock round her. The boy with the bicycle rides up proudly, if a bit wobbly, and stops and watches. '*Vuoi del pane, per gli uccelli?*' she asks him, giving him some of her crust to feed the birds. The boy takes it and smiles at her gratefully as he tries to entice

the pigeons to take it from his hand. Deirdre is looking at the boy intensely, strangely, and to Callie's surprise, she looks as if she's about to cry again.

'What's wrong, Deirdre?'

'I'm sorry. Look, I'll go, leave you in peace.'

'For Christ's sake, sit down. Here, have a tissue, I've got one somewhere.'

The boy, sensing warily Deirdre's sudden intensity of mood, cycles away, causing the pigeons to fly noisily into the trees and onto the buildings. Deirdre says, 'That boy. He reminds me so much of my daughter.'

'Your daughter?'

'She's about his age, too, maybe younger. Four.' Deirdre sniffles, blows her nose.

'Where is she?'

'Home, in England. Staying with friends. I hated leaving her, but Angela refused to take her along, said she needed a proper holiday without kids. And Angela insisted I come; she won't travel without me. Well, either me or a man, but she hasn't one in tow now.' She makes a strange sound, half bitter laughter, half sob. 'Nor do I, so I shouldn't talk. Kathy's father left me before she was born, I haven't a clue where he is now. We live with Angela, you see. She supports us both.'

Callie leans back on the bench and closes her eyes for a moment. She mistrusts these moments, when a tour member confides in her as if they were old friends. It's a false intimacy, based on illusion, on complete strangers who have nothing in common being thrown together for twenty-four hours a day for a short period of time. Very often the confidences are regretted later.

Despite this, she opens her eyes, turns to Deirdre and says, 'Why do you stay with Angela? You're young, healthy, you can get a job and a place to live somewhere else. I know it would be terribly hard, but

thousands of single mothers do it. There's day care, childminders—'

'She's all I've got,' Deirdre cries.

'Hey, calm down, OK? It was only a suggestion.'

Deirdre is so agitated that others in the *campo* are looking at them, wondering what is wrong. Her voice is strained as she says, 'My father left Angela six months after I was born. I've seen him once, tracked him down, to tell him he had a granddaughter, but he didn't want to know us. Angela gives us a home, and a job that I can do from there, where I can look after Kathy myself. I don't want her with childminders.'

'It's sometimes necessary,' Callie says gently.

'I didn't have parents, OK? You've seen Angela, she's been the same since I can remember. How can you count her as a parent? I grew up alone and fast, far too quickly. I'm not going to leave my daughter to the same fate. I want her to have a family, even if that family is only me.'

As they have been talking, the boy on the bicycle has come back with some crusts of bread, which he has found somewhere. He offers them to Callie and Deirdre shyly. '*Per gli uccelli.*' For the birds.

Together the three of them scatter the crumbs and the pigeons quickly recongregate. The boy's grandfather has been joined by his wife, and the two amble over, exchange a few words, and are pleased to hear Callie speak Italian. The old man puts one hand on the boy's shoulder, the other round his wife's, says it is time to go home to lunch. '*Arrivederci,*' the boy calls back to them as he cycles away, his grandparents slowly following.

Callie says, and the words surprise not Deirdre, but herself, 'I thought that was what I didn't want: what those two old people have. I bet that all their loved ones, family, friends, live right on this island, and have for generations. Just like my parents in their village, and I hated it. But I'd forgotten about people. If you're

forever pulling up roots and starting again, you lose people along the way. Those three . . .' Callie gestures towards the old couple and child. 'No partings, no goodbyes, no meeting people and learning to like or even love them, and then watching them disappear from your life for ever.'

Deirdre doesn't say anything, but nods sympathetically. 'Oh shit,' Callie says, 'I'm getting maudlin. Oh hell, I shouldn't swear in front of the clients.'

An ungrateful pigeon, having just eaten a good deal of Callie's pizza, flies up into a tree overhead and shits on the comet on her Comet Trail Travel regulation white blouse. 'Oh fuck,' Callie says.

Deirdre grins, then Callie does, then they both begin to giggle. 'If you knew what hell these are to wash and iron. Trust Comet Trail to give us uniforms that are impossible to travel in.' They both laugh again as Callie tries to wipe the mess off with a tissue.

When it's time to go back and meet the others, Deirdre says, 'Thanks for sharing your lunch hour with me. I haven't been so relaxed since this tour started.'

'I enjoyed it, too,' Callie says, amazed that this is true. Usually the last thing she wants to do is spend free time with her group members. Pleasant and interesting though many of them are, they are still clients, still strangers. Too much time with strangers, however nice, can be extremely wearing. Lonely too, in the end.

As they head back into the centre of Murano, Deirdre says, 'Can I come up to your room sometime? Show you some photos of Kathy?' Her voice is sad, pleading.

Callie, knowing she shouldn't, struggling to maintain her professional detachment, without which she cannot cope with her job, of course says yes.

That night Callie sits and nibbles bread sticks in the Hotel Isabella while her group eat *lasagne verdi*. She is able to get away by nine o'clock, and runs out into the Campo Santo Stefano and round the corner to the Riva

Toma. Patsy is in her room, sitting on the floor and calmly painting her toenails.

'I thought I was supposed to pick you up at nine,' Callie says.

'This won't take long. I bought some sandals today and they absolutely require scarlet toenails.' Patsy paints the last nail and waves her toes in the air to dry.

Her new shoes do not surprise Callie, who by now has got used to the strange paradox of plain, square Patsy, who never wears make-up, whose clothes are unimaginative to the point of dullness, but whose feet are pampered and indulged in a manner that hints at obsession. Indeed, they are well shaped and attractive, unmarked by age, or the hours she spends standing on them. Her one luxury is expensive Italian shoes, which she spends hours of her free time finding. Callie admires the sandals which, though low-heeled and obviously comfortable, have elegant silver straps and two discreet buckles round the ankles.

'Don't look so edgy,' Patsy says. 'I told Giovanni we'd be there anytime between nine and half-past. You said their place is only across the bridge. Sit down for a minute, relax.'

But Callie cannot. She paces the floor, looks at herself impatiently in Patsy's full-length mirror, wondering if she should have worn her long black summer dress instead of the short flowery print she has chosen. 'Is my dress too sheer? ' she asks Patsy anxiously. 'It's such a thin cotton.'

'You look great. Too good for a married man.' Patsy begins to put on her sandals.

'I'm not interested in married men, you know that,' Callie snaps.

'Touchy, touchy!'

'Sorry. Don't know what's up with me. I found myself telling Deirdre — you know, the Vamp from Hell's daughter — first about Tommaso, then at great length about the loneliness of touring, something I've

never ever felt before. It must be bloody Venice, getting to me at last. I'm going to tell head office to scrap Venice for me, for a year or two; I want my next year's tours to be somewhere less ephemeral, less watery. Somewhere solid, built on rocks and earth, substantial.'

'Maybe you should.' Patsy stands up and admires her feet in the mirror. 'Hm, love these shoes.'

'Doesn't the city get to you sometimes?'

'Not often,' Patsy admits.

'It's not *real*. It's all about a splendour and glory that doesn't exist any more. It's a constant reminder that nothing, *nothing*, is permanent. Doesn't it bother you?'

'Not much.'

'But then you have permanence in your life, as you said the other day. You have a husband.'

'Yup,' Patsy grunts. 'And a good job, like you.' She gives her toenails one last critical look. 'I'm ready, should we go?'

The two women walk out of the hotel and back into the Campo Santo Stefano, zigzagging across the square to avoid various members of their groups, and crossing over the Accademia bridge. It is not yet dark, but a deep twilight hangs in the air like soft velvet drapes. Above the domes of the Salute pale clouds are slowly being glazed with pink. The Grand Canal is quiet, all traffic momentarily stopped, and the only sound is the lapping water against the buildings on either side of the bridge, and the calling of swallows as they fly over the water in great swirls of motion. They can hear their own footsteps in the silence. Inside Callie something is deeply touched. She knows she can never ask not to return to Venice.

'There is the *palazzo*, where we are dining tonight,' Callie says, pointing to the right. 'The one with the two pillars and the archway on the water. You can see into the courtyard, and look, there is the terrace balcony, just above the water.'

As she says this, she sees someone come out on the balcony and light a candle on the table. He looks up, as if expecting to see her there on the bridge, and spots her and waves.

She waves back. Patsy is already beginning to walk on, but Callie stays leaning against the railing for another moment, looking at Tommaso. Then, slowly, she follows Patsy down the other side of the bridge towards Ca'Valier.

6

Callie and Patsy ring the bell of the massive front doors. Though the front of the *palazzo* is on the water, the back leads on to a small *calle* by a side canal. 'Do you know,' Patsy says, 'that just about the only casualties Venice had in the last war were the two hundred civilians that fell into the canals during blackouts. You can see why.'

Callie laughs. 'That's why you're a better tour leader than I am: all these wealth of facts at your fingertips.'

Patsy laughs, too. 'I can't stop it, can I?'

'I hope you're not going to lecture the Venturi brothers on Venice.'

'Maybe just on Goldoni. I've picked up enough facts about him to impress even my least impressionable punters.'

They are both still giggling, feeling girlish and high-spirited on their first proper social evening event away from work, when one of the heavy black doors is opened and Tommaso appears. Callie's laughter is the first thing he registers, and it moves him again, so much so that he holds her hand too long in greeting. Finally he pulls himself away to greet Patsy. '*Ciao*, Patsy. Welcome to Ca'Valier.' He is still wearing his prescription sunglasses, Callie notices, though the night is darkening rapidly.

There is a scent of wisteria in the night air, mingling with jasmine from the garden. Giovanni, in pale-blue jeans, a white shirt and a beige jacket, is in the kitchen putting fresh sage leaves in a pan of

butter, to fry quickly for the pasta later. He kisses them hurriedly and says, 'Some last-minute preparations to the antipasti. Tommaso will take you on the terrace for drinks, and I shall join you in a moment.'

On the balcony, Patsy exclaims over the view. The Grand Canal is bustling now, with two *vaporetti* heading in opposite directions converging on the Accademia landing stage, and a flotilla of six or seven gondolas, crammed with Japanese tourists, floating right in front of their perch. The gondolas are grouped together so the passengers can see and hear the musicians in the centre one, an accordianist, a fiddler and an elderly Italian singing – not badly – 'Santa Lucia'. When the song ends, the gondola passengers applaud, and so do Tommaso, Patsy and Callie. One of the gondoliers shouts up, '*Ciao, Tommaso*,' and waves. Tommaso waves back and the gondolas drift away down the canal.

He brings them drinks from the drawing room just inside: Campari and fresh orange juice for himself and Callie, and a gin and tonic for Patsy. 'Giovanni is drinking prosecco in the kitchen. It is obligatory when he's cooking for special guests.'

Giovanni joins them. It's quite dark now, and the lights on the canal gleam and glisten on the black water. There are some, not many, lights on in the windows of the *palazzi* up and down the canal, but many are dark, empty. On the water itself, the dim red light of a solitary gondola lights the darkness. 'This beats the Hotel Riva Tomá,' Patsy says. 'Some place you've got here, Giovanni.'

Tommaso is setting the table on the terrace. 'We need more candles,' he says, indicating the solitary flame cradled in a blue glass holder. 'I'll get some.' When he returns, Callie sees that he has changed his glasses. They are ordinary clear lenses in tortoiseshell frames, and they somehow make him look more English, less

Italian. The colour of his eyes is still obscured in the darkness.

Giovanni is delighted with his guests, for all three eat with abandon. They begin with prosciutto and fresh figs, which disappear at once, and the next course, *spaghetti alle vongole*, is set upon in an appreciative silence. 'I bought the clams fresh this morning, at the Rialto market,' Giovanni says.

'Bliss,' Patsy says with her mouth full.

There's salad of rocket leaves and tomatoes to accompany the meal, and a couple of bottles of prosecco. For dessert there is crème caramel. 'Ohh,' Patsy sighs with pleasure. 'I do love puddings.'

Later, when the table is cleared and they are drinking espresso, Callie says, 'Do you always cook like that, Giovanni? It was delicious.'

'Always I have three courses.'

'Even when you are alone?'

'Especially then. It is so easy to let oneself go when one is alone.' He looks thoughtfully out into the night. A few stars are out, competing with the sparse lights on the canal. Callie cannot imagine Giovanni ever letting himself go, over anything.

Giovanni looks at Tommaso and a soft arrow of affection darts between the two brothers. Giovanni says, 'Of course, it is much better with Tommaso here. He accommodates my love of food, of cooking.'

'He means I eat everything I see in front of me,' Tommaso grins.

After a few comfortably silent moments, Patsy says, 'Giovanni, did you ever find that reference of Goldoni's, the remark he was supposed to have made to that actor? You mentioned it yesterday and said you had hoped to track it down.'

Giovanni leaps from his chair on the terrace with great excitement. 'Ah, Patsy, of course, I have not told you yet. It was the great Pantalone actor of the *Commedia dell'Arte d'Arbes*, whom Goldoni was

speaking to. Come with me to my study and I will show you what I have found.'

They disappear together into the house. 'I still can't get over those two,' Callie says. 'Such an odd friendship.'

Tommaso shrugs. 'Ah, Callie, all friendships are strange, eh? People, too. When I first met Patsy yesterday I would not have thought she was a woman to paint her toenails scarlet. Or wear silver sandals.'

Callie looks at him curiously. 'You are very observant.'

'I have to be, in my job. So much can go wrong with underwater work, and ultimately I am responsible.'

There is a long moment of silence between them, punctuated by the soft lapping of the water against the building. The scent of jasmine and wisteria, still lightly palpable, mingles with the smell of the water, of wet brick and marble, of the lilies still placed in their bowl on the table inside the open door. It is almost too much, too rich, too sensual after the wine, the food, the hypnotic canal and Tommaso's presence, which is permeating Callie's skin, mingling with her blood and bones. She stands up and goes to the balustrade enclosing the terrace. Tommaso stands up, too, and leans over the wall with her. It is high tide, and the five or six steps that go down from the courtyard to the water are completely covered. From somewhere in the distance comes the sound of a boat's horn.

'I was wrong to come here,' Callie says. 'I don't want to leave.'

'Then don't,' Tommaso says. 'Don't.'

'It's even harder to leave places if you let yourself become too attached to them.'

Whatever Tommaso starts to say is lost as Patsy and Giovanni return to the terrace. Patsy says, 'Callie, do you know the time? We'd better get back. At least there haven't been any urgent phone calls for us here, any

emergencies. Hopefully our lot are all tucked up and asleep in their respective hotels.'

The brothers walk them home. It is well after midnight, but there are still people lingering on the street, mostly couples who cannot tear themselves away from the soft Venetian night. 'I have to say,' Patsy announces as they walk through the lamplit Campo Santo Stefano, 'that Venice is not a bad place for lovers.'

She says this so detachedly, so pragmatically, that the other three laugh. And once again Tommaso hears that laugh with a longing he cannot remember ever having experienced.

'*Arrivederci*, Callie,' Giovanni says as he kisses her cheeks at the steps of the Hotel Isabella.

'See you tomorrow,' Patsy says. The Hotel Riva Tomá is further on, just off the *campo*.

Callie says goodbye to Patsy then turns to Giovanni. '*Ciao,* Giovanni. Splendid meal. *Molte grazie.*'

'*Prègo. Ciao!*' He and Patsy begin to walk away towards her hotel.

Callie turns to Tommaso. '*Arrivederci*, Tommaso.'

'*Ciao*, Calypso.' They stand a moment, facing each other. Tommaso kisses Callie, as she knew he would, and it is not a kiss on both cheeks as it was when he greeted her, which is also as she had anticipated. He says, 'Please. Can I come in with you?'

Callie does not let herself think. She turns and walks inside, knowing he will follow her. She gets her key from the all-night receptionist, who is new and doesn't know her, and she goes down the corridor to her room on the ground floor. Tommaso is right behind her.

Her spartan room is cell-like in its tidiness, its lack of clutter or personal momentoes. A window overlooks a tiny garden crowded with unkempt shrubs and a solitary mimosa tree. Callie opens the shutters, then the window. A light drizzle has begun to fall. Still without letting herself think, she turns to Tommaso. She is

aware of the sweet scent of mimosa, released by the rain, as they make love for the first time.

It is four thirty, the first pale light of morning creaming the night sky. Through the open window comes a cool breeze, and the first tentative calling of birds. 'Tommaso, wake up,' Callie says. 'You must go.'

He stirs, opens his naked eyes. 'Green,' Callie says softly. 'They are green.'

They focus myopically on her, warm with a sleepy smile. His hands reach for her and pull her down again onto the bed.

But Callie is thinking now. 'Please, Tommaso, get up, get dressed. It's getting light.'

'I love the light, I can see you in it,' he says, taking in the sculpture of her body, its curves and angles, its mixture of white and brown, the places where she has been exposed to the sun juxtaposed with those which have remained under cover.

But she is already putting on a dressing gown and handing him his clothes. 'I've never done this before, I don't know what possessed me. Sneaking a man into my room like, like . . . like I don't know what!' Words fail her. She is a professional tour manager, she has never mixed her lovers and her job; nor indeed has she mixed friendships with work. Both end unfortunately every time. Friends made on a tour turn out to be totally different back home; they fall into their allotted roles, put on the masks, are not the people they were on holiday.

Friends made at home in England were just as difficult to keep. Callie had tried, when she first acquired the house in Kent, to join a local film club, and met a few kindred souls there. One or two of them had invited her out, but the busy summer season had begun and she'd had to refuse. By the time winter came and things had slowed slightly, Callie found that she had, understandably, been forgotten by her new

109

acquaintances, and by then she didn't have the energy to begin again the slow process of making friends. She was tired, drained after months of travelling, of being constantly with strangers, and needed the slack season to find some space and time alone, to recover.

And lovers. Callie glances at Tommaso as he puts on his clothes and wonders what she is doing, becoming involved with a man while on tour. She has always had strict rules about this. Once, she became infatuated with the newly divorced manager of the hotel in Seville where she was working, but though he seemed to be reciprocating her affection, she scrupulously avoided him. When the tour ended, she took advantage of the week's break she had and stayed in Spain instead of going back to England. She and the Spaniard had had a tumultuous affair, but it had burned itself out as quickly as it had begun.

After that, she has been careful not to become involved with anyone connected with her work. It has been over a year now since there's been a man in her life. She tells herself that this is why she fell into bed with Tommaso so quickly, though she knows it's deeper than that. She says to him now, 'This is strictly against Comet Trail rules, against the hotel rules, against *my* rules. I was a little crazy last night. I hope that new night receptionist doesn't remember you, doesn't realize you aren't a guest.'

'We both broke some rules last night. More important ones than hotel rules.'

Callie stops walking round the room and looks at him sombrely. 'Yes. We did.' She means to say, And it will not happen again. But she doesn't. Instead, she says rather bitterly, 'But you're used to breaking rules, aren't you. Remember you've already told me that you've cheated on your wife before. This is the first time I've broken *my* rule. I told you from the beginning I don't sleep with married men.' She turns and walks to the window. A tabby cat is staring at a sparrow

sitting on a broken stone urn covered in damp vines. She says, 'I should say, I *didn't.*'

He does not touch her, nor does he move nearer to her as he says, 'I've had affairs, Callie. I'm not going to try to justify those to you. But I did have one very important rule myself. Not to get involved, not to fall in love.'

As he says this the cat, tail swishing, crouches to leap on the unaware sparrow. 'No!' Callie cries. 'No.'

Tommaso joins her at the window to see what has made her cry out. Then he says softly, 'I've broken my rule too, Callie. We are both undone.'

'No,' Callie says again, but this time it's not to the cat, who is sulking under the window, but to Tommaso. 'Don't tell me things like that. It's too soon, you can't mean them.'

Tommaso is silent. To him it is not too soon; he feels as if he has wanted this woman all his life, has loved her all his life. During the night, when they were making love a second time, this very same tabby cat, a tom, had yowled with either pleasure or pain, and the sound had first startled them, then made them laugh. Tommaso had held her laugh to him like a piece of soft velvet, or precious silk, dearer and finer than all the rich fabrics in the many small shops of Venice.

He says, 'I do mean them. And it frightens the shit out of me, too.'

They are both quiet for a moment. Then he goes on more calmly, 'We've started working on the Zattere, on the stone quay. I have two sets of divers beginning in just a few hours, and I'll need to be on site almost all day. But I'll be at Ca'Valier for lunch, from twelve thirty onwards. If you are free, please come. We can talk.'

He leaves before Callie can answer, opening the door of her room silently. Luckily, the night receptionist is in his tiny cubicle in the room behind the desk, sound asleep, and doesn't see. Tommaso unlocks the door,

111

walks down the few steps and is in the *campo*. It is totally empty, except for the statue perched on its pedestal, and the cat who, bored with the garden, is washing himself at the base of Nicolò Tommaseo, the *Cacalibre*. But as Tommaso leaves the Hotel Isabella, a curtain twitches on the first floor overlooking the square.

'What is it, Ellen?' says a whining voice from one of the twin beds. 'Why are you up? It's only five o'clock.'

'Go back to sleep, Candice. I am just opening a window; we need some air.'

'Oh dear, is it safe? We're not very high up.'

Ellen ignores this. She wonders where she has seen the man before; he looks familiar. Then she remembers: he is the Italian with the sunglasses, the one their tour manager was talking to outside that little wine bar on their first day in Venice.

Ellen knows the stranger is not on their tour; she also knows he is not staying at the hotel. The few guests other than Comet Trail tour members seem to be solely German or American. 'Well, well,' she murmurs.

'What, Ellen?'

'I said, good night. Or good morning. Whatever, I'm going back to bed.'

Ellen does so. As she tries to get back to sleep, she feels oddly happy. Venice is certainly living up to her expectations.

When Tommaso leaves, Callie takes a shower, puts on her cotton pyjamas and determinedly gets back into bed, intending to sleep. It is, of course, impossible. At six o'clock she gets up, dresses and creeps out of the hotel, skulking past the sleepy receptionist, who will be relieved at eight o'clock and is looking forward to the end of a boring night.

Only a couple of people are in the *campo*: a man carrying a briefcase walking towards the *vaporetto* landing stage, and a solitary jogger, definitely a tourist.

It is cooler today, and a grey mist makes the air seem opaque, like gauze.

Callie heads in the opposite direction from the bridge and the *sestiere* of Dorsoduro and instead goes towards Piazza San Marco. She doesn't see another person; the shops and buildings are tightly shut. On the Ponte San Maurizio she stops to look into the shallow canal. The water is a creamy green, its surface smooth as a bubble. A white mist rises quietly from the water; pigeons coo.

The Campo San Maurizio is also empty, but from a side alleyway comes the smell of fresh coffee. As Callie walks across the *campo* a lone church bell strikes once. She walks down Calle Zaguri, across another bridge to the Campiello della Feltrina and across the Ponte Duodo o Barbarigo, where a small votive light is burning at a crucifix outside the church. A man carrying a cardboard tray of fresh bread passes, and then no-one at all until she gets to the Ponte San Moisè, where a lone rowboat, its oarsman hardly more than a shadow in the white canal mist, glides silently through the water.

Callie stops, stares at the disappearing boat, at the patch of water. Her mind seems unnaturally clear, unlike the opacity of the air, the canal. She is not thinking of anything; she feels in a state of complete calm, transcendency. She knows she is not very far away from both joy and pain, but right now she is above them both.

She passes the ponderous Baroque church on the *campo* and goes down the Salizzada San Moisè into the Piazza San Marco. Here the early morning mist has cleared and the sun is streaming in behind the campanile. It's not quite seven o'clock and the piazza gleams like a gold nugget, the sunlight and shadow working together with the buildings to create a sense of richness and purity. There are no more than five or six people in the vast square: a solitary nun, encased in

white, walking slowly, silently, towards the *piazzetta*; a lone photographer, standing awed in the middle of the piazza; two workmen with old-fashioned witches' brooms, sweeping the square from the night before.

As Callie walks slowly down the length of the square towards the Basilica, she hears another solitary bell from a distant church. As if in answer, the bells of San Marco begin to peal exuberantly. Callie looks up at the campanile and the joy breaks through her like the spring tide, flooding her with sharp, salient happiness. It is an omen, she thinks, for me and Tommaso.

'Napoleon said this was the greatest drawing room in Europe,' says a voice in Callie's ear.

'Archie, for heaven's sake!' Callie shouts as she whirls round. 'You frightened the life out of me.'

Archie cannot be more apologetic. 'I'm sorry, I thought you saw me, you were looking in my direction as I approached.'

'I was miles away.'

'Yes, I'm sorry, I shouldn't have disturbed you. I thought you saw me. I'll leave you now.'

'No, no, I'm fine.' Callie, with great difficulty, pulls herself together, becomes the tour manager again. 'What are you doing out so early?'

'I often wake early and take a walk to dissipate my morning stiffness. Isn't the piazza amazing at this hour? So empty and pure. Hardly any people, yet in a couple of hours it will be teeming.' He gazes across the empty square, then his face suddenly lights up. 'Why look who's coming towards us. It's Ellen! How delightful.'

He walks towards her as Callie moans softly, a tiny sound, half laugh, half cry of despair. Much as she likes them both, she feels trapped, suffocated, meeting two of her group members at this hour of the morning when she needs to be alone with the feel of Tommaso on her skin, on her body, still fresh. The joy she has just experienced now plummets and desolation wraps itself round her like a snake.

He is married. The thought she has been suppressing now overwhelms her, and she feels sickened, wretched. But not, as she should, for Tommaso's wife, for the unknown woman she has just grievously injured, but for herself, for she knows, without a doubt, that she is deeply in love with him.

Ellen and Archie are enthusing over the coincidence that brings them both here at this hour. 'I couldn't sleep either,' Ellen says, glancing surreptitiously at Callie, noting that her face is both ravaged and radiant, an unsettling combination. Oh, what a splendid night she must have had, Ellen thinks. Does she know how rare such nights are? Does she know what a precious gift she has just had?

Archie is talking about the Basilica, commenting on the light glinting on the statue of St Mark and the angels. 'Ruskin gloried in the Basilica. He said the crests of the arches are like a marble foam; sculptured spray, he called them. I would have enjoyed talking to him.'

'Only about architecture, I hope,' Callie says without thinking. 'I believe his personal life was rather peculiar.'

Archie looks pained, and Callie immediately feels guilty. 'John Ruskin wrote some amazing stuff about Venice, I agree,' she says to mollify him.

Ellen says, 'Did you know Napoleon said this was the grandest drawing room in Europe?'

Callie stifles a yawn as Archie says, 'Ah, but do you know the second part of what he said? That it is only fit that the ceiling of the drawing room should be the sky.'

As Callie is trying to think how to get away from them, Archie says, 'There is a café open just off San Marco's, through the *sottoportego* next to Quadri's. Should we have a cappuccino?'

Ellen says, 'What a good idea. It's still an hour before breakfast.'

Callie declines the invitation to join them, and sees they are not too bothered. They go off towards the café as Callie wanders slowly down the *piazzetta* to catch the *vaporetto* back to the hotel.

On the near empty boat she stands at the railing for the short distance to the Accademia. The sky is blue and pink and white, coating the water with reflected colour. As the *vaporetto* passes by Ca'Valier, she sees Tommaso on the balcony, dressed for work, drinking coffee and staring out into the canal. Although the boat comes close enough for him to see her, recognize her, he is looking past it, towards the *cupole* of the Salute and the Basin of St Mark. His coffee seems forgotten as he stares into the distance.

'Tommaso,' she whispers, and though he cannot hear her over the noise of the *vaporetto* and the water sounds of the canal, he turns and sees her.

Neither of them wave. They look at each other carefully, as if scrutinizing each other for future reference, until the boat passes and they can see each other no longer.

Callie is late for breakfast, for when she'd got back to the Hotel Isabella she'd lain down on the bed for a few moments and, exhausted physically and mentally, she had fallen asleep. There is a spare place at the table where Deirdre, Angela and Sylvester are sitting, and Callie joins them. Sylvester says, 'You look like something the cat dragged in.'

Angela smirks. Deirdre says to Sylvester, 'That's not a nice thing to say.'

Callie thanks the waiter for the pot of coffee he brings her and says evenly, 'Sylvester and I go back a long way. He's been on so many of my tours he treats me as one of his mates. Right, Sylvester?'

'We kid each other,' Sylvester agrees, twitching his body in the silent spasm that passes as laughter.

'I'd hate to be one of your mates,' Deirdre snaps, and

Callie thinks, I wish she were as forthright with her mother. She sips her coffee, which is muddy and bitter.

'Sylvester's right, you do look rather peaky,' Angela says, scrutinizing her through slanted eyes. Her shoulder-length hair is down today rather than pulled up in one of her elaborate styles; it is sleek and perfect, and Callie cannot believe she slept in that hair. She stares at Angela's long gold earrings, which sway in a hypnotic manner every time the woman moves her head. The vamp is in black and gold today: a long linen dress, with slits up the side and a plunging neckline. A large gold brooch sinks in the crevice. She looks dressed for Harry's Bar or the Cipriani, not for the Accademia gallery, where they are going this morning.

The thought of shepherding her wayward group round the gallery, usually one of her favourites, today fills Callie with exhausted dismay. 'Are you OK?' Deirdre looks at her with concern.

Ellen, Candice and Archie are sitting at the table next to them. Archie says, 'You're working too hard, my dear. You were up and out very early today. You young people need your sleep.'

Candice, who still is distressed after waking up to find Ellen gone, with no apologies whatsoever when she returned just before breakfast, flushed and somewhat excited, says plaintively, 'Oh dear, whatever will become of us if you get ill, Carolyn?'

'Callie,' Callie says automatically, as Sylvester sneers at the same time, 'Calypso.'

Ellen is silent. She knows why Callie is in such a strange state today, would like to say so and comfort her. She herself has felt her tired heart stir this morning; she has seen the piazza at dawn, the Basilica cloaked in pearl and gold; she has taken coffee with a kind, attentive gentleman, who talked to her of art and architecture, of Ruskin and Carpaccio, as if she counted, as if he cared for her opinion. As if he cared

117

for *her* – Ellen – because of who she was rather than what she could do for him.

The feeling this gives her is so intoxicating, yet so comforting, that if this is what Callie wants, and gets from that man who walked out of the hotel at five this morning, then Ellen is happy for her. A rush of both affection and understanding breaks through her and floods towards Callie. 'I'm sure our tour manager is just fine,' she says loudly to both tables. 'I think she looks lovely. Let her be, all of you.' She gets up, walks over to Callie and lays her hand comradely on her shoulder.

This unexpected act of kindness finally undoes Callie. Without speaking, she gets up from the table, walks hurriedly out of the dining room and collapses on her bed as the emotions of the past twenty-four hours crowd in on her like both demons and angels.

An hour or so later, Callie is up and dressed in her
Comet Trail regulation uniform: knee-length navy
skirt, crisp white cotton blouse, with the comet
emblem blazing across the right breast, and light navy
jacket, which she keeps on today for the air is slightly
cooler after yesterday's rain. On a tour such as this, she
often abandons her uniform for more comfortable,
casual clothes, but more and more these past few days
she is using it as a costume, to hide the person behind
the tour manager, the confused, uncertain woman she
fears is beginning to seep through.

Only half her group members are going to the
Accademia gallery; the others have opted for shopping,
sitting in the sun and writing postcards home. Minnie
and Dexter, experiencing the joys of reunion after their
rift over Dexter's cappuccino with Angela in Murano,
decide to stay at the hotel. They are languid after their
night of married sex, which is really no different than
the unmarried sex they had been having for the year
before their marriage.

Everyone hoped Angela would have remained
behind, but she is there, wearing an elegant black straw
hat to complete the outfit she wore at breakfast. That
woman stands out like a carnival character, thinks
Giovanni as he passes the group in front of the gallery
waiting to go in. At first he doesn't see Callie in her
Comet Trail uniform, so different from the thin flowery
thing she wore last night. Then she turns and their

eyes meet. 'Giovanni,' she says, '*ciao*. Are you off to the Casa Goldoni?'

'*Sì*, yes, I am. So much work to do . . .' he trails off vaguely.

There is a moment of awkward silence. Callie would like to thank Giovanni again for the delicious meal last night, for the trouble he went to, but she's aware of her group around her, listening curiously. She is aware, too, that Giovanni must know that Tommaso didn't return to Ca'Valier after he said good night to her.

Giovanni knows. He had taken Patsy to her hotel and walked through Campo Santo Stefano expecting to see Tommaso there, waiting for him. But the *campo* was nearly empty, as was the bridge. When Giovanni unlocked the door of Ca'Valier and found the apartment empty as well, a tight ball seemed to encase itself in his chest, like a small hard fist.

He knows, of course, that his brother has had at least one affair, perhaps two. It has never been spoken of, and Tommaso has been always discreet, but Giovanni somehow knows these things. Perhaps it is nothing more than knowing his brother, and knowing Sandra. Giovanni has great affection for Sandra, while at the same time doubting her capacity for passion. As a man in whom passion no longer exists, is spent, Giovanni can recognize this. Sandra is in too much control of herself: her body, with the disciplined workouts to make her fit for important tennis matches; her work, where she seems to be praised highly; and her family, which she handles with efficiency. Giovanni has enjoyed his holidays with his brother's family; he loves his two nephews devotedly, and enjoys being spoiled by Sandra, though he sometimes wishes she didn't insist on cooking for him. Sandra would never dream of letting Giovanni or anyone else in the kitchen; she prides herself on being the quintessential super-woman, handling career, children and the tennis club with precision and intelligence. Perhaps that is why

she is not such a good cook, Giovanni thinks; she has no passion for it, just as she seems to have no passion for Tommaso, though there is love there, certainly.

Tommaso, on the other hand, has always been intense, volatile. Yet Giovanni had hoped that this disparity between them would bring balance, that with compromise, Tommaso and Sandra would be compatible.

When he first suspected Tommaso of being with another woman, he had momentarily feared for the marriage. But as his brother seemed untouched by the affair, Giovanni, though not approving, had been relieved. This affair he knows is different. He was not unaware, last night, of the tension between Callie and Tommaso. And this morning, at breakfast on the terrace, his brother had said, 'I should have walked home with you last night, Giovanni. I should have walked away when I still could.'

Outside the Galleria dell'Accademia, the silence between Callie and Giovanni is becoming disconcerting. Finally he says, '*Allora. Io vado. Ho molto lavoro. I have much work to do.*' He is aware that he sounds abrupt, and rushes with great relief past the gallery and down the Calle Gambara, away from Callie, from Tommaso and Ca'Valier, away from all the uncertainties of the messy, chaotic present and into the certainty of the past. His beloved playwright will restore his balance: the jaunty, kind and humorous Goldoni, who knew better than anyone about delusion and artifice, who threw away the physical masks of the *commedia dell'arte* to write about real people with other, more subtle, kinds of illusions. Goldoni will soothe him, protect him from the uneasy emotion he is feeling over the events of last night. With a sense of urgency, he rushes through the *sottoportego* to San Barnaba, across bridges and down alleyways into the *sestiere* of San Polo. Finally, with great relief, he walks across the Campo San Tomà, down the Calle dei Nomboli, and, at

last, as if arriving at a place of great refuge, to Palazzo Centani. Standing in the fine Gothic courtyard of the house where Carlo Goldoni was born, Giovanni takes deep breaths, as a man trying to master a severe anxiety attack, and prepares his mind for work.

Callie, flustered after her encounter with Giovanni, hustles her group into the gallery. Angela exclaims the loudest over the paintings, in a manner that suggests she is the one who cares least about them. She poses dramatically in front of the largest canvas, fully aware of the attention she is attracting from other visitors to the Accademia. In the later Renaissance room a group of Germans look at her and point, and wonder aloud if she is someone famous. Callie doesn't care in the slightest what the vamp thinks of Veronese or Tintoretto, so long as she is happy and doesn't upset the group. Deirdre, in beige shorts and a brown T-shirt, her hair newly washed and more fluffy, and not as limp as usual, looks far less tense. She is able to enjoy the museum because her mother is, for the moment, happy. Get a life, Callie thinks as she watches her. Leave Angela, and get a life.

Callie leads her group into Room Twenty-one to view the *Legend of St Ursula* cycle by Vittore Carpaccio. Archie begins telling Ellen about the paintings, sitting her on the long polished wooden bench so that they can look and talk at the same time.

Sylvester, sitting next to them, says, loudly, to the room at large, 'For fuck's sake, there's nothing worse than an old bore who thinks he knows about art.'

There is complete silence for a stunned moment. Archie's face flushes, but he doesn't speak. Then Ellen says steadily, 'Yes, there is, Sylvester. There is something a great deal worse: a rude, ill-mannered lout with the sensitivity of a goat.'

Now it is Sylvester's face which goes dangerously red. He opens his mouth to retort, but Callie is

suddenly standing over him, blocking him from the older woman. 'I've had enough, Sylvester,' Callie says quietly. 'I have put up with your nasty behaviour not just on this tour, but on all the others, and I'm not prepared to do so any longer. Unless you apologize to Archie, I am phoning the Comet Trail head office and requesting you be released from this tour. I shall tell them that you are a persistent troublemaker and that I can no longer be responsible for the disruptions you cause to the rest of my group.'

Once again, the Carpaccio room in the gallery is silent as everyone listens to this scene. Sylvester stands up and takes a step towards Callie, his hand raised slightly as if he is about to hit her. Callie says quietly, 'I mean it, Sylvester. I'm not bluffing.'

Sylvester hesitates and drops his hand. He begins to bluster, to say she can't do that, he's paid his money like everyone else, they can't just throw him off the tour. Callie doesn't say a word, but nor does she drop her eyes from his face. Finally the splutters come to an end. There is something in Callie's eyes that looks determined, dangerous. Sylvester enjoys his holidays with Comet Trails; he has found, through trial and error, that they are not only the best value for money, but the most varied and enjoyable. He doesn't know if Callie really does have the power to ban him from further tours, let alone expel him from this one, but he's not sure that he wants to take that chance.

'Oh, have it your way then,' he snarls at last, as Callie doesn't back down. 'What the hell do I care.' He turns to Archie. 'Sorry, OK?'

He is less than gracious, but Archie says, with dignity, 'I accept your apology.'

Sylvester retreats and slinks away into the next room. Callie says her piece about the paintings, and the others wander about to gaze at them again. Angela, peering at a detail, cries, 'Look at the neat little bum on that archer in the red tights; God, it's been years

since I've had access to buttocks like that.'

Archie and Ellen are still sitting on the bench. Archie says, 'Thank you, my dear, for defending me so gallantly.' He is filled with a huge tender gratitude for her, and not only for the way she stood up to Sylvester for insulting him. It is the way she seems to care about the things he cares about: paintings, architecture, his silly little obsession with Ruskin. Only one other person has ever shared these things with him, and that was his wife. Venice has made him lonely for her, more so than usual. He'd been torn between seeing Venice and his favourite works of art once again – knowing that the city's melancholy would sadden him – or cocooning himself at home, protected from the Serenissima's insidious nostalgia perhaps, but also from her beauty.

In the end Archie had seemed to hear his dead wife saying, 'Go, you daft thing. You're not getting any younger, you know. Go for me, if not for yourself.'

But it is Ellen, not his wife, who is speaking now. 'Sylvester was terribly wrong, you know, that horrid young man. You are anything *but* boring, Archie. It's a long time since anyone has infected me with such enthusiasm. For so many things – Venice, its treasures. But not only that. You've made me enthusiastic for life again.'

Neither of them speak for a moment. Both are overwhelmed: Archie, at what she has just said; and Ellen, by the fact that she has said it. Embarrassed now, she stands up to study one of the paintings. 'What wonderful detail. The dogs, the little boats . . . You feel you are right there at the close of the fifteenth century. No wonder you love them so much, Archie.'

Archie looks at her, sees her looking with genuine rapture at the first painting in the cycle, *The Arrival of the English Ambassadors*, and feels uplifted. It is his favourite in the *St Ursula* cycle, but for once it is not the painting that is lightening his old heart, but

something else, something less cerebral, something human and solid and here now, not contained in a painting from the past. The face he turns to Ellen is beatific.

Candice, who had been cowering in the corner during the row with Sylvester, sidles over to Ellen and stands as closely as if she were attached at the hip. 'I'm afraid I don't know much about art,' she says, 'but I know what I like.' She looks doubtful, belying her words.

Angela, draped on the bench in front of the Carpaccios, says, 'Perhaps I will write a novel about St Ursula. It would make a bloody good historical romance. It's got everything: a princess called Ursula, proposed to by a pagan prince – love, passion, all that. But the poor darlings haven't a chance, because he's a pagan, she's a Christian. Two different backgrounds, families opposed. There is a feud—'

'I think that's been done,' Ellen says shortly. 'Shakespeare. *Romeo and Juliet.*'

Angela ignores the interruption. 'So the prince promises to convert. Then . . . I forgot what happened next. Callie, what did you say happened then?'

'St Ursula makes a pilgrimage to Rome with eleven thousand virgins. How are you going to fit eleven thousand virgins into your book, Angela?'

The vamp stands up, looking at the paintings calculatingly. 'The virgins will be the best thing about the book. They got attacked by the Huns before they got to Rome, right? Just imagine the scene! Think of all the sex you can throw in, all those virgins being raped. But you could create a secondary story round one of them. Say she falls in love with one of the Huns, and he falls in love with her, tries to save her. And Ursula, maybe she doesn't really love the prince at all, but secretly lusts for the king of the Huns.'

'She's a *saint*, Angela,' Deirdre says mildly. 'Saints aren't allowed to lust for anyone.'

'They are in fiction, darling.'

When they finally leave the Accademia, the group seems happy for once, except for Sylvester, who is skulking at the fringes, unusually subdued. Outside the gallery Callie tells them, 'You are on your own now. There are no excursions planned this afternoon, so you're free to do as you like. Tonight there is a Vivaldi concert in the courtyard of the Ca' Rezzonico, the *palazzo* which once belonged to Browning's son, Pen, and where Robert himself died. For those of you who want to go, the cost is thirty thousand lire. We'll meet after dinner in the hotel about eight. The concert starts at nine.'

After the usual questions, comments, queries, the group disperses. Deirdre looks rather longingly in Callie's direction as she dutifully follows Angela, who is saying, 'I'm starving, darling. The hell with my diet. Where shall we have lunch? I'm quite excited about this book, you know. I think contemporary fiction has had its day. What the reader wants is history.'

'With plenty of violent sex thrown in, of course,' Deirdre says. Angela misses the sarcasm. 'That goes without saying. Do you know, I think this book is going to be the turning point for me. Why didn't I think of writing fiction before? The money, darling, think of the money. No more of these God-awful tours, it will be the Hotel Danieli next, Deirdre, I can feel it.'

Deirdre has heard all this before, but is wise enough not to mention the fact. She casts a hopeless look at Callie, shakes her head and follows Angela across the Accademia bridge.

Callie knows she should cross that bridge, too, go back to the hotel and sleep this afternoon. Instead, she turns right in front of the museum and walks round the corner to Ca'Valier, hoping Tommaso will be home for lunch by now. She presses the buzzer and, almost immediately, he opens the door into the courtyard for her.

'That was quick,' she says. 'You shouldn't run down those marble steps, they're lethal. On practically every Italian tour someone slips on marble steps. Luckily, only one was seriously hurt; she had to have stitches in her leg and spent the rest of the tour in her hotel room.'

'You're babbling,' Tommaso says, kissing her. 'And I wasn't upstairs. I've been sitting here in the courtyard waiting for you.' He takes her hand and leads her towards the apartment.

It is cool in the courtyard. Much of it is covered over by beams and a low roof, but in the open part in the middle, the branches and leaves of the japonica tree create shade and shadow. The air smells of rain. Together, they climb the steps leading to the living room. On the table the white lilies gleam in the darkening room. A black cloud has covered the sun, and through the open window the water of the canal is dark brown.

Callie looks round for Giovanni. 'He's not here,' Tommaso says. 'He went to Casa Goldoni for an hour or so this morning, then suddenly decided to go to Padua. He has a colleague there; he'll be gone a few days. He left a note.'

Callie nods. She is not surprised. The situation must be awkward for him. 'I suppose Giovanni knows your wife? Your sons?'

'Callie, please, not now.'

'Does he? He must.'

'Yes, of course he does.'

'So what did he say, then, when you came in at five this morning? Or did you sneak into your bed while he was still asleep and pretend you had been there all night?' She does not wait for an answer but goes out onto the balcony. At the mouth of the canal, the sky above the Salute is dark yet luminous, with brushstrokes of deep amber tinging the storm clouds. The water is stained brown and orange, with a sheen of

silver from the odd metallic light. It looks eerie, unreal. The wind is cold and Callie shivers.

'Come in,' Tommaso says, standing next to her. 'Please.'

Callie doesn't move; and together they look out over the water and see lightning streaking the black sky over the distant lagoon. The strange yellow colour deepens. The sound of bells coming from the direction of San Marco roll through the sky and, as an echo, thunder peals above them. Although it is midday, the colours tinting the sky and canal give the sensation of a supernatural nightfall.

'Come in,' Tommaso says again. 'You are cold, I see goosebumps on your arms.'

Callie feels the wind freshening on her face and sees a gondola rocking crazily in the rough water, its gondolier hurrying back to his mooring, no passengers now. Except for the lone gondola, the canal has emptied; not even the ubiquitous *vaporetti* are visible. 'Come on, Callie.' Tommaso tries to steer her gently into the house.

'I have fallen in love with you,' she says, and the words are almost drowned out by the bells, the thunder. 'It makes me so angry. I haven't been in love for years, and never in Venice, and it has to be with you.' She turns to him at last, and he is filled with pity at her red eyes and the circles under them.

'I haven't been in love for years either,' he says, but does not add aloud, and the last time was with my wife, when we first met. What he does say is, 'But I'm glad it's with you.'

Callie says, 'Tommaso, please, would you take off your sunglasses? I've forgotten what your eyes look like.'

He smiles, suddenly joyful. 'Come inside and I'll remind you.'

But when they lie down on Tommaso's bed, the open windows looking out over the scented garden, the rain

falling on the lavender, Callie does not see his eyes at all. Exhausted by emotion, sex, love, the sleepless night, she lets herself relax in Tommaso's arms and is asleep immediately, before he has a chance to even kiss her properly.

They both sleep deeply for a couple of hours. When they wake the storm is gone and the scent of rain-washed flowers trickles in from the open window. Tommaso looks at his watch and says, 'Hell, I told the men I'd be back at three, and it's past that now. I've got to go, Callie.' He is out of bed and rushing about finding shoes, splashing water on his face. 'You stay here, if you like. I'll try to get away early.' He puts on his dark glasses.

'I work, too, remember? I'm meeting Patsy at five to sort out some excursions we're putting on.'

'Tonight then.' Tommaso is combing his hair, buttoning a clean blue shirt. 'Come over tonight.' He is not looking at her but at his reflection in the mirror.

Callie is hurt by his abruptness, the casual way he is making plans for them. Emotions are running too deep in her yet to treat them with insouciance.

'I can't,' she says shortly. 'I'm busy.' She puts on her own shoes. 'See you, then.' She starts to leave the room.

'Callie, stop it.' Tommaso has not moved, but his voice is sharp, and it forces her to turn round. 'I am feeling exactly as you are now, but I have to force myself to keep those feelings under control, at least while I am at work. Like you, I have a job to do. Like you, people rely on me.' His voice softens. 'I can't fall apart on them, *cara*, nor can you. Even though this thing, this momentous, wonderful, frightening thing has happened, *is* happening, we still need to preserve at least an outward show of normality.'

He looks at her with such love that Callie can see it, even behind the dark glasses. She says, 'I truly can't come tonight. I have to have dinner with my

group, then take them to a Vivaldi concert.'

'Come later then. After the concert. It doesn't matter what time.'

Callie nods. Together they walk out of the house into a sunny day. The rain has scrubbed the city and cleansed the air around it. The sky is so clear it looks like thin blue glass, and the buildings are spruced, freshened.

Tommaso says, 'Walk me to the Zattere, you have time before meeting Patsy. I suddenly don't like leaving you, Calypso.'

They walk down the Rio Terrá, past the small Campo Sant'Agnese, where some small boys are kicking round a soccer ball. They turn right at the Gesuati church and go along the wide walkway by the Giudecca canal, which looks like blue-grey enamel after the storm. Across the water the buildings of Giudecca seem like a painting drawn with sharp coloured pencils. The outline of the Redentore, the church built by the Venetians in the 1500s to give thanks for deliverance from the plague, is stark against the glass sky.

'I love the weather in Venice,' Callie says. 'It's so whimsical, so flamboyant. Just like the city herself.' In her pleasure of the moment she feels rested, and with rest has come the simple but profound pleasure of discovering herself to be in love, and to be loved also in return. She takes Tommaso's hand, naturally, without even thinking of it.

He holds it tightly for a few moments, but then deliberately withdraws his hand. Surprised, she looks at him. They are approaching the quay where the divers are already at work. Two of them are in the water, the other two poised to go down next. A pontoon laden with equipment is tied to a mooring near by.

Suddenly, Callie understands. The men on the job are Tommaso's friends, colleagues at any rate; they know he is married, some of them might even know his wife.

'I am sorry,' she says quietly to Tommaso. 'I had forgotten there are rules for this sort of thing. You will have to teach them to me.'

Tommaso looks pained. 'Don't, Callie. Please.' He touches her lightly on the cheek, and the touch says more to the men on the quay than any hand-holding would have done. 'Later, yes?' he says.

'Fine.' They smile at each other, then Callie breaks and starts to walk away. '*Ciao*, Tommaso,' she calls lightly and lifts her hand in a slight wave.

'*Ciao*, Calypso.' He waves, too.

Paolo, one of the divers standing on the quay, says with exaggerated innuendo, 'Ah, *bellissima*.'

Tommaso surprises him by not grinning, not cuffing him playfully on the chin, not adding his own comments on the physical attributes of the woman he was walking with. '*Che Dio gliela mandi buona*,' Paolo says to the others when Tommaso is out of hearing. 'God help him, it looks serious.' The others cluck their tongues in sympathy.

Callie has a couple of hours before she has to meet Patsy, so she walks to the end of the Fondamenta Zattere Ponte Lungo and then down a series of alleyways, some so narrow that you can touch the crumbling brickwork on either side at the same time, without even stretching your arms out to their full length. Without remembering how she got there, she finds herself in the Campo Santa Margherita, a large, elongated *campo* dotted with tiny shops, cafés, market stalls. There is a shop selling natural food products, a bookshop, a ramshackle store with piles of cheap bras, underpants and socks. It is a popular *campo*, with the university near by, the busy fruit and fish stalls in the centre. The tables and chairs outside the cafés are crammed with people eating, drinking and talking; the sounds of the square are happy ones: children shouting in play, adults laughing, people talking

131

animatedly. A canary in a cage outside one of the houses is full of song, and a small terrier barks teasingly at a muzzled German Shepherd.

Something about the scene touches Callie, and, suddenly moved, she sits down on a bench under a leafy shade tree in the middle of the *campo*. For a moment she cannot sort out her thoughts, cannot quite identify what it is that is affecting her so profoundly. She looks around her. Although, of course, the square is milling with summer tourists, it is still primarily a meeting place for the Venetians, for students, housewives, children; retired men and women out enjoying the sun and the company of each other; workers who have left their offices and shops early, or are taking a break for a quick espresso in one of the outdoor cafés. Callie watches and, without warning, she is overcome by a yearning so intense it makes her feel momentarily ill. She wants to be part of it, one of the women who know this *campo* as they know the lines on their ageing husband's faces, one of the women who come every day with young children in tow, bargaining with the man selling zucchini flowers at the vegetable stand, with the woman hawking squid and fresh tuna at the fish stall.

And as she thinks this outrageous (for her) thought, she understands what it was that touched her so poignantly as she walked into the *campo*. It was a memory of the past, of her own childhood, of the small village in England where she grew up, where her own mother walked across the village green every day and bought milk and the morning newspaper at the same shop, her stamps at the same tiny post-office counter that doubled as a greengrocer.

Stunned, Callie sits on the bench in the Campo Santa Margherita for a long time, feeling the past change shape, its shadows becoming real and solid, its shackles no longer chains but wings. I have not understood, she thinks. I didn't know that it is better to soar

to the sky like a tree, branches free and touching the wind, but roots deeply in the earth, than to flutter like a butterfly from one ephemeral flower to another.

Callie sits, dazed, until it is time for her to meet Patsy.

The concert at Ca'Rezzonico that evening is a success, the wide courtyard setting delightful in the elegant *palazzo*. The weather remains dry and warm for the event, and Callie's group seem unusually contented after it is over. They decide to walk back to the hotel, for the night air is sweet, the music still gently echoing in their ears. There is no need to walk back in a group, so some of them linger, others walk quickly on ahead. Archie's hip is hurting him again, so he soon falls behind, but Ellen notices and waits for him, much to Candice's chagrin. 'But Ellen, it's quite dark. We don't want to lose the others.'

Ellen says firmly, 'You go ahead with Callie. I'll wait for Archie. He's just coming through the *sottoportego*.'

Candice peers down the street and, sure enough, Archie is slowly limping along through an archway under a building. Candice, undecided, sees Callie and the others getting ahead of them. Ellen says, 'Quick, or they'll be gone,' and Candice turns and rushes to catch them. 'Oh dear,' she puffs to Callie, 'I do feel dreadful, not waiting for Ellen and Archie. But I don't like being out in the dark.'

Callie had hoped to detach herself from what remained of her group, who were beginning to straggle, and go straight to Ca'Valier, but now she is stuck with Candice. There is no way she can leave the woman to find her own way back to the hotel. Candice is in a talkative mood and the walk seems to take for ever. Finally Callie sees her into the foyer, endures another ten minutes of compulsive chatter, and at last watches her go to her room.

Callie leaves the hotel and quickly walks away. As she goes across the *campi* Santo Stefano and San Vidal, she sees Ellen and Archie standing on the Accademia bridge, watching an orange moon, ripe like a nectarine, hanging succulently over the outline of the Salute. Ripples of pale gold are reflected in the water like yellow snowdrifts.

Callie hopes they will not see her scurrying past, but they do, and stop her to talk about the concert. 'How is your hip, Archie?' Callie asks. 'These constant bridges with all the steps must be the worst thing for it.'

Archie makes light of his pain. Ellen says, 'Is Candice back at the hotel?'

'Yes, I saw her to her room.'

Ellen looks relieved and suddenly relaxed, as if a great burden has been lifted from her. 'Then I don't need to hurry back,' she says.

Callie smiles. 'No, no need. Stay out and enjoy the moon.'

There is a slight awkward silence. Callie is aware that it is after eleven and that she is going in the opposite direction from the hotel. She braces herself for one of them to ask where she is going, but curiously, neither of them do. Archie is too polite, not wishing to seem inquisitive, and Ellen knows. 'You, too,' she says to Callie. 'You, too, enjoy the moonlight.' She smiles at her, but Callie doesn't notice the complicity in her smile.

Once again Tommaso is waiting for her. 'For the first time ever I hated Vivaldi,' he says as he runs upstairs with her. 'He kept you from me all evening.'

The doors to the terrace are open. 'The moon is rising quickly, it will be silver soon. Shall we have a drink outside and watch it?'

'I'd love to, but I can't. Two of my group members are on the Accademia bridge, and if we go out they'll see me. I know it's dark and they probably wouldn't see us clearly, or recognize me if they did notice us, but I can't

take the chance.' She looks at him helplessly. 'Is there any place in all Venice we can go that is private?'

Tommaso takes her hand. 'Yes, and it's even better than the terrace, even though there is no moon.' He takes her by the hand, leads her into the house and to his bedroom. 'The last time I was here, I slept so soundly,' Callie says. 'Was it only this afternoon?'

'And do you feel like sleeping now, Calypso?' he asks, beginning to slide her skirt slowly from her hips.

'Funny you should say that, Tommaso. Suddenly I feel wide awake.' And with a fury that shakes them both, she tumbles with him onto the bed and kisses his body with a rough intensity that seems more like rage than desire.

'Easy, Calypso,' Tommaso murmurs. 'This is only flesh you are pummelling, not stone.'

Something breaks in Callie and she tries to pull away from him. 'I hate you,' she cries. 'I love you, but I hate you too, because I shouldn't love you, because you can't love me honestly and openly, because you will leave me in the end.'

'Hush, *cara*. There is only *now*, all right? For this moment there is only now.' He pulls her gently back.

She knows that there is no other way. With a shudder her anger dissolves, and all that is left is love.

Tommaso wants her to stay the night, sleep in his arms as she did that afternoon, but she insists on returning to the hotel. It is now after one in the morning, and they have finally left the bedroom and are standing on the balcony. The night sky is thick with cloud, and lightning sporadically lightens the dark. Tommaso has pulled on jeans and a shirt, and Callie is wearing an old dressing gown of his.

'Don't go back. Stay the night,' Tommaso says.

'I can't, I really can't. I shouldn't have stayed so late, I didn't tell anyone where I was. It was very unprofessional of me. If something had happened, if there

had been an emergency, a problem with one of the group, no-one would have known where to find me.'

'Patsy is just round the corner from you. Your hotel would contact hers if anything went wrong.'

'And then Patsy would be frantic, wondering where I was.' Callie goes inside and begins to get dressed.

'All right.' Tommaso gives up. 'I'll walk you back.'

'Don't, you mustn't. Someone will see us.'

Tommaso is already dressed. 'I thought I was the one who needed to be discreet,' he says wryly.

'I'm not supposed to have men on a tour,' Callie says, grabbing her handbag.

This annoys Tommaso. 'You make me sound like a one-night stand.'

He follows Callie down the stairs, through the court-yard and through the heavy doors onto the street. The air is damp, though no rain has as yet begun. Thunder growls like a dog in the sky above them, and there is no-one on the Accademia bridge as they slowly climb the steps, arms tightly round each other. Lightning is smashing the sky to fragments all around them. 'It's beautiful,' Callie whispers.

'Like you, Calypso.'

'I'm not beautiful. It's Venice blinding you, making you believe I am something other than I am.' She feels sad as she says this.

They walk in silence down the bridge. Under the mimosa tree at the edge of Campo San Vidal they stop and kiss. The scent of the damp tree fills the space between them as they reluctantly pull apart.

When they reach the hotel, Tommaso says, 'I can't bear saying good night to you tonight. I can't bear part-ing.' He holds her tightly. Rolls of thunder break over them like waves, but they are oblivious.

Callie finally pulls away. '*Ciao*, Tommaso. *Ti amo.*' She runs inside, knowing that if she stays a moment longer she will never let him go.

*   *   *

A few days later, on a *vaporetto* going to the Lido, Patsy says to Callie, 'Are you going to tell me, or will Giovanni be the first?'

Callie, who has been staring at the water, turns to face her. 'I'm sorry. Of course I'll tell you about it. I was waiting for the right time. I couldn't blurt it out in the middle of the Doge's Palace, or as we took our groups round the church of the Frari.'

'I saw Giovanni last night, when he got back from Padua. We met for a drink.'

Callie looks despondently out into the lagoon, at the cloudless sky, the sun reflecting on the green water like shards of crystal. 'I suppose he told you about me and Tommaso?'

'Shit, Callie, give us a break. Giovanni's not a gossip. He was preoccupied, though. Something was worrying him, and for once it wasn't Goldoni. When I asked him, he said he was concerned about his brother, but didn't say why.'

'Oh God.' Callie groans and lowers her head into her hands. 'What a mess.'

'You said it. Are you going to tell Aunt Patsy all about it then? You'd better be quick; we're not that far from the Lido. C'mon then, confession time.'

Callie turns in her seat to double check that none of her group members are within hearing distance. 'Patsy, don't play games, OK? It's Tommaso, you know that. You were there at the beginning, remember? We've been together every free moment since that dinner. Yes, we are having an affair, and yes, I know he's married, and yes, I know I'm a shit and so is he for doing this thing, but I love him.'

Patsy says calmly, 'Yup, I know all that. So, I'm sure, does Giovanni.'

Callie looks miserably at Patsy, who seems fresh and solid and wholesome in her clean white blouse with the Comet Trail logo blazed across it. 'Don't lecture me, Patsy. Please.'

Patsy shrugs. 'Look, Callie, it's none of my business, OK?'

'But you disapprove.'

'What do you expect me to do? You disapprove, too, you told me so before it even began. Come on, we're here.' She stands up as the boat docks.

Callie says, 'I didn't want this to happen. Nor did Tommaso. But it did, Patsy. OK?'

Patsy softens. 'I know, love,' she says kindly. 'And so, I'm sure, does Giovanni. We're both worried; him about his brother, me about you. Now let's forget it and concentrate on our jobs.'

The boat has stopped at the Santa Maria Elisabetta. Patsy and Callie shepherd their groups down the wide, tree-lined shopping street. 'Remember, there are cars on the Lido; it's not like Venice where there is no traffic. You can't stand in the middle of a street staring at something, or you're liable to get run over, if not by a car then by a bicycle.' Callie smiles as she says this, for she is nearly hit by an elderly couple cycling in tandem.

'When can we swim?' Minnie shrieks from the middle of the group. 'I'm dying for a swim. I bought a new bikini in Venice.'

'At vast expense,' grumbles Dexter. This is only the end of the first week of his honeymoon tour and he is appalled at how much money they have spent. Or, rather, how much money Minnie has spent. This marriage lark has some disadvantages, he muses.

At the entrance to the public beach the group splits up. Angela announces to everyone that she is going to have a drink at the Hotel des Bains. The way she says it implies an intimate knowledge of the sumptuous old place. Sylvester says, 'You just want to find yourself a toyboy, like Thomas Mann in that stupid movie.'

'And you,' Angela retorts, 'want to sit on the sand and leer at the bimbos.'

'I intend to do more than leer, Angela.'

'You should be so lucky.' She appraises him disparagingly. Sylvester is dressed in camouflage shorts, a matching T-shirt and a straw gondolier's hat. 'Come on, Deirdre, let's get away from the riff-raff.'

Dexter says hopefully to Minnie, 'Perhaps we should join them? I'd like to see this famous hotel.' He looks at Angela, rather lustfully for a married man.

'No, Dexter, I've brought all our swimming things, we're going to *swim*.' Minnie takes his hand and pulls him towards the water, which is calm and muddy looking. The sand looks grey, like fine crumbling concrete.

The others are either spreading towels on the beach or heading, behind Angela, to the Hotel des Bains. Callie and Patsy are free for a couple of hours, and sit in the shade under a grapevine at the café on the beach directly in front of the hotel.

'I think the Lido has a dreadful beach,' Patsy says, not for the first time. 'I can't think why anyone would want to swim here.'

In front of the restaurant garden where Patsy and Callie are sitting there are several rows of beach huts, newly painted and obviously in use. In between they can see the beach and some of the members of their groups. Archie, Ellen and Candice are strolling, fully clothed, up and down the beach; all three are wearing cream-coloured cloth hats. Dexter and Minnie have come out of the water and are flopped down on their towels. After a few minutes Dexter, peering at Minnie and seeing that she is asleep, casually gets up and wanders away. Callie watches him disappear between the beach huts, past their sheltered arbour and up the steps towards the Hotel des Bains. 'I wonder what he's up to?' Callie murmurs.

Patsy slips her feet from her latest new pair of shoes, a wedge heel in the softest yellow leather, and admires her feet. Her toenails are painted the palest pearly pink today, and look innocent, childlike. She says, 'So you and Tommaso – what are you going to do?'

Callie says, 'What can we do? Nothing.'

'Have you talked about it?'

Callie looks pained. 'This relationship is hardly a week old. We've scarcely talked. But I knew before I began that he has a wife, family. I knew, too, that he's had other affairs. He won't leave his wife. I wouldn't want him to.'

It's difficult for Callie to say this, but she has forced herself to think about it. She and Tommaso, in the first grip of passion and the first discovery of each other, have avoided any talk of the future. She knows it must stay this way; she also knows she mustn't let herself harbour false illusions, false hopes. 'There are enough illusions in Venice,' she says. 'It would be very easy for me to have my own. Living happily ever after with Tommaso, that sort of thing. If I ever start talking like that, hit me a few times.'

Patsy finishes her cold drink and chews up the ice left in the glass. 'Don't worry.' She slips her shoes back on and looks at Callie. 'As long as you are clear on that,' she says sombrely. 'You and Tommaso. Married is married, OK?'

Callie closes her eyes. 'OK.'

'End of lecture. Now, I'm going to wander up the Elisabetta. There are some fantastic shoe shops there. Want to come?'

'I don't feel like shopping. I'm going to sit on that stone wall over there, under the trees, and try to read my book. I'll meet you back at the landing stage.'

As soon as Callie settles herself by the steps going down to the beach, Minnie, bright red from the sun, strides up to her in her new green bikini, a towel tied round her middle. 'Where's Dexter?' she says without preamble.

Callie says, 'I don't know, Minnie. Perhaps he's taken a walk.'

Minnie sees Deirdre crossing the road from the Hotel des Bains to the beach. 'Where is your mother?' Minnie

demands loudly as Deirdre joins them. 'And my husband?'

'She was at the Hotel des Bains with me, sitting on the veranda. Then Dexter joined us. I decided to come to the beach.'

Without another word Minnie rushes up the steps to the street and crosses over to the hotel.

'Uh oh,' Callie says.

'Uh oh,' Deirdre repeats. They both raise their eyebrows, and Deirdre says, 'It's the only time I can get free of Angela, when she fancies some man or another. Except when she's sleeping or shopping.'

'She fancies Dexter?' Callie is incredulous.

Deirdre shrugs. 'For the moment.'

Callie groans. 'Deirdre, do you know the trouble that kind of thing causes me on one of these trips? I don't need it.'

'Sorry about that. But once Angela sets her mind to something, there's no stopping her. Frankly, it's much easier to be in her company when she has someone to flirt with.'

They walk idly down to the water's edge, their shoes off, feet cooling in the shallow sea. As they stand there, Minnie and Dexter walk by, on their way to swim, but obviously in the middle of a row. Minnie is shouting, 'I saw her, Dexter, leaning over in her wicker chair, nipple hanging out, and you just sitting there, staring at it.'

Dexter attempts humour. 'Now why would I want to stare at a wicker chair, Minnie?'

This is a big mistake. Callie and Deirdre hastily turn and walk the other way until they can no longer hear Minnie shrieking at her newly wed husband. Unfortunately, this leads them past Candice, who is sitting alone on a towel. 'Oh, Callie, I'm so relieved to see you. I think I'm burning. I covered myself with factor-twenty sunscreen, do you think it's enough? I wanted to ask Ellen, but she's in the water, paddling with

Archie. They've taken off their shoes and stockings.'

She says this as if they have stripped naked and are frolicking merrily up and down the Lido. Callie murmurs politely and, desperately needing to be alone, tries to walk away, leaving Deirdre with Candice. She is immediately confronted with the spectacle of Sylvester following a young Japanese woman down the beach, obviously making a nuisance of himself from the angry look on her face.

Callie wants to run and hide, but there is nowhere to go on this crowded, hot muggy beach. Her group is falling apart, and what is worse, *she* is falling apart, too. She knows she should waylay Sylvester before he gets arrested for harassment, soothe Candice, deflect Minnie and Dexter, but she cannot do any of these things.

All she wants is to see Tommaso. The need for him is so strong that she breaks away from the others and, without explanation, begins to run as fast as she can along the damp shore.

8

While Callie is running down the sands of the Lido, Tommaso is in Ca'Valier with his brother, having their lunch in the garden, on the stone table facing the wrought-iron fence and the Grand Canal. They are sitting under the sleek dark leaves of a large bay tree, by a clump of lavender. Behind them is the pergola, dripping with jasmine and honeysuckle.

'Giovanni, *per amor di Dio*, don't start, *per favore*. I have had one shit of a morning. The outboard engine on our supply boat wouldn't start and the men weren't able to get more cement, or diesel. Then the fucking rubber tube that the grout runs through to fill in the underwater cracks got blocked, and had to be cleaned at once because it goes hard in the hoses. I tell you, it's been hell. I do not need to come home for lunch and be lectured by you. *Lasciami in pace*, Giovanni. *Non intrometterti.*'

Giovanni has finished the spinach torte he brought back from Padua last night. When he'd arrived at Santa Lucia Station, he'd taken the *vaporetto* from the *ferrovia*, but when he got off at the Accademia stop, he realized he didn't yet want to go back to Ca'Valier. It was just past nine, and Callie would be there. Not wanting to face her and Tommaso just yet, he walked over the bridge to the Hotel Riva Tomá, where Patsy was free and willing to go out for a drink with him.

He is now, on the surface, calmly eating the fresh raspberries that he bought from the fruit and vegetable canal boat at Campo San Barnaba, on his way home

from Casa Goldoni this morning. Inwardly, he is far from calm. He ran away to Padua on a whim, to get away from Venice, from the emotional and sensual turmoil around him: in Tommaso; in Callie; in the Serenissima herself, that most seductive of cities, with her glittering water, her rich façades, her shops of silks and velvets, of glass and jewellery, masks and disguises.

'Finish your lunch, Tommaso. *Per favore.*'

'*No, non ho molta fame ora.* I'm not hungry.'

Giovanni wills himself not to be distracted from his own lunch, and slowly takes another bite of the raspberries. They are exquisite. When he has chewed and swallowed, he says, 'I am not interfering, Tommaso, whatever you say or think. I come home from Padua late last night, and this morning I hear from our neighbour Maria Teresa that a strange Englishwoman has been here every night, arriving late, and staying so long that no-one has seen her leave.'

'Fucking Venice. Such a small, nosy, narrow-minded, petty little town.'

Giovanni finishes the last raspberry carefully. 'That is not the point, Tommaso. The point is, that Maria Teresa knows you are married. She has met Sandra and the boys, remember, years ago, when you brought them to meet our parents; she still asks about her, asks when your family will come again to Venice. I am just warning you to be careful. Do as you wish, but be careful who you hurt.'

Tommaso's rage goes, leaving him limp and drained. He drinks the coffee Giovanni has made and sits down on the stone bench next to him. For a moment they don't talk, as the loud warning siren on the *motoscafo* of the *Vigili del fuoco*, the firemen, shrieks down the canal. In the quiet that follows Tommaso says, 'I wouldn't hurt the boys. Nor Sandra. Sandra doesn't like Venice, doesn't like going away anywhere during her holidays. She prefers being at home, playing tennis

every day. And the boys, they have their own concerns now. They won't be back here for a long time, so they'll be safe from the gossips like Maria Teresa. They won't suffer, I promise you.'

Giovanni pours himself more coffee, takes his cup and begins pacing round the garden, on the pebbles between the flower beds. How he hates this, but his love for Tommaso is too strong for him to remain silent. 'Even if it is as you say,' he begins, but his voice registers doubt, 'that they will be untouched by this, *you* will not be. You will be hurt with this woman, I can see this.'

'Oh, so now you are the Delphic oracle, eh?'

Giovanni is suddenly weary. The canal seems even noisier today. Another siren, another racing boat with a blue flashing light whizzes by – an ambulance, this time. After it comes a flat green rubbish barge, several *vaporetti,* a *motoscafo* carrying a cement mixer, and another siren, that of the boat of the *polizia* now racing past. The noise rings in Giovanni's head, makes him even more weary. He says, 'Tommaso, *tu prendi in giro*, you poke fun, you laugh at my concern, but this is no joke. Remember I am uncle to your sons, I know your wife—'

'This has nothing to do with my sons,' Tommaso says testily. 'As to Sandra, you haven't a clue what a marriage is all about.'

A shadow passes through Giovanni, is reflected on his face. 'It may not have been a marriage to you, Tommaso, but to me—'

Tommaso has already come to Giovanni, has clapped his hand on his brother's shoulder, then pulled him towards him in a rough embrace. 'I'm sorry, Giovanni. I didn't mean that, you know I didn't.' He breaks away and walks over to the wrought-iron gate that leads to the canal. 'Interfering, nosy neighbours; what is the matter with people? Minding everyone's business but their own—'

'Tommaso, calm down.' Giovanni, trying to steady his own agitation, walks over to the gardenia bush, plucks a flower and puts it in the buttonhole of his light linen summer jacket. 'You keep getting away from the main issue.'

'Oh? And what in the name of the Madonna Mother of God is that, eh? If not all these scandal lovers trying to cause trouble?'

Giovanni inhales the scent of the white flower, slowly, deliberately. How difficult it is, talking about these things. He says at last, 'Having affairs is one thing, Tommaso. Falling in love is another.'

'*Che cosa vuoi dire?* What do you mean? Did the Venetian neighbours tell you that, too?'

'No, there was no need. There are certain things – this one you have brought home here, to our parents' house.'

'Her name is Callie. Can you please refer to her by name.'

'You have not done this before, Tommaso. Brought a woman to this house.'

'I haven't just brought any woman. I brought Callie. She is not just any woman.'

The intensity with which Tommaso says this makes Giovanni wince. He says, 'Are you going to leave Sandra?'

The words cut the air between them like razors. Tommaso says, his voice like stone, 'I have no plans, nor desire, to leave my family.'

'I see.' Giovanni begins to put plates on a tray, carefully, methodically. 'So you are, instead, going to leave the Englishwoman. When the affair is over.'

Again, the razors. Tommaso shivers in the hot afternoon. 'I hadn't thought of that either.'

Giovanni looks at him steadily. 'It is either one or the other, Tommaso. Maybe you should face up to that.'

Tommaso says softly, 'You know about married men,

Giovanni. How torn they can be. Have you no sympathy?'

Giovanni's hands grow white beneath his brown skin as they clutch the tray heaped with the debris of lunch. He says steadily, 'It is because I know, Tommaso, that I am speaking to you like this. I am not without compassion, both for you and for Callie. That is why I am warning you. Be careful.'

Together they go into the kitchen. Before they part, Giovanni to the Casa Goldoni and Tommaso to his work site, Giovanni says again, 'Be careful.'

Patsy is saying the same thing to Callie as they meet for a drink before dinner. They are sitting outside in the Campo Santo Stefano, at Paolin's, drinking Venetian spritzers: white wine, fizzy mineral water and Campari. 'Your group is falling apart,' Patsy says after Callie has told her about her disastrous day. 'And so are you, by the sound of it. You'd better be careful.'

Callie takes a long swallow from her icy glass, and looks across the *campo* at the pigeons on the statue of the *Cacalibre* and the tired tourists sitting at its base. 'I'm bushed, Patsy. I'm with Tommaso every night after I finish with the group. I hardly sleep, I'm so screwed up emotionally it's not true. I know I'm not doing my job properly either. Do you know, yesterday I couldn't remember what church we were in; I just had this mental block and I totally forgot what I was doing. Not only that, but I didn't give a damn. All I could think of was when I'd be seeing Tommaso again.'

Patsy shakes her head warningly. 'Watch it, OK? You sound right on the edge.' She gets up to leave. 'Gotta go, one of my group has a skin rash, I promised I'd go with him to see if we can find something at a pharmacy.'

Callie lingers, unwilling to leave the shade of the awning, the buzz of the square, and go back to the Hotel Isabella and her group. Looking across the

campo she sees Deirdre walk across from the direction of San Marco. Deirdre is alone and doesn't see her, and Callie is at first relieved, then oddly disappointed. Her intitial relief was the normal one of needing to be alone, away from her group, but her disappointment is more complex. She is beginning to *like* Deirdre, not in the superficial way she either likes or dislikes one of the touring group, but in the deeper, more affectionate, way one does before an acquaintance turns into a friend. Despite her involvement with Tommaso, Callie has kept her promise to visit Deirdre in her room when Angela was otherwise engaged, to look at the photo album she has carted all the way from England, full of photos of her little girl.

On impulse, Callie leaves the café and intercepts Deirdre by the statue. Deirdre looks surprised, then pleased. She says, 'I was just making my way back to the hotel. I went inside the Basilica again, on my own this time. It knocks me out, all that gold mosaic.'

'It's amazing,' Callie agrees. 'Look, should we sit down for a minute? It's too nice to go inside, and dinner isn't for another twenty minutes.'

They sit down on the steps at the base of the statue, facing the Palazzo Pisani. Next to them a Dutch couple sit wordlessly rubbing their blistered feet, shoes and sandals lying scattered like pigeon droppings. Callie says, 'How did you manage to get some time on your own?'

'Angela went off somewhere with Dexter, I'm afraid. Minnie was exhausted and went to her room for a nap. I hate to say it, but I think Dexter and Angela planned this. God knows where they've gone.'

Callie frowns. 'Oh boy. Trouble.'

'Yup. Sorry.'

'Not your fault.'

Deirdre says, 'Do you know where I went after the Basilica? To buy a cat mask for my daughter. I met that old American couple in the shop; they were buying

more stuff for their grandchildren. Lavender was so sweet, helped me to pick out something for Kathy.' She opens the bag she is carrying to show off the mask, black and feline. 'She'd love it here, all these wonderful mask shops and the workshops where they make them.' She smiles at Callie, suddenly shy. 'Stop me if I talk about her too much. I don't usually, only with you and Pogo and Lavender. They keep telling me that I mustn't feel so guilty about leaving her behind for three weeks, but I can't help it, even though she seems happy enough. The friends she's with have a little girl her own age, Kathy's best mate, so she's got someone to play with.'

Deirdre talks, and Callie listens sympathetically, without the usual detachment she forces upon herself when dealing with her group members. Indeed, as Deirdre describes her love for her daughter, Callie is overwhelmed by an empathy she has never experienced before, a certain knowledge that she too could feel this way about a child, if the child was hers and Tommaso's.

The thought crushes her. She has never wanted children before, not with any of her other lovers, not when she was younger, nor when she passed the tricky age of thirty-five, the age when many women feel the time has come to make some kind of a decision about children before it's too late. She's not sure she wants them now; all she knows is that when Deirdre talks about her daughter, she feels she could love a child of Tommaso's as unreservedly as Deirdre loves Kathy.

But she knows, too, that the decision to have Tommaso's child will never be hers to make, though that is not what is distressing her. What is shattering, is the realization of just how deeply Tommaso has affected her in the short time she has known him.

Deirdre has finished talking, and Callie, desperately locked in her own tumultuous thoughts, says to herself, I will tell her about Tommaso; she will be

sympathetic. That is what I need now. Not lectures to be careful, nor disapproval, but the plain empathy that only a friend can give.

But before she has a chance to do so, Angela and Dexter suddenly come into view, laughing at something together. Dexter looks over at the Hotel Isabella, doesn't see anyone he knows, and surreptitiously pinches Angela's bottom. She laughs, mockingly pretending to slap his face.

Deirdre says, 'I'd better go and break that up before Minnie sees them.'

'I'll go with you.' They get up and walk over to the couple. Deirdre mutters as they approach, 'Bloody married men – all the same. Can't resist an easy bit of stuff.'

Her words hit Callie like stones. Serves me right, she thinks, for wanting to confide in one of the clients. She's aware that she has nearly made a dangerous mistake. She doesn't know Deirdre; she has been lulled by the intimacy of travelling into the illusion that she did.

Shaken, she leaves the others and goes into the hotel alone.

Callie doesn't go to Ca'Valier that night, nor does she go the next lunchtime. She rings Tommaso from the hotel hurriedly and tells him truthfully that she is innundated with problems, with a sudden rush of group activities. He is monosyllabic but accepting. They do not make plans to see each other again. And so the next time they meet, twenty-four hours later, they have been apart for the longest period of time since they met.

It is evening, and Callie is in the Piazza San Marco with some of her group: Archie and Ellen, Deirdre, Pogo and Lavender, who seem to be as much a part of her group these days as the others. The Americans had found Callie at the Hotel Isabella just as she was finishing dinner and insisted on taking her for a drink in

the piazza. Callie had at first protested. 'Do you know how much a coffee costs in St Mark's Square?'

'Honey, I don't begrudge paying it,' Lavender had answered. 'You can sit there for as long as you like over one coffee, no-one rushes you. And you not only get live musicians and a concert, you get a great view, the lights on the Basilica, the buildings, plus a real buzz with all the people there in a festive mood. I think it's great value.'

'Besides,' Pogo took over, 'we'd like to give you a little treat, a bit of a thank-you for all you did for us when I fell into the Giudecca. Say, why don't we ask Tom to come along? Why don't we just go over to his place right now and drag him out? We'd like to thank him again, too.'

Callie says quickly, 'He's very busy with his work. Maybe you can ask him another time.' She knows she cannot cope with Tommaso and her tour people at the same time.

San Marco's is brimming with noise and colour. It is midsummer and the spring tide is high, bringing the waters of the lagoon into the *piazzetta* and the piazza. There are several inches of water in front of St Mark's Basilica, and some French students have taken off their shoes and are paddling in it, laughing and shrieking. Everywhere there are deep pools of water, which seems to add to the carnival atmosphere as people skirt round the flooded areas or try to jump over the smaller puddles.

They are sitting at the Lavena café, having chosen it instead of either Florian's or Quadri's because Pogo insisted the musicians at Lavena were livelier. Indeed, the two violinists are playing a rousing Russian polka, with an accordionist and flautist and a cellist. Callie watches them, then looks beyond them to the Basilica. The dimming evening light is pearl-grey and pink, translucent, reflecting on the gilt on the façade. The angels' wings on the statues are polished golden by the

sun. Outside the enclosure of tables and chairs, where she sits with her group, a crowd has gathered to listen to the musicians, and in the dry part of the piazza, a young Italian couple is dancing.

'Come on, sugar,' Pogo says to Lavender. 'Do you remember how to polka?'

'My wife liked to dance,' Archie says. 'I was never very good at it.'

'I love dancing,' Ellen says. 'My husband doesn't.'

She sounds wistful. Archie registers this and says, 'My dear, as I said, I'm not very good, but I'm always willing to try. Will you have a whirl with me? I can't quite manage a polka, but we can shuffle along somehow.' He is quietly glad that his hip pain is in remission tonight.

They leave the outside enclosure of the café, to join the other dancers in the piazza. Deirdre says, 'Ellen must feel as I do tonight. Crazy with freedom from our charges.'

'Odd, though, that Candice, Minnie and Angela all have headaches.'

'Not odd at all. Minnie gets migraines, has had one since returning from the Lido, apparently. Candice is always ill with something or other. And Angela is faking.'

'Really? But why?'

'*Think*, Callie.'

'Oh hell. Of course. To get rid of you, so that she and Dexter—'

'Exactly.'

The others return breathless and happy. Lavender gasps, 'Isn't that long-haired violinist wonderful? I just love this place.'

'You're in good company,' Callie says. 'This was Wagner's favourite café, too.'

A voice behind her says smoothly, 'Always the tour manager, Calypso. Don't you ever relax?'

She doesn't have to look up to know who it is.

Lavender is shouting, 'Well, hi! Hi there, Tom! We haven't seen you in ages, except when we walk by that quay you're working on. And I darn well won't let Pogo get too close! Come on over and sit with us. You know Archie, and this is Ellen, and Deirdre, and of course you know Callie.'

Tommaso is in the company of one of his divers, Paolo, whom he introduces. Paolo recognizes Callie from the site, when she walked Tommaso back to work that day. He notes the way they react to each other, Tommaso and the Englishwoman, and thinks, *Oh, che incosciente!* What an idiot Tommaso is, letting a woman get to him so.

Lavender and Pogo insist on buying the two men drinks, and will not be refused. Paolo speaks no English, but conversation begins boisterously enough, with Pogo and Lavender describing in a combination of halting Italian and sign language how Pogo was rescued from the depths of the Giudecca Canal. Paolo, though he was there and saw it, listens and smiles. Ellen watches Callie and Tommaso carefully, saddened by the troubled look in his eyes, the wariness in hers. Not so soon, Ellen thinks, not so soon. She hopes they will not waste Venice. They are here for a fleeting time; every moment must be accounted for. She would like to say this to Callie, but, of course, she cannot.

The musicians take a break and the violinist Lavender so admired comes to their table, for he is a friend of Paolo's. The other musicians join them, and in making room, Tommaso and Callie are pushed closer together. As the others talk and joke, Tommaso says quietly, 'Am I wrong, or are we avoiding each other suddenly. You didn't come to Ca'Valier after dinner tonight.'

'And if I had, you'd have been out.'

Both register these two facts.

Callie says, 'I made myself stay away. I couldn't face your brother, to start with. And then one of my group

153

members said something about married men, and it got to me. It's no good, you know.'

'It *is* good. That's why it's so fucking difficult.' He pauses, checks that they are not being overheard. 'Sandra phoned yesterday. We speak two or three times a week, mainly so that I can talk to the boys.'

'You don't have to explain to me,' Callie says stiffly.

'I'm not. I am telling you that I, too, felt torn, after I spoke to my family. I was almost relieved, you see, when you stayed away.'

The others are calling them back into the conversation, and they are forced to join in. Callie thinks, with a great rush of pain, So this, then, is it; but Tommaso has reached out for her under the table, and is holding her hand tightly. Finally the musicians get up again to play, and there is a rush of movement as everyone decides it is time to go. Lavender and Pogo must head for the station and the last train back to Mestre, and Deirdre, uneasy about Angela, decides to take the *vaporetto* with them as far as the Accademia stop. Ellen and Archie decide to walk back to the hotel. Tommaso's friend Paolo excuses himself to join his girlfriend, who has just arrived, and Callie and Tommaso are at last alone.

Tommaso wants to say, Come back with me to Ca'Valier, now. But he does not. Callie wants to say, I'm going home with you, Tommaso. But she does not.

They are no longer holding hands, not even speaking. The musicians are playing Vivaldi. Callie says steadily, 'Do you know that the church of La Pietà, round the corner on the Riva degli Schiavoni, where Vivaldi directed and wrote music, was originally a home for orphans?'

'I'm not one of your tour group, Callie.'

His voice is odd, strained. Callie listens to the music for a few seconds, then says quietly, 'What are you then, Tommaso? What exactly are you to me? And for that matter, what am I to you?'

Tommaso doesn't speak. The music is livelier, grows to a crescendo. Every time I hear Vivaldi, I will remember this, Callie thinks. She says, 'I'll tell you what we are to each other, Tommaso. Nothing, *niente*. Oh, we can go on about love, but in the end what is love without some kind of promise, some kind of commitment? Neither of us has the right to ask for that from the other, nor do we have the right to give it.'

She is standing up, preparing to leave. The music crashes around her as she says, 'Tommaso, it was a mistake. We were both a bit crazy. It was sweet and wonderful, the week or so it lasted—'

'Six days, Calypso. I don't think we can count the last twenty-four hours.'

'Tommaso, don't. Don't make jokes.' The catch in her voice makes him want to go to her, hold her, but she says, 'It is easier for me if we call it all off now, right now. And it will be for you, too.'

Then she is gone, running through the underwater part of the piazza, her sandals squelching, in her haste to get away.

Paolo, watching from another table, wonders if Tommaso will follow her. He sees him half stand up, then sit back down. Callie is out of sight in an instant, having ducked down the Calle San Basso, at the side of the Basilica, and out of the piazza.

It is best this way, Tommaso tells himself as he signals the waiter and orders another beer. It is, without a doubt, completely for the best.

Paolo breathes a sigh of relief. Having a woman is one thing, falling in love is another, for a married man at any rate. With a wave, he motions Tommaso to join him and his girlfriend at their table.

At the Hotel Isabella Ellen looks out the window and sees Callie, alone, walking towards the entrance. Her bowed head and the slump of her shoulders contrast sharply with the vivacious figures still lingering at the

outside tables of the restaurant opposite the hotel. Then she raises her head slightly, and Ellen can see her face in the pink and amber light of the three-headed lamp-post, her cheeks wet and glistening.

Ellen thinks, I wouldn't be young again for all the tea in China.

The hot weather breaks suddenly, and with the dropping of the temperature there is fog, and a misty, drizzling rain. Callie's group, which has been moaning about the heat, is now whinging about the wet. Callie goes dully about her job, avoiding Dorsoduro whenever possible, except when she is scheduled to take her group to one of the churches or museums in the district. Once on the way to the Scuola Grande dei Carmini, she passes Tommaso sitting with Giovanni, in a café in the Campo San Barnaba. The two brothers are having a late lunch, and Callie is crossing the *campo* with her group, heading for the fruit and vegetable barge moored on the canal round the corner.

The drizzling rain has begun again, having stopped briefly in the morning. Tommaso and Giovanni, dry under the café awning, glance at the cluster of wet tourists walking past, not yet seeing who it is. Then Giovanni says, 'Tommaso, I believe that is Callie, with the yellow umbrella.'

Tommaso has never seen Callie at work, though, of course, he has seen hundreds of tour guides leading their charges from one important landmark to another in the city. She hasn't seen him, not yet, so he can watch her unobserved. Right at her heels a fat, pallid man with shorts and a dirty white T-shirt is trying to get under her umbrella, for the rain is coming down harder now. On the other side, an attractive but hard-looking woman, heavily made up and unsuitably dressed in a tight red skirt and stiletto heels, is holding her own umbrella but shouting something vitriolic at Callie. Tommaso cannot hear what she is saying, but

understands from the woman's face that she is angry about something. Callie looks tired, strained, unhappy. Others keep plucking her elbow, trying to get her attention; everyone seems disgruntled. Tommaso starts to stand up but Giovanni says softly, 'No, let her be.'

As he sits down again, Tommaso sees Callie look his way and start slightly as she recognizes him. She stares at him, either in panic or in despair, he is not sure which, and then she turns sharply and walks away from him.

Giovanni says kindly, 'Does she still affect you so much?'

'*O Dio!* It's only been a few days. What kind of a bastard do you think I am, eh? That I can get over a woman in so short a time?'

Giovanni smiles, just a little. 'I have known you to get over a woman in an hour, Tommaso.'

'You know this is different. I didn't need to get over the others, there was nothing to get over. And before you think the worst of me, let me tell you that *veramente*, truly, there was nothing for them to get over either. All that was agreed upon before anything was begun.'

Giovanni gets up, puts down some lira for the bill. 'That sounds so cold, so calculating. So unlike you, actually.'

'Some things are necessary, Giovanni. I never liked it much. But I needed the women, they needed me. Have you never known what it is like?'

Giovanni allows himself a wry smile. 'Not with women, no, you know that. But it is not so different with men, I suppose. My problem is that I want it all. Not just sex, but warmth, friendship, compassion, harmony. That is why I am still alone. Too fussy.'

Tommaso shakes his head, clasps his brother's arm fondly, and the two men part, Tommaso to walk back to the Zattere, where a boatload of concrete is due to arrive at three, and Giovanni to Casa Goldoni. The

museum is not far, but it's still raining and he's glad he has his black umbrella. There aren't many tourists about today, most are huddled inside museums, churches or their hotel rooms. It's really quite chilly for late June, Giovanni thinks.

As he walks along the Larga Foscari to the Campo San Tomà, he thinks of Tommaso, of the way his brother's whole demeanour changed after he had seen Callie. Giovanni thinks sadly about the last time a man looked at him like that, or indeed, the last time he himself had felt that strongly about someone. It has been a long time. The old familiar melancholy begins to pervade him, and he wishes he were home in Milan, not here in Venice, where rain on wet marble and watery reflections of peeling buildings in the narrow canals only remind one of the ephemeral nature of things.

The narrow alleyways are empty, the pitted bricks of the buildings on either side are wet, pungent. The yellow-green waterway alongside Casa Goldoni bristles with raindrops, but the playwright's house itself, with its warm golden bricks, its splendid well-head in the courtyard, looks comforting, beckoning. Giovanni rings the bell, and the proprietor, whom he knows well, lets him in with his familiar welcoming voice. *'Buongiorno. Che tempo brutto.'*

Giovanni agrees wholeheartedly that it is a nasty day. Putting his umbrella in the stand, he feels the spirit of the kind, gentle, fun-loving Goldoni gently prodding him, lifting his spirits. Upstairs are the first editions of the plays, with their wit and mischief, their frolicking plots and deluded characters, waiting for Giovanni to peruse, to comment upon, to translate into a new modern version.

I may not have a lover, a partner, but I have my beloved Goldoni, Giovanni thinks with great satisfaction.

As he settles to work, he decides that he would rather have his problems with the Venetian playwright

any day, than Tommaso with his Englishwoman.

Tommaso, at work on the Zattere, stands in the *moto-scafo* at the site, trying to concentrate on the work in hand, while the rain pockmarks the water. As he watches the pontoon, the square raft used to transport the materials for the job, his mind keeps wandering to Callie, to the look of sheer distress she had given him when she spotted him in the Campo San Barnaba. Paolo calls to him, asks him a question about the high-pressure jet wash which is being used to clean the marine growth off the stone that is being repaired. Tommaso is so preoccupied with thoughts of Callie that he doesn't hear him. Paolo shouts again, louder.

This time Tommaso hears and forces himself back to the present, to work. As the rain falls on him and the motor launch, as the men shout and try to unload the equipment, hampered by the weather, Tommaso swears loudly, furiously, '*Figlio de' na mignotta!*'

Paolo, who is waiting to relieve the diver under the surface, says mildly, '*Hai ragione*, Tommaso, the rain is a son of a bitch, true, but it's not stopping the under-water work. This shitty city is so soggy anyway it doesn't matter much if the sky is wet or dry.'

'Fuck the rain,' Tommaso says. 'Fuck Venice, too, for that matter.'

Paolo shrugs and prepares to dive.

The drizzling, misty rain changes to thunderstorms in the next two days, bringing warmer weather, but unpredictable chaos in the skies over the lagoon. Callie wakes early in the morning, five or six, to hear gargles of thunder interspersed with the bells of the churches over the city.

After work, Tommaso sits on his terrace and watches the lightning pierce the black sky above the Basin of San Marco, as he did once with Callie, the water underneath him rough and choppy. The sky turns dark amber, purple with the storm. Giovanni comes out and says, 'Do you want a drink, Tommaso?'

'No,' Tommaso replies shortly. Then, '*Grazie.*'

'Dinner will be ready soon. We'd better eat inside tonight. It looks like rain.'

Tommaso, standing at the marble balustrade around the terrace, doesn't turn but remains staring at the sky, the water. He isn't hungry, but Giovanni has prepared cannelloni, then risotto di secole, a Venetian risotto made with leftover bits of roasted beef or veal. He makes himself go inside, to try to put some normality back into his life.

Callie's group, free this evening after dinner, is split into those staying in the hotel, hiding from the approaching storm, and those who are out revelling in it. Candice, of course, is in her room, flinching with every rumble of thunder, cross that Ellen is out wandering somewhere with Archie and leaving her to the

storm. She is uneasy about Ellen, about this relationship that seems to have developed between her and that man. Of course they are merely acquaintances, thrown together by this wretched tour she wishes she'd never come on, but still, Ellen is a married woman. She wonders if she should tell Rodney. Or Ralph, come to think of it.

In the end she does nothing, merely gets into bed and pulls the covers up, waiting for the storm to pass.

Sylvester is in one of the bars in the Rialto area, trying to get friendly with two young Englishwomen. He invades their space, crowds in on their table and makes rude jokes, until one of them finally says, 'Piss off, will you?' Undaunted, he shrugs and waits for someone else to come along. Someone does, but it's only Deirdre, the daughter of that tasty but bitchy Angela, and Sylvester doesn't fancy Deirdre in the slightest. Still, she's better than nothing, he supposes. He decides to chat her up, begins to move from the bar in her direction, when he notices she's with that weird old couple, the Americans who are always tagging along with the group. It's not on, he thinks as he retreats back to the bar; they've got no business hanging round Comet Trail tours; it should be reported to head office.

The thought of head office makes Sylvester uncomfortable. He still hasn't got over Callie's threat to turf him off the tour. If that happened, he'd be blacklisted from other Comet Trail excursions. Silly old cow, he thinks malignantly. He has a good mind to phone head office himself, complain about the tour manager, about her rudeness and bad temper. That would teach the silly bitch, he thinks, his body twitching in a spasm of silent laughter.

But then he remembers the steely look in Callie's eyes that day in the museum, the deadly seriousness of her threat, and knows he dare not take the risk. He

likes the feeling of importance he gets from being an experienced traveller on these trips, able to tell the others what Comet Trail holidays are really all about. He also likes going back to his job at the college and bragging about the arty places he's been to, like Venice or Florence, to the snooty girls in the art department. Galling as it is, Sylvester knows he'll have to tread carefully with Callie for the rest of the tour, and not only that, with all the other tour managers on his various Comet Trail trips, for Callie is sure to say something about him.

The thought frustrates him so much that he quickly orders himself another drink.

Angela is out tonight, too. She is walking along the Fondamenta Zattere Ponte Lungo with Dexter, watching the lightning smash the sky above the Giudecca Canal. Minnie, exhausted after an afternoon buying cheap clothes at Standa, the low-budget department store on Strada Nova, Dexter in tow with his Visa card, has gone to their room with two aspirin and a bottle of mineral water. At dinner, Minnie, delighted with her purchases, tried to make Dexter promise to return the next day, to buy a handbag to go with her new clothes.

'Steady on, Minnie,' Dexter had said shortly. 'This holiday is costing us a fortune.'

'Holiday?' Minnie's voice changed from fire to frost. 'I thought this was our honeymoon. Our once in a life-time honeymoon. I can't believe you are starting a row with me on our *honeymoon*.'

Dexter, in a foul mood because there was fish on the menu again, had replied in an untactful way that, if this was a honeymoon, he hated to think what the marriage would be like. Soon a major quarrel was being witnessed and enjoyed by the rest of the group. At the end of it, Minnie rushed to Callie's table, demanded that Callie find her more aspirin because she was out and was fast developing another headache, and why

the hell was there never enough hot water before dinner so they could have a decent shower for once in this rotten hotel?

Dexter is thinking unkind thoughts as he walks down the Zattere with Angela. There is a high tide again and water is splashing the pavement. Angela squeals playfully and jumps to keep from getting her thin high sandals wet, and the leap lands her in Dexter's arms. Somehow she stays there for a few moments, cleavage pressed against his chest, and he gets a whiff of musky scent, which mingles with the smell of seaweedy things from the canal. Dexter remembers he's a married man, something he has forgotten once or twice before with Angela, but the way she's clinging to him now suggests more than the odd pinch. He pulls away, albeit unwillingly. Then he remembers how many pounds Minnie's shopping spree has cost him today, and how ugly the clothes she bought were, and how she didn't pay the slightest attention to him when he told her truthfully what he thought of them. He pulls Angela back towards him and says, 'It's going to pour with rain in a minute. Should we cut down this side street and take a short-cut back to the hotel?'

He doesn't intend to go back; he has noted that the alleyway is dark, deserted. He pulls Angela into the Calle Trevisan, beneath a dark *sottoportego*. She offers no resistance as he takes her back into his arms and begins to rummage through her cleavage. The thunder roars, lightning flashes, and, as Angela puts her hands on his belly and moves them down his thighs, he thinks, *Shit*, marriage was never like this.

Patsy and Callie are sitting out the storm in their separate hotel rooms. Patsy, at the Riva Tomá, is repairing the polish on her toenails and thinking of her husband, Stuart. She has to admit she doesn't think of him often on a tour. She likes her job enormously and is

extremely good at it, and one of the reasons is that she doesn't let herself be distracted by thoughts of home and her husband. She loves her husband, but is quite happy to be without him for weeks at a time. Luckily he has his own interests – his garden, mainly, and his computer. The first is his hobby, the second his job; both give him much pleasure. He has always been a solitary man.

Patsy is thinking of him now because she has tried to phone him for two nights in a row and he has not been in. She phones him once a week on a tour, when they talk amiably for twenty minutes or so. The uneasy thought hits her that perhaps something is wrong, for he doesn't usually go out in the evenings except to garden, and then he takes the mobile phone. She doesn't like to ring later, for he goes to bed early. Patsy stares at her drying toenails and reminds herself that no news is good news, that if Stuart were ill, she would have been notified. Comforted, she hobbles into the bathroom, pours some bath salts in the tub and runs her bath.

Callie, round the corner at the Isabella, is trying to have an early night, but the storm is keeping her awake. The rain that finally came was torrential but didn't last long; it has already stopped, the thunder dying to nothing more threatening than a distant gurgle. Callie has taken a sleeping tablet, something she rarely does, but it doesn't seem to be doing any good. Her head, her limbs, her body, her heart, feel heavy, dead, but she cannot sleep, for she cannot stop thinking of Tommaso. She misses him. She hardly knows him, her mind says, but her heart and body tell her that this is useless rationalization.

She tries to read, but it's hopeless; tears brim onto the page in the middle of comic scenes. She turns the light back off and finally dozes for a couple of hours, but is awake again at four. She lies in bed and waits for

daylight, for the sound of birds. When it comes, she opens the curtains in her room and looks out over the scruffy patch of garden. The cat is there, wide awake and posing, like one of the winged lions carved and sculpted all over Venice.

At six she goes out, unable to bear her room any longer. The morning is misty, white shapes rising from the canals like spirits. There's not a soul anywhere, only the ghost shapes on the water as she crosses over the Accademia bridge. She deliberately doesn't look towards Ca'Valier, but on the other side of the bridge, towards San Tomà. A nearly empty *vaporetto* slices the mist on its way to the Rialto. She doesn't know where she is going, but it's not to Tommaso. She needs to be outside, to walk, to move. Uneasily, she knows it is herself she's trying to get away from as well as Tommaso.

She turns right at the Accademia and angles round some side alleys until she is walking on the *fondamenta* opposite the church of San Trovaso. The mist on the side canal is frothy, like the milk on a cappuccino. She passes the *enoteca* where she and Tommaso had their first lunch together, on the bridge over the small canal. She quickens her steps and passes the *squero*, the gondola workshop, where the boats are made and repaired. Finally she is at the Giudecca Canal, on the Zattere. Here the mist is thicker, but stained with pink from the hidden rising sun. It is six-thirty in the morning.

Callie walks along the empty *fondamenta*, the water lapping fitfully at the walkway, until she finds herself at Tommaso's work site. There is no-one there, of course, but there are signs of work in progress for 100 yards along the quay. There are underwater tools, a cement mixer and pump, a rubber tube going into the water. And safety fencing, of course, now the survey is over and the job itself is well underway: a three-foot metal-mesh interconnecting fence round the whole

area. Callie stops and smiles wanly, wondering if the fence would have deterred Pogo had it been up when he fell in.

She doesn't move for ten, fifteen minutes. She cannot be near Tommaso, but she takes comfort in being near his work. The mist is chilly for the tail end of June; she's glad she took a sweatshirt. The island of Giudecca is invisible across the canal and few boats are out at this hour. An old man with a cane and a muzzled mongrel makes his way past Callie, nods and then disappears down a side street. There is no-one else on the entire *fondamenta*.

Except Tommaso. Callie turns from staring out at the water to see him walking towards her, only a few yards away.

He says, 'You're not planning on jumping in, I hope? I've already had to rescue one foreigner from the Venetian waters this summer.' His words are light, but his voice is gruff.

Callie says, 'Bloody Italians. So vain they not only wear their sunglasses in the midst of thick fog, but they think every Englishwoman they make love to is going to throw herself into the Grand Canal when it ends.'

Tommaso smiles, slightly. 'You're a crap tour guide. This is the Giudecca Canal.'

'I know, you fool. It doesn't have the same romantic ring as the Grand Canal. That unknown mistress of Byron's, the other jilted lovers in Venetian history – they didn't throw themselves into the Giudecca. It had to be the Grand Canal or nothing.'

Tommaso takes a step closer to her. 'I didn't jilt you, Calypso.'

'No? Perhaps not. I suppose we did the jilting together.'

They look at each other thoughtfully. 'Well,' Callie says.

'*Sì. Allora.* What now, Callie?'

But she has no time to answer, for he is holding her,

166

and whether it was she who made the first move, or he, neither of them will later remember.

Giovanni wakes at eight-thirty, puts on his dressing gown and goes across the landing to the bathroom. As he passes Tommaso's bedroom door, he sees that it is tightly shut. Giovanni stops. His brother never shuts the door of his room, not when he's alone.

On the stairs, in a discarded heap, Giovanni finds a crumpled blue sweatshirt, with the trail of a comet blazed across the front.

With a heavy heart, he goes to the kitchen and makes a pot of coffee for three.

When Tommaso and Callie emerge, reluctantly but fully dressed, a few minutes later, the coffee is still hot. Giovanni is tactfully in the kitchen, as far away as possible from the upstairs bedrooms.

'I have made coffee,' he says. His voice is dull.

Callie and Tommaso drink a small cup each, black with a teaspoon of sugar. Conversation is stilted, unreal, as if their voices are muffled by the mist still hovering in the garden, on the canal. Very shortly Callie has to race back to the hotel and make a brief appearance for her group at breakfast before taking them to the Correr Museum in San Marco. As Tommaso opens the door into the courtyard, Callie cries, 'Oh look, Tommaso, there, by the statue of old Signor Valier, or whoever it is. A cat!'

'Ah, Bambi.' He leans down, begins to stroke a fat, fluffy black cat with a white striped face. Callie joins him. 'Tommaso, is he yours? Or Giovanni's? Look at his face, it looks just like a mask.'

'Bambi belongs to no-one. He's the neighbourhood cat, moves from home to home, never settles anywhere for long.'

As they go to the outside door, Bambi strolls down the courtyard and yowls at the door they have just

shut. Within seconds Giovanni opens it, and when Callie turns for one last look at the cat, Giovanni is cradling him in his arms, stroking him, as if he were a long-lost child.

'You're late,' Patsy says to Callie as they meet under the statue of Nicolò Tommaseo. They are walking together to the Piazza San Marco, having combined their two groups.

'Only five minutes. Is everyone here? Let me count mine; I think only thirteen have signed up. God, Sylvester's coming. Does he never give up?'

'He buys art postcards and sends them to the students at his college,' Patsy says. 'He told me the other day. "The chicks get turned on by all that arty-farty stuff," were his exact words.'

Callie groans, but even Sylvester cannot make her unhappy today. She has seen Tommaso, made love with him until it was time to rush back for breakfast and made plans to see him later in the day. For the moment, that is enough. For the moment, nothing else matters.

They lead the group to the Museo Correr, the civic museum. Archie is disappointed because his favourite Carpaccio is *in restauro*; Candice has a crisis over the grotesque depictions of a Bosch painting; Sylvester says that everything in the whole museum is shit-boring. Minnie and Dexter, who are heartily sick of museums and churches, but came along because they got tired of arguing over where they should go instead, are hissing at each other as they pass from room to room. Dexter, guilt making him more irritable than usual, checks his reflection in glass cases holding old coins and ancient Venetian jewelry, and wonders why Angela didn't appear for breakfast this morning. Too exhausted, he thinks smugly. He feels a macho pride that it has something to do with him, with his performance under the *sottoportego* last night when

Minnie was in bed with her migraine.

Despite the cantankerous complaining of her group, Callie maintains a cheerful calm. 'I must say you look perkier today than you have for days,' Patsy says when they are outside in the Piazza San Marco, their groups at last dispersed for lunch. 'Quite bright-eyed and bushy-tailed, as they say. Are you on drugs?'

Callie laughs. 'No. Yes. Oh, Patsy!' She tries to look shamefaced, but it comes out radiant.

'Bloody hell. You didn't. I thought it was over.'

'It was, Patsy. Then we met, sort of accidentally—'

'Does Giovanni know?' Patsy is blunt.

'Yes. I saw him this morning, before breakfast. Look, I know he doesn't approve, I could tell the way his mouth was set this morning, tightly as if I were the original whore of Venice.'

'Do you blame him?'

'It's none of his fucking business.'

It is, as usual, crowded in St Mark's Square, and several people turn to stare at Callie as she says this last sentence louder and more vehemently than necessary. The morning fog has lifted and the sun is hot, penetrating. Callie turns and begins ploughing through the groups of tourists, Patsy at her heels.

'That's your first big, big mistake,' Patsy cries. 'Thinking that what you and Tommaso are doing is no-one else's business. It's Giovanni's, because he's *family*. He dotes on his two nephews, I've seen their photos, long before you came on the scene. Sandra's, too, for that matter. She's a real person, Callie. I saw her standing, smiling at the camera, her arms round the shoulders of her two sons. She looked nice. Pretty, too, with curly blond hair—'

'Don't, Patsy, just don't.' Callie tries to walk away.

'Stop sticking your head in the sand.' Patsy follows her, beetling a path through the pigeons, the tourists. 'They exist, OK? His sons exist, his wife exists.'

Callie stops and faces Patsy. 'Look, you've made it

169

perfectly clear that you don't approve. I told you when this thing began that I didn't approve either, so I don't need either yours or Giovanni's judgement. I tried, Tommaso tried, to stay apart, then to break it up before we got in too deeply. It didn't work, but I'm not stupid enough or selfish enough to try to have him for ever. I just want a bit, OK? That's the way it is, Patsy. Now stop bugging me.'

They stare at each other with hatred for a moment. Then it passes, and their old affection for each other replaces the animosity. Next to them a Milanese businessman on a mobile phone, frantically waving his arm at his unseen caller, frightens the pigeons, and hundreds of them take off in a huge flapping of wings. 'Bloody birds,' Patsy says, 'I can't understand why the Venetians are so fond of them.'

Callie quotes, in her best tour-leader voice, 'There are several different stories as to how the pigeons came to St Mark's Square in Venice. One is that they belonged to one of the Doges—' Patsy pokes her to shut her up, and they both laugh, relieved as the tension is broken. Patsy says, 'Look, I'm starving, shall we go find some lunch?'

Callie hesitates. Patsy says, 'Sorry I asked. You're going to meet Tommaso, of course.'

'Come with me. I'm meeting him at Ca'Valier. If Giovanni's there, maybe the four of us can go somewhere.'

Patsy shakes her head. 'No, no way. You're kidding yourself, Callie, pretending that we can all double date or something, like everything is fine and open. I'm under no illusion as to who he is, even if you are. See you later.' She stalks away, across the piazza, scattering both pigeons and tourists with her determined stride.

Callie is late getting to Ca'Valier. Tommaso, waiting in the courtyard, says, 'I was terrified you'd changed your mind and decided to jilt me again. Don't do this to me,

Calypso.' He kisses her under the japonica tree, not giving a damn about Maria Teresa or any of the neighbours.

Callie says, 'After this morning? Do you think I can leave you, after this morning?' Her voice is deep with love.

Tommaso takes her into the kitchen, where he gets a bottle of prosecco from the fridge and pours them each a glass. 'To celebrate,' he says. 'Finding you in the mist.'

'I never asked what you were doing there at six-thirty in the morning.'

'Same as you, couldn't sleep. I decided to try to concentrate on the job instead of you, so I walked over to check on a piece of equipment.'

'Oh dear. You never did.'

'There was time later.' He hands her a glass.

'Where is Giovanni?'

'He left a note, saying he won't be home for lunch. I think he's being tactful.'

'Or disapproving.'

Tommaso is silent. He cannot deny his brother's disapproval. 'It's only because he wants what he thinks is best for me.'

'Which isn't me.'

Before Tommaso can answer, Callie raises her glass. '*Salute*, Tommaso. No, don't say anything, please; don't try to justify how Giovanni feels. He's right, he means well. He's only trying to protect you from the sirens, after all. Remember, I'm Calypso, the other woman.'

Tommaso clinks his glass to her glass. '*Salute,* Calypso. Not just the other woman. The only woman. *Ti amo,* Callie.' He puts down his glass and kisses her. 'And in English: I love you, Callie.' He has never said this to another woman, only to Sandra, his wife. And he has not said it to her for a long time.

Callie nods, unable to speak. 'Last night . . . this morning, I mean . . .' She cannot go on.

'I know. I feel it, too.'

She struggles to find words. 'It was truly making love. I've used the term before, thought I had done it before. But it wasn't, I see that now. Oh, it was good with some of the others, and I cared for them, and sometimes I thought I was in love with them – but it wasn't making love. This morning, that was making love.'

Tommaso cannot answer. The enormity of what they are saying to each other hums in his ears, echoed by the sound of purring from the window ledge. As he and Callie embrace, the mask-like face of the black-and-white cat stares at them sombrely, for once unnoticed.

The first week in July is hot, humid. Tommaso and Callie make love in the early mornings, when the breeze from the canal comes into the garden, and from there into Tommaso's bedroom, smelling of jasmine, honeysuckle and wisteria; and smelling of the sea, too, which fills the hot canals with the freshness of a new tide. Callie and Tommaso lie naked on the bed, soaked in sweat, cooling in the morning breeze.

They make love as soon as she arrives, usually at about six, before any of her group are up. At eight Tommaso gets out of bed, goes down the marble stairs to the kitchen to make coffee and brings it upstairs on a tray for the two of them before Callie has to return to the hotel.

Giovanni drinks his first coffee of the day alone in the kitchen, or on the balcony, letting the other two have their time together. He doesn't approve, but he will not condemn. His worry over Tommaso is huge and deep, and it is affecting his work on Goldoni.

Sometimes Callie comes at night, especially when Giovanni is out, at a concert perhaps, or having an after-dinner drink with Patsy in one of the bars at Campo Santa Margherita. Then Callie races over to

Ca'Valier as soon as she finishes her dinner with the group, and stands with Tommaso on the balcony, drinking Campari with either orange juice or soda, and watching the swallows, dozens of them, swoop and dive above the canal, catching their evening meal of insects. They listen to birdsong and look into the green water of the canal to see perfect reflections of the city, the *palazzi* turning pink, then amber, in the water as the light fades.

Tommaso always asks Callie to stay the night, but always she says, 'I can't, Tommaso. I'm supposed to be on call twenty-four hours a day. If there were an emergency, if one of my group needed me, I'd be in big trouble if I wasn't there.' Even for those few evening hours, she leaves her phone number with Signor Alberti, who is a man of the world and knows he can get her at Ca'Valier in the morning, too, if need be.

And so at midnight, like Cinderella, Callie leaves. Sometimes Giovanni comes home first and they have coffee together, talking politely about Goldoni, about Tommaso's work, about Callie's group. Giovanni is grudgingly beginning to like Callie, but he likes Sandra, too. There are no more dinner parties for the four of them, Callie and Tommaso, Patsy and Giovanni, though Giovanni would dearly love to cook again for such appreciative eaters. It isn't right, somehow. It would not show respect for Tommaso's family.

One night, when Giovanni knows Callie is taking her group to a concert in Castello, he asks Patsy to come to dinner again. Tommaso has gone to Milan on business and will not be home until late. Giovanni prepares a magnificent meal of zucchini flowers stuffed with cheese, rolled in flour, and fried in olive oil. Next they will eat *gli spaghetti ai gamberetti all'olio*, spaghetti with shrimp in olive oil and fresh basil and garlic.

The meal is perfect, as always. Giovanni and Patsy eat mostly in silence, concentrating on their food. It's late, because Patsy had to sit through a meal with her

group at the hotel, and it's quite dark on the balcony. Three or four stars are out, and over the water the red light of a gondola glides through the night like a shooting star.

Only when the meal is over does Giovanni say, 'Does your friend Callie speak to you, Patsy? About Tommaso?'

'No, not since we had a bit of a row about it. She knows I don't like it, that I'm wary.'

Giovanni says carefully, 'I don't mean to pry, or to interfere. My brother does not talk to me either; he feels it is not my business. He is right, of course, but I worry. His family, you see. You don't think . . . that is, he wouldn't leave them, would he?'

Patsy stares out into the night, discreetly stifling a belch. 'I don't think so. I mean, I don't know your brother, but Callie said from the start that she didn't want to break up a marriage. I think they are making the most of what time they have, which isn't much. Her tour in Venice ends in another ten days.'

The relief Giovanni feels is overpowering. His brother has said that he has no intention of leaving Sandra, and if Callie feels the same, the family is safe. Giovanni thinks of his nephews, thinks of Sandra, and decides to visit them this Christmas. He is asked every year, but seldom goes, not liking to intrude on a family celebration. But, of course, he is family; both Tommaso and Sandra have said it often enough.

He will go this year, *di sicuro*, for sure. With a great lightening of heart, he excuses himself to Patsy and goes downstairs to the kitchen to collect the dessert.

The next morning at eight o'clock, Tommaso does not go downstairs to make the coffee. Instead, he turns to Callie and holds her tightly. When he speaks it is to say, 'I can't leave you, *cara*. I can't see a future without you in it. I'll tell my wife as soon as the job is over, as

174

soon as I get home. You understand, it's something that cannot be done on the phone.'

Callie, in his arms, cannot breathe for several seconds. When she inhales again, she takes in the clean scent of Tommaso's sweat with the smell of sea and sex and stone and jasmine.

At breakfast, Giovanni hears Tommaso repeat the
words he spoke to Callie that morning. Callie has gone
back to the hotel and Tommaso is sitting with Giovanni
on the balcony. It's almost nine and the Grand Canal is
already humming with traffic. Flat, low boats carrying
red tomatoes, yellow peppers, boxes of peaches and
nectarines, crates of zucchini flowers, head from the
Rialto Market to the hotels round San Marco. A *Vigili
del Fuoco* boat shrieks up the canal, the firemen alert
and ready in their bright-orange protective clothing.

Giovanni, distracted, tells himself he has misheard
Tommaso. '*Non capisco*, Tommaso. What do you
mean, you are going to speak to Sandra? But you talked
with her only a day or so ago.'

Tommaso looks out towards the domes of the Salute,
red-tinged in the early morning sunlight. He registers
the patterns of light and shadow above the open lagoon
in the distance. Putting down the brioche that
Giovanni has just bought fresh from the bakery down
the street, he says 'I am going to speak to Sandra as
soon as I get home. About Callie.'

The canal is suddenly quiet, as if it, too, is as
shocked as Giovanni. For a few moments no boats blas-
pheme the air with hoots and motors and the hard
slash of sliced water. The morning sound of the birds
seems loud, raucous. The shriek of a seagull, the call of
swallows, the twitter of sparrows, seem to create dis-
cord rather than harmony.

A tiny sparrow, its reddish-brown head gleaming in

the morning light, sits cheekily on the marble stone of the low terrace wall, waiting for crumbs. Tommaso breaks off some of his pastry and carefully places it on the stone. Bambi, the cat, whom Giovanni had let in that morning, walks onto the balcony and eyes the sparrow furtively. 'No, Bambi,' Giovanni says softly, and the cat, offended, flicks his tail and goes back to the bedroom.

At last, Giovanni makes himself look at his brother, who is still staring out at the *cupole*, pearl-grey in the morning light. 'But why, Tommaso? Why?' Even as he says it, he knows the answer is obvious.

Tommaso stands up, leans against the railing and looks straight ahead, at the *palazzi* lining the water opposite Ca'Valier. The one in front of him is the place where Henry James stayed when he was in Venice, and Monet, and Whistler, too. A few buildings down is the smaller *palazzo* where the poet Gabriele d'Annunzio wrote; his jealous mistress, the actress Eleanor Duse, taking up residence opposite to keep an eye on him. Past the Accademia, there is Byron's old residence, and Wagner's – the list goes on and on. Tommaso hasn't thought about this for a long time, but for some reason he does now. He finds it comforting how unimportant it all seems, the passions of these intense people who lived and worked and loved in Venice, as he is now. Time will make what he is about to do seem unimportant, too.

He says, still looking across the water, 'As you know, I talk to the boys often when I am away, I miss them. Sandra and I talk, too, but I have to say, I've never longed for her like I have for them. It's the same for her. She has a busy, fulfilled life.' Tommaso allows himself to think for a few moments of his wife's life, so active, so involved. Loving and devoted to her sons, she has nontheless been able to create a good life for herself, fully enjoying her job, throwing herself steadfastly into her tennis. A picture of Sandra comes unbidden

into his head: running off the tennis court, dressed in white shorts and a T-shirt soaked in sweat: bouncy, jubilant over a particularly sweet victory, shouting, 'Did you see that, Tommaso? Did you see that last serve?' before rushing over to her partner to savour their winning game.

'I know Sandra is a good mother.' Giovanni is determinedly eating his second brioche, pouring himself another cup of coffee. He will not, he tells himself, let his breakfast be spoiled by Tommaso's revelation. He is shaken enough already, without the added trauma of missing a meal. He doesn't need food so much as fuel, although his skinny, wiry body requires it, but for some kind of stability, order, security in his life.

Tommaso says, 'Sandra and I, as you know, had our children late. We were married young, still teenagers, not even twenty. We fell in love rapidly, too rapidly, married too quickly.'

'I thought you were happy,' Giovanni says, staring miserably at his half-empty coffee cup. 'You seemed so. The marriage has lasted.'

The marriage has lasted. How stiff, how inadequate the words sound, Tommaso thinks. How lacking in passion.

Giovanni is saying again, 'It has lasted, Tommaso. Your marriage. Through some difficult times. Surely it must be a good one.'

Tommaso says sadly, 'It's not easy, to build a good marriage when one of the main reasons for marrying comes to nothing.'

Giovanni knows his brother well, remembers clearly those long, difficult years when Sandra alternated between black despair, when she could not conceive a child, and near hysterical elation when she thought that this time it had happened. He says, 'But Sandra had her baby in the end. Your son Antonio was born.'

'Yes, eleven years later.' Tommaso thinks of those eleven years, the long waits in consulting rooms and

clinics, Sandra's increasing agitation, alternating with depressive resignation. He thinks of her first pregnancy: the exuberant joy mingled with terror that something would go wrong. But nothing went wrong, thank God; the birth was surprisingly easy, the baby perfect.

'Such a beautiful *bambino*, your Antonio,' Giovanni smiles, and the thought of his oldest nephew calms him after the agitation of Tommaso's news. He eats the rest of his pastry, then continues, 'I was overjoyed to be an uncle. For your sake first, of course, but then selfishly for my own. I knew I would never be a father, so your sons were – are – as dear to me as my own would be. When Marco was born soon afterwards, less than a year, I was as thrilled as you were. Do you remember, we met in Paris a few days later and drank champagne together?'

'That was a good evening. You were at the university there, and I flew out from England to see you, just to celebrate together, before going on to a job near Rome.'

The smile fades from Giovanni's face, slowly like a long twilight. 'That is why I am so concerned now, Tommaso. It will hurt your boys, this . . . this separation,' he finishes lamely, not knowing quite how to refer to the disaster that is about to befall his beloved brother and family.

Tommaso shakes his head. 'I talked to them both, just the other day. They are ten and eleven now, full of life, of their friends, of their summer vacation. They are off to a summer camp, and Sandra will be with them; she's an instructor there. It's a sports camp, you see. The boys will learn cricket, I suppose.'

Giovanni laughs out loud. 'Your boys are so very English. Cricket already? So grown, so soon? *In quattro e quattr'otto*, in the twinkling of an eye! Our parents would have loved to watch them grow. Pity they are not here to see it.'

'But *you* are. You've not seen them for some months,

you must come out to England to stay with us.'

As soon as he says this, he remembers. He amends his words. 'Stay with me and the boys, Giovanni, wherever we are.'

'Sandra will have the boys, you know that.'

'Yes. But I will see them, have them, whenever I am home, and soon, on their holidays, they will be old enough to travel alone, meet me in Italy, perhaps.' He looks at his brother carefully. 'Meet *us*. Callie and me.'

'I see.'

'Do you?' Tommaso, agitated, stands up again, would like to pound the rough marble of the balustrade with his bare hands, but tries to maintain some control. 'I believe you must do; you have loved, I know that. Then you will understand when I say that she is like the sun to me, Giovanni. As if I have been living the last twenty years in shadow, and suddenly there is sunlight. You would have me give up the sun, after years of darkness?'

Giovanni, remembering sunlight, the kind that penetrates your heart and soul and bathes you in tender radiance, shakes his head. 'No, Tommaso. I could not ask anyone to give that up, once they have known it.'

They are silent for quite some time, listening to the traffic on the canal, deep in their own private thoughts. Finally Giovanni forces himself to ask, not looking at Tommaso, 'And Sandra?'

'When I spoke to her, two days ago, she was like the boys, full of her own life, a life which has nothing to do with me.'

'Surely you do not resent that?'

'Of course not. But I realized, as I was talking, how little any of them need me.'

You are wrong, Giovanni thinks, his morning's brioche sitting heavily in his stomach, churned by the acid of worry. You are wrong, but you won't listen to me any more, I can tell by the way your face is set

– tightly, grimly, like it did when you were a child and determined on a difficult course of action.

Sure enough, Tommaso is looking at his watch, announcing that he must go to work. Giovanni makes one last effort. 'You have known Callie such a short time, Tommaso. Would it not perhaps be better to wait, be sure before you take such a drastic step? Be sure that what you feel for each other is real, *non è tutto una mostra*, not make-believe?'

Tommaso looks steadily into his brother's eyes. 'I am sure, Giovanni. It doesn't feel like I have known Callie for a short time; it feels as though she has always been part of me. That is why I cannot leave her.'

There is nothing more Giovanni can say. He doesn't look at his brother as Tommaso says goodbye and leaves quickly for work.

The public boat to Torcello is large, uncrowded, comfortable. Callie and Patsy board with their group at the Fondamente Nuove, an hour or so after Tommaso's conversation with Giovanni, and settle themselves on the top deck, where there is a roof to protect them against the sun, if it should trouble to come out from behind the clouds. The seats by the open railings are three across, and on the other side of the boat Callie sees Angela squeeze herself in next to Dexter, who, dressed in drab green trousers and shirt, looks like an olive between two slices of bread, for both women are wearing white. Angela, in a smart linen jacket with matching skirt, shudders at Minnie's crushed cotton sundress with the sad bow-tied straps in a length that is neither long nor short, but something blandly in between. She smiles sympathetically at Dexter for having such a frumpy wife.

Callie is sitting next to Patsy, on the opposite side of the deck. She sees Angela simpering at Dexter, sees Minnie scowling at the water, which has become choppy and ruffled like an unironed silk shirt. It's

181

deep blue today, tinged with iron-grey.

Sylvester, a few seats down, mutters softly, so that Callie won't hear, 'Poxy tour guides, they don't half pick the days to go on excursions. Feels like a hurricane's coming up; it's gonna rain buckets in a minute.'

Candice, sitting between Archie and Ellen, looks anxious. Ellen says, 'Don't fret, you've taken your anti-seasickness pill, and I assure you there isn't going to be a storm. The weather forecast is good; I asked Signor Alberti this morning. This is merely morning cloud.'

Callie is looking out over the lagoon, still stunned by Tommaso's announcement that he is going to leave Sandra. Patsy says, 'Something's up; you're not only on another planet, you've been acting like you're never getting off. You actually smiled at Sylvester a few minutes ago. Is it the thought of visiting the island of Torcello again? And I thought you were such a jaded tour manager.'

Callie notes the irony in her voice, but doesn't reply. Instead she looks at the water, staring intently at the flat, muddy islands and a monk in his brown robes driving a motorboat. She's silent because she cannot shout out to Patsy, or anyone, what has been whirling round and round in her head since she left Tommaso this morning: that she's not going to lose him. She would like to cry it to the world, to the boatload of tourists, the residents on the island of Murano that they are just approaching; she would like to pour it out to Patsy, and to Deirdre, to anyone who will listen. But she cannot, not yet, not until it actually happens.

And she wants it to happen; she will not lie to herself. She didn't ask for this, she never once asked Tommaso to leave his wife; nonetheless, it has happened. When he told her this morning – was it only a few hours ago? – she was stunned into silence, and couldn't answer. But there was no need for her to speak; Tommaso knew, had always known, how she felt about him. They lay holding each other as outside

the great bells of Venice began their morning peal. Finally she said, still muffled in his arms, 'Tommaso, are you sure?' and when he answered, simply, '*Sì, sono sicura,*' she nodded, his use of the Italian somehow making it more true, more real, than when he had said it in English.

She left soon after, as she had to be at breakfast early to get her group to the Fondamente Nuove in good time for the boat to Torcello. Now on the boat she feels unreal, dazed. Watery, as if she has become part of the lagoon. As the boat steams away from Murano and goes out into the open water, the clouds drop away, freeing the sun, and the cool wind turns into a warm breeze. The boat goes slowly, passing reedy mud flats and tiny uninhabited islands with the crumbling remains of what look like once-splendid buildings. They pass Burano, island of lacemakers and fishermen, where the boat stops. Torcello is not far now, but by the time they get there it is eleven thirty, and hot. 'Only mad dogs and Englishmen are out in this,' Sylvester grumbles, forgetting that only an hour or so ago he was complaining about the wind and clouds and possible rain.

It is a hot ten-minute walk in the near-noon sun to Santa Maria dell'Assunta. Inside, the cathedral is cool, tranquil. Callie's group stops moaning about the heat to listen to her say, 'The building dates from about 1008, and is a fine example of Veneto/Byzantine architecture.' She goes on to point out some of the features, then lets them wander round the church to look on their own.

Alone for a few moments, Callie takes in the pale pearl-green of the marble pillars, the mosaic floor, the graceful, ancient serenity of the church, and feels transformed. Joy sparks her nerve endings, ignites her whole body, yet at the same time a strange peace descends on her. She can see every detail of the cathedral in great clarity, vivid colour, as if it were magnified a hundred times. So this, then, is love, she

thinks rapturously, gazing at the magnificent twelfth-century mosaic Madonna and Child on the ceiling. She has seen the mosaic over a dozen times, yet never has she seen the figures stand out so majestically in their sea of gold.

She leaves the church quietly, wanting to savour what has happened to her, but all too soon she is joined by the others. The sun, even hotter, dazzles her still further, and she lets Patsy take over the talking. Patsy points out the stone seat that the judges of Torcello used to sit on. 'The locals say that if you sit on it now, you'll be wed within the year.'

With much show, Angela sits regally in the seat. Candice says, 'Oh, Angela, but I thought you were married.'

'And so I was, darling,' Angela answers playfully. 'Several times. Deirdre is legitimate, I made sure of that. I quite enjoy the married state, it's a diversion.' She looks at Dexter and laughs. 'Especially other people's.'

After Torcello, they take the boat back to Burano. When they disembark, Patsy tells the two groups, 'It's lunchtime now, but the shops selling lace will be open.' She tells them how to get to the main square, with its restaurants and cafés, and arranges to meet them in two hours.

'You OK?' Patsy asks when they have dispersed. 'You seem a bit flaky.'

'I'm fine. Just too much sun, I suppose.' She is still in the odd state that had descended on her in the cathedral, a paradoxical state of exhilarated serenity.

'Should we get some lunch?' Callie asks, struggling to appear normal, even though she's not hungry.

Patsy looks disconcerted. 'Actually, I've got a date for lunch.'

Callie stops and stares at her. They're walking down one of the side streets of Burano. The brightly painted fishermen's cottages, a riot of cheery blues, yellows,

deep pinks and lavenders, are a welcome change from
the grand, faded buildings of Venice. Patsy goes on,
'With Giovanni. He has friends on Burano, colleagues
from Milan who have rented a cottage here for the
summer.'

'Oh. Right.'

'Sorry, but when they asked me, I didn't know we
were combining the two groups. Originally you were
going to Padua today, and to the islands next week.'

'Look, it's no problem, honest.'

'I'm sure if you want to come,' Patsy says slowly,
'Giovanni won't mind.' But she can't keep the doubt
from her voice.

The last person Callie wants to see is Giovanni. 'You
go, have a great time, and I'll see you back at the boat.'
She quickly changes the subject. 'Did you ever get hold
of Stuart, by the way? I meant to ask you earlier. You
were trying to phone him again last night.'

'Yeah, I did. He's fine. He must have been in the
garden when I called before, forgot to take the phone
with him. He's getting absent-minded, my Stuart.'
Callie notices again the complacent expression on
Patsy's face when she talks of her husband, as if he
were a jewel that she kept tucked away, to take out
when she was home. Callie wonders if she herself will
look that way, in years to come, when she talks about
Tommaso. The thought stuns her.

Tommaso. Callie begins walking slowly back
towards the quay as she lets herself think solely about
him. She has been too rushed; this is the first time she
has been alone since she returned from Ca'Valier this
morning. She is glad Patsy has gone off, is delighted to
have a couple of hours to herself. She walks back to the
quay, and finds a bench under the shade of some pine
trees, in a patch of rough grass near the landing stage.
There's an ice-cream vendor near the quay, and she
buys a *gelato* and takes it back to her seat. The shade is
welcome, and so is the quiet. She has known Tommaso

less than two weeks, and they have both made a decision to make a life together. It has never been discussed, was never even considered a possibility, but suddenly it has happened. Callie feels no doubts, no qualms. It feels right, it feels sure.

She lets herself think, tentatively, of the future. A *home*, perhaps? Italy? Tommaso has said he misses Italy. She could live here, find work here, she is sure. She finds she is grinning like a mad old lady, sitting on her bench under the shade trees. She is thinking of a home, a cat, a pot plant. She must surely be mad: she has spent the last twenty odd years running away from a home, from all the stifling barriers she had thought were synonymous with the word. And here she is, all this time later, realizing that she had got it all wrong. She had spent years pitying her parents for being chained to their beloved house and garden and village, not realizing that she herself was the one who was shackled, to a life barren of deep emotion, of any kind of honest commitment.

Her thoughts are interrupted by a loud cry, someone calling her name. It's Minnie, who has spotted Callie and is running towards her. 'They've gone off,' she shrieks, then bursts into tears.

'Who?'

'Dexter and that horrible woman.' The tears stop as abruptly as they began, giving way to fury. 'We had a fight, just an eensy one, over lunch. Just because I ordered ice cream as well as tiramisu, and fresh strawberries on the side. Just because it turned out to be more expensive than the main course, Dexter got on at me.'

Callie sighs and shakes her head. Minnie, oblivious, carries on. 'Well, I couldn't take his comments lying down, now, could I? I don't want him to think he can bully me, you know. So we had this fight, and then, well, then he stormed off. Just like that, left me right in the middle of the restaurant, all by myself, and I

hadn't even finished my ice cream.' The horror of it brings tears to her eyes again.

It was Sylvester, apparently, who had told her half an hour later, as she was wandering disconsolately round the island, that he had seen Angela and Dexter go off together on an earlier boat. 'I'm not staying in this dreadful city another minute, I'm going home,' Minnie wails to Callie. 'You can call the airport as soon as we get back and arrange a flight. I don't care what it costs, Dexter will pay. Serve him right.' She sniffs.

She hangs around Callie for the next hour or so, until its time to leave Burano, as does Sylvester, who says he's bored, and Candice, who tells them she's sure she has sunstroke, and would Callie take her right to the hospital when they get back. Callie sits her in the shade with Ellen and says she's sure it isn't sunstroke. Deirdre also arrives early, looking for Angela, not knowing she has run off with Dexter. Archie is sitting on another bench under a tree and looking pale and frail; he's having one of his bad days. Ellen leaves Candice and sits by him. 'Your hip's quite painful today, isn't it,' she says sympathetically.

He starts to say, as he always does, that it's fine, quite all right; Archie doesn't like to distress people by telling them of his ills. But something in her eyes, a spark of genuine compassion, compels him to say, 'Yes, it is. Very painful.'

It's such a relief to say it, to admit it. Ellen merely nods, but is still looking at him with such sympathy, such – yes, he's sure of it – affection, that, moved, he takes her hand.

Candice, on the bench opposite, sees this, sees how Ellen doesn't move away, doesn't disengage his hand. She half gets up, but sits down again in confusion. Ellen is *married*, she thinks. What would her husband, Ralph, say? What would he do? More to the point, what should *she* do? For surely Ralph would expect her to do something. And her own Rodney? What

would he advise her? Should she speak to Ellen?

As usual, she does nothing, just sits and stares miserably at the lagoon. How she hates Venice, its slippery buildings, its eroded stone, its labyrinth of tiny, dark, empty alleyways that lead nowhere, or to dead ends, to slimy green water. Steps lead straight into canals, streets go into tiny, shadowy courtyards, with nothing but feral cats with torn ears staring at you. Candice is relieved to admit how she hates Venice, her smug buildings, her smelly water, her seductive shops selling sensual fabrics, gaudy glassware, strange marbled paper, or those dreadful masks that seem to leer and sneer wickedly as one goes past.

Perhaps she can return to England earlier. The thought cheers her, and she rushes over to Callie to ply her with questions about the next plane home.

Back at the hotel, Callie manages to convince both Candice and Minnie that it would be ridiculously expensive to fly home early. Then she finds Angela – drinking gin and tonic at the café opposite the hotel – and discovers what she has done with Dexter. Apparently they have spent the past hour, while the others were still in Burano, in Angela's room, but Callie is not about to tell Minnie that. Dexter appears at dinner both guilty and smug, and so full of himself that he exerts all his charm on Minnie, to placate her. Deirdre is overwrought and appalled at the behaviour of her mother, and Archie is so white with pain that Callie wonders if she should get him a doctor.

At last the nightmare evening is over, and Callie leaves the hotel to walk over to Ca'Valier. She longs for Tommaso; she feels that she, too, will be near tears, like half her group members seems to be, if she doesn't see him soon.

But as she's leaving the hotel, she hears her name called, and Archie, face distorted with pain and fright, is clutching her arm, saying, 'That was Lavender on the

phone. She's in a bad way, Callie. Pogo's in hospital. He had an attack, his heart, earlier today. Lavender cannot speak Italian, not well, she says she doesn't know what to do, what is happening. I said I would come. My Italian is non-existent. Callie, please—'

'Of course I'll come,' Callie says, not waiting for him to ask. 'Where is he?'

'In Castello, at the civic hospital, the Giovanni e Paolo. Apparently he suffered chest pains on the *piazzetta* this morning, when we were at the islands, and Lavender forced him to go to the hospital. Thank goodness she did.'

'We'll walk, it will probably be quicker. No, I forgot your hip. We'll go the Zattere landing stage, catch the Number Fifty-two *motoscafo* to San Zanipolo.'

As they set off, Ellen rushes out behind them. 'I'll come, too. Please. I can't sit in the hotel wondering what is happening.'

Callie is about to tell her that there's no need, but then she sees the look on Archie's face: warm, grateful, loving. There is a need, of course there is. She has been so wrapped up with Tommaso, she hasn't really taken much notice of how attached Ellen and Archie have become to each other.

As they walk over the Accademia bridge, a thin sliver of a moon appears in the darkening sky, not far from the balcony where she had hoped to sit with Tommaso tonight, talking about their future. The terrace is empty; he will be waiting for her inside or in the courtyard, but there is no time to let him know she won't be coming. She'll phone him as soon as they reach the hospital.

The late evening sky radiates silver and gold and pearl, a fitting background for the pale new moon. How Venice flaunts her beauty, Callie thinks distractedly; faded though she is, she's still splendid, and she knows it. She glances one more time at Ca'Valier and resolutely walks on, leading the other two towards the Zattere.

11

They are lucky with boat timing, and arrive at Campo Santi Giovanni e Paolo fairly soon. As they approach, Ellen says, 'This is the hospital? It looks like a massive church.'

'It was once the old Scuola Grande di San Marco,' Callie says. As she leads them inside, through the vast foyer with its sumptious marble columns, cracked but still-elegant tiled floor, Ellen feels great relief that it is not she who's in charge. How easily she has relinquished her role as leader, as organizer; how relaxed she feels, being herself for once.

Callie seems to know exactly where she going in this huge place, and indeed, she knows the hospital well, having been here before with group members on other tours who had been suddenly taken ill. She leads the other two through several open courtyards crammed with wayward trees and shrubbery, down long corridors, in and out of archways, until finally they are in a four-bed ward, where Lavender sits with a subdued Pogo.

For the next hour, Callie finds doctors, nurses and officials, talks to them in detail, and helps Lavender to fill in forms and sign papers. Luckily the couple took out fully comprehensive insurance before leaving the States, so there'll be no financial repercussions for them. And even more fortunately, Pogo's prognosis is excellent. He did suffer a heart attack, according to the ECG tests, but it was very slight, more a warning than an indication of a serious heart condition.

'You should be out of here in a couple of days,' Callie tells him, and Lavender weeps with relief. 'But you must take it easy, rest. No lifting things. And no driving that camper van of yours, not yet.'

'But we were going to head South as soon as your group leaves,' Pogo says.

'Lavender will have to drive, then.'

'I can't, honey. Never learned.'

Callie says gently, 'Well, perhaps you should consider going home. You don't want to exert yourself, Pogo, not for a while. The doctor will be giving you tablets to take, but you must look after yourself.'

By the time they leave it's late. Callie is concerned about Lavender and where she will go; the last train to Mestre and the campsite has already gone. She thinks of Ca'Valier, and says, 'You can stay at Tommaso's place tonight. He would be happy to put you up, I'm sure.'

But Lavender refuses, saying she will stay right there, in the chair beside Pogo's bed, and nothing any of them says can dissuade her.

Callie parts from Archie and Ellen at the Accademia, having walked there with them from the *vaporetto* landing stage on the Zattere. She is in Tommaso's house, in his arms, within minutes. 'You are here, thank God,' he says inanely. 'Before you phoned from the hospital, I was crazy with fear, thinking you were leaving me. Then, when you phoned, I wanted to go right there to meet you, but you said you hoped to be away soon.'

'It took longer than I expected.'

'I was so worried. I thought, she's never coming back to me. I wanted to go out, find you, but I was afraid we would miss each other.'

They are downstairs in the kitchen, the window open to a breeze from the garden. The familiar fragrance of night flowers mingles with the smell of good strong coffee as Tommaso pours them each a cup.

Giovanni is in bed asleep; it is well after midnight.

Tommaso asks about Pogo and says, 'I like that funny little couple. They come by the work site often, you know, and stop and watch the work and ask me how it's going. And they want to know, truly; they are not just saying it.'

'They're interested in so much, they care about so much. Everyone loves them for that reason.'

They sit at the kitchen table and drink their coffee. Tommaso, so garrulous when Callie first arrived, is suddenly unnaturally quiet. Callie puts down her cup and says carefully, 'I know this morning, when you told me you would leave Sandra, that you meant it. But I also know that perhaps you said it too hastily and, after a day's reflection, have changed your mind.'

Tommaso starts to speak, but Callie stops him. 'It's all right if you do. Or rather, not exactly all right, but I would understand. And accept, of course.'

'I've told Giovanni. Afterwards, I felt great relief, as if by speaking of it, it has become true. No doubts, Callie.'

Relief washes through her, cleanses the pain her words had caused her, like the sea tide cleanses the canals each time it rises. 'You were so quiet, sombre, I thought—'

He goes to her, holds her. 'I was stunned, I think. It's such a big thing for me to do, leave my family. No, no, don't speak, I want to do this thing, I *choose* to do it. But it won't be easy.'

'It will be painful, Tommaso. For all of you.'

But not, he realizes, as painful as giving up Callie. 'Don't go back to the hotel tonight, please,' he says, suddenly terrified once again that he will lose her.

In his arms she smiles shakily. 'I'll phone the Isabella and give the clerk this number in case of an emergency. I need to be with you, too. Do you know it will be our first whole night together? We can't really count the time I sneaked you into the hotel.'

'The first, then. The first of many.'

192

Bambi, coming into the kitchen, meows loudly for food. 'Should we bring him up to bed with us?' Callie asks, stroking him as Tommaso opens a tin of cat food.

'No. No cats in bed.'

'In the house, then? Tommaso, please, can we have a cat?'

Her words make the future suddenly vivid, real. Tommaso, forgetting the cat, scoops her up in his arms and whirls her round. '*Sì, sì, sì, va bene*, of course we'll have a cat. A dog, too, if you like.'

'I'm not fussed about a dog. And with both of us working, a dog might be a problem. But a pot plant. Oh, Tommaso, can I have a pot plant?'

'You can have a hundred pot plants, if that's what you want. But only if you come upstairs with me, right now.'

Laughing, high on love and promises for the future, they race together up the marble stairs, leaving Bambi on the kitchen table trying to dig out with his paws the cat food still in the open tin.

Callie wakes to the bells of San Trovaso coming through the open window, and bird calls in the garden. She props herself up on the pillow to look out at the clump of lavender right under the window and the deep purple flowers of a hydrangea bush beyond the lavender. She sits up higher, to catch a glimpse of deep-blue canal water beyond the iron garden gates.

'Tommaso, wake up, it's so beautiful! God, I love Venice. Look, see the colour of the canal. Yesterday it was soupy green, today it's the colour of the sky. Tommaso, I slept so well, didn't you?'

Tommaso, not his best when he first wakes up, grunts unsociably and tries to go back to sleep. Callie delights in this little cameo of real life and lets herself think of what it will be like to wake up next to Tommaso morning after morning. Blazing with

happiness, she grabs his dressing gown, brown cotton, faded, slightly grubby, puts it on and goes down to the kitchen.

Giovanni is up, wearing a blue silk dressing gown, carefully measuring coffee into the cafetière. If he's surprised to see Callie, who has obviously been here all night, he doesn't say. All he says is, 'Will you and Tommaso have your coffee on the terrace?'

Callie looks at him, but he is avoiding her eyes. She says, 'Yes, if you join us, Giovanni.'

He meets her eyes, finally. His own, behind his small, round owl glasses, look helpless, almost panicky. Callie says, 'I know this is difficult for you. It is for me, too, but especially so for Tommaso. Neither of us wanted this to happen. But it has, Giovanni, and there's no going back, no returning the clocks to the time when we could have stepped away from it. If there ever was such a time.'

Giovanni says nothing.

Callie goes on, 'I know your brother would like it if you joined us for coffee, and so would I.'

He doesn't answer but turns and leaves the room. The coffee is sitting on the table, ready to pour. Callie waits a few moments, but he doesn't come back. Finally, she takes three cups, pours the coffee, finds a tray and carries it upstairs to the terrace. She calls Tommaso, who sleepily puts on a pair of shorts and joins her at the table.

'How clear the light is today,' Callie says. 'The air feels fresh, clean. Look at the detail of the *palazzi* across the canal, look at the reflection of them in the water.' She is making small talk, determined not to let Giovanni's snub spoil her mood.

Tommaso nods and squints behind his dark glasses in the bright morning sunlight. Then he looks at Callie and says, 'Are you really here? Did you really spend the whole night in my bed?' He goes to her and kisses her. 'Good morning, Calypso.'

Giovanni walks onto the terrace just as Tommaso does this. He looks embarrassed and turns as if to go away again, but Tommaso is too quick; he goes to his brother, embraces him gruffly and says, 'We are celebrating the light on the canal, Giovanni, come join us, your coffee is here.'

Giovanni does. For a few minutes he sits there stiffly, polite but obviously not happy. But Callie and Tommaso are in a zany euphoric mood, and soon he begins to smile, then to relax. By the time Callie says she has to go back to the hotel, he is feeling much more cheery, for their mood is certainly contagious. And when Callie kisses not just Tommaso, but him, too, as she leaves, he finds himself patting her shoulder avuncularly.

'*Ciao, Giovanni. E grazie.* Thank you, ' she whispers, and his heart does a tiny flip as it wantonly changes sides and goes over to the enemy.

The next four or five days are hot, very hot, and humid, debilitating. Callie's group is prickly, but Callie herself is in a bubble of bliss that nothing can burst, not even a series of minor disasters that occur one after the other.

It starts with not one but two casualties. First one of the group members breaks his wrist fooling around in a gondola, and then a middle-aged woman travelling with her sister is taken ill with food poisoning. What with Pogo as well, Callie is in and out of the hospital in between her usual duties.

The food poisoning is blamed on Signor Alberti's food, though the attack was found, later, to be caused by a prosciutto sandwich bought near the Rialto and left out in the sun too long. Signor Alberti has to be appeased for the slander to his restaurant, his chef, his hotel, his reputation, which takes some doing. Then a purse is lost by one of the group members, which entails a visit to the *questura*, the police station, and

another to the lost-property office in Ferrovia Santa Lucia.

Callie handles all this in a state of unnatural calm, as does Tommaso, who is coping with his own work crisis. The grout used to fill the cracks underwater has been leaking out, for the cracks have not been sealed properly. Too much grout has been wasted and lost without filling the holes. It's the kind of thing that drives engineers mad, and Paolo, at the site, waits for Tommaso to explode. But, oddly, he does not. If this is because of that Englishwoman, then long may she stay in Tommaso's heart and in his bed, Paolo thinks gratefully.

She is very much in both during these heady days. Despite their problems at work, Callie and Tommaso find time to be together. Unless there is a special evening programme planned, or an emergency, Callie eats quickly with her group, then rushes to Ca'Valier. Together they explore Venice, and though each know the city well, together it is new and fresh in their eyes. The canals are greener, the buildings more lush, the light more exquisite than it has ever been before.

They are less circumspect now about their relationship. Ellen and Archie see them sitting at Florian's holding hands one night, listening to the musicians, drinking *un'ombra*, a small glass of wine, like any one of the thousands of lovers in Venice. Ellen chides herself for having been so concerned about Callie; all hints of strain are gone; she is relaxed, calm, obviously happy. 'Whatever happens to them in the future, they have this, they have *now*,' Ellen says to Archie as they walk across the piazza.

And so do I, Archie thinks, his arm linked in Ellen's. To *feel* again, after the numbness which followed the grief after his wife died, is no bad thing, though the irony of it does not escape him. Life stirs within him as he grows old and approaches death. He decides

that, all and all, he would rather go out vibrantly, emotions engaged and functioning, defying his poor old body and the pain it causes him, to the last.

Deirdre, walking with Angela through the tiny Campiello dei Squellini late one afternoon, sees Callie and Tommaso standing under the shade of a mimosa tree, arms round each other, looking at a cat in the middle of the square. Luckily Angela has spotted a shop and has gone inside without seeing them. Deirdre, about to follow her mother, hears Callie calling her. 'Meet Tommaso,' Callie says, introducing him proudly.

So this is the married man, Deirdre thinks, whom Callie mentioned once, that day in Murano, then clammed up about. The attraction Callie had mentioned has obviously evolved into something more. Deirdre is pleased for Callie. Most likely the married man is separated, lives apart from his wife, whatever. She hopes Callie will be happy, and tries to convey this as they chat for a few minutes.

Callie understands, is appreciative. She decides she will try to keep in touch with Deirdre when they are all home again; this time she's sure their acquaintance can develop into something deeper, stronger. How easy friendship is when you have roots, stability, she thinks. And the promise of a cat, and a plant.

Deirdre leaves, to join Angela in the shop. When they come out again, Callie and Tommaso are gone.

Candice spots them one night in the candlelit restaurant in Campo Santo Stefano, right opposite the hotel. Callie and Tommaso are sitting in the outdoor enclosure, tucking into spaghetti with a seafood sauce. 'Goodness,' Candice exclaims to Ellen, who is with her. 'Callie is eating another dinner.'

'Nonsense,' Ellen retorts. 'If you noticed, Callie didn't eat a thing at the hotel, just sat with us and

drank mineral water. You must be more observant, Candice.'

Ellen knows she is being more caustic than she should with Candice, but she's cross because she is not with Archie. There aren't that many nights left on the tour, and she's wasting it walking round the *campo* with Candice, who insisted on a constitutional before bed to help her sleep.

Ellen looks at the couple one last time, to see them raise their wineglasses and lightly tap them together. Unsettled, she abruptly turns and marches Candice back towards the Hotel Isabella.

'I love this restaurant,' Callie says as they sip red wine from a bottle of Bardolino that Tommaso had bought to celebrate. They've been celebrating for days now, for the moment trying to live in the present, not thinking of what has to be got through before they can be together permanently. However, reminders seep into Tommaso's consciousness each time he phones his boys at their summer camp, which he has been doing more often than usual. Sandra, of course, talks too. She tells him short anecdotes about the other staff members at the camp and describes the children in her charge. He can almost see her there, holding the phone to her buoyant, curly hair, most likely wearing a tracksuit and her favourite pair of old white trainers. He can see her smile, as she tells him of the tennis competition the instructors organized, how it teemed with rain and the match had to be stopped just as she was one game ahead in the last set. He can see her, but she is fading. He feels detached from her, though closer than ever to his sons, whom he suddenly longs to see.

Callie and Tommaso eat and drink, saying little, still overwhelmed by the fact that they are together. The candle on the table flickers slightly in the light warm breeze that gently exhales over the *campo*. Although

by now it is ten-thirty, all the tables outside are full, and the language spoken is mostly Italian, for this is a restaurant favoured by locals. At a table near Callie and Tommaso, a well-dressed Venetian couple, elegant and beautiful, are finishing dinner with their two sons, also impeccably dressed. Tommaso stares at them for some minutes.

'Do they remind you of your sons?' Callie asks.

'Yes. Well, not their clothes, my boys look much more disreputable than those two. But they have the same moplike head of hair, the same round faces.'

'I look forward to meeting Marco and Antonio. I know I'll like them.'

'And they will adore you.'

Yet as he says this he's not sure. They adore their mother, too. They will resent Callie at first, but he hopes it will not be for long.

Tommaso looks away from the two boys with their parents and says to Callie, 'If you don't want dessert, should we walk? It's a beautiful evening.'

They stroll towards Campo Sant'Angelo, towards the Rialto, passing through the market place, empty of stalls and people. They head towards the *sestiere* of Cannaregio, walking single file down thin alleyways under tall, pocked brick buildings, shutters closed tightly against the night air. They catch thin slithers of moon behind slowly moving clouds, and when they're tired of walking, they sit on cracked stone well-heads in tiny *campielli* and touch in the shadows. Then they move on, and walk some more.

They find themselves in the Strada Nova, the wide street hushed and empty, shops and restaurants shut. They stroll aimlessly through the ghetto, passing the kosher food shops in the Campo Ghetto Nuovo, the synagogues. They carry on, not caring where they're going, as long as they're going there together. Finally they pass through a *sottoportego* that leads to a dead end, to steps disappearing into a canal, where the

moon is making mosaics of green and gold and silver on the water.

Here they stop again, sit for a long time on the top step, totally alone under the archway of the buildings, the narrow *calle* leading to the steps. The houses lining the water are shuttered and dark, quiet. They kiss again, lightly, then more urgently, until slowly, naturally, they are making love, the water lapping gently at their feet and their bodies rocking rhythmically in tune with the ripples slapping against wet stone. It is a silent lovemaking, mysterious and deep, and, when it's over, they cling to each other wordlessly, the moonlight making mosaics on them now, fragmenting them into opalescent shards as they gaze without moving into the patch of silver water.

When at last they get up to move on, a very slight drizzle is falling, but it feels cool and comforting on their hot bodies. They aren't far from the Ponte Scalzi, and as they approach the bridge the gleaming lights of a *vaporetto* appear, a halo of mist and fine rain surrounding it.

'We'd better take this,' Callie says. 'Do you know how late it is? And it's starting to rain harder.'

The boat is like a ghost ship, only them and two other solitary passengers. They pass through the covered cabin and sit on the benches in the open space at the back.

The journey down the Grand Canal is slow, quiet. The rain is persistent now and they're soaked through, but they do not go inside. They sit close, touching, watching the patterns that the drops make on the water, seeing the reflection of lamps dancing on the dark canal. The occasional light of a *palazzo* window peers on them through the mist, its faded façade masked by the rain. There is nothing on the canal but their one boat, safely taking them home through the dark silent night.

* * *

Someone else is awake, too, while Callie and Tommaso walk home from the Accademia landing stage. Dexter and Minnie are lying in bed, awake and exhausted, having just completed a marathon round of sex. 'Bloody hell, Min,' Dexter pants. 'What's in those headache tablets you've been taking?'

'Hmm. You complaining?'

'Hell no. I'm just knackered.'

Minnie stares at the ceiling, at the flickering reflection of the candle she lit earlier. Her new black nylon nightie, bought that morning on the Strada Nova, is flung crumpled on the floor, but it has served its purpose, as did the near-empty bottle of massage oil she also purchased. 'So what do you think of married sex now?' she purrs in Dexter's ear, gently blowing into it.

Dexter groans. 'Give us a break, Min, I'm spent. I gotta get some sleep.'

Minnie leans back victoriously. Having watched Dexter flirting outrageously with Angela for the past couple of weeks, she has tried tears, scenes, anger, but nothing seemed to work. This morning she spotted the nightgown in Standa, and bought it as a last desperate attempt, never really believing Dexter would fall for something so embarrassingly simple. With the lacy black number tucked in a bag under her arm, she tried to remember every magazine article she'd read entitled 'How to Keep Your Man' and 'What Men Like in Bed'. Grimly, for she thought that after marrying Dexter she would be finished with this sort of nonsense, she set about making her other purchases.

Dexter had been suspicious at first, accusing her of being unfaithful during the year of their engagement, for where else would she have learned tricks like *that*? Certainly not from him, he'd said indignantly. Rubbing oil into his belly, she murmured that of course she hadn't slept with anyone other than him since the day they met, which was true, of course. But the seed of

201

doubt had been sown, and would lay fertile for a long time in the compost of his rather sandy heart. Minnie, thinking about this, decides that it's not a bad thing to keep him guessing; he's taken her for granted for far too long.

Dexter, asleep next to her, begins to snore.

After no more than three or four hours sleep, Callie's morning begins badly. As soon as she has had a shower back at the hotel and joined the others at breakfast, Deirdre comes over to her table. 'Callie, I'm sorry, but there's a problem. Angela's in a foul mood, and I am afraid she's after your skin. I just thought I'd warn you.'

'Where is she now?' Callie pours a large cup of Signor Alberti's strong, poisonous coffee from its silver pot and puts two sugars in it. 'And why is she upset with me?'

'Because you weren't around at about midnight last night. Look, Callie, I'm so sorry about this, I tried to stop her—'

'Never mind, just tell me what's up. Why did she want me? I left phone numbers, that of Patsy's hotel, and the place where I stayed the night.'

'I know, I know. Signor Alberti told her all that and offered to ring you himself. Look, she was just spoiling for trouble.'

'You still haven't told me what the problem was. Why did she want me in the middle of the night? Was she ill?'

Deirdre looks embarrassed. 'She wanted to move hotels. There and then.'

'What? She's crazy. Why?'

'Because of Dexter, but I'm not supposed to tell you that. She was supposed to meet him last night; he was going to sneak out of his room when Minnie was asleep. She's usually dead to the world by ten, apparently. But he never showed up, left Angela stranded for

two hours in some hotel bar where they were supposed to meet.'

Despite herself, a smile begins to twitch on Callie's face. Deirdre catches it and giggles. 'Oh, Callie, you should have seen her face when she stormed back here at midnight. What she really wanted to do was pound on Dexter's door, but of course she couldn't with Minnie there.'

'So she did the next best thing and demanded to see me.' As Callie says this, she looks across the dining room to see the Vamp from Hell striding splendidly and furiously across to their table. 'Oh shit,' Callie mutters.

'So you've deigned to come back to the hotel, to your group, to your responsibilities,' Angela cries theatrically. 'I've just phoned Comet Trail Travel, told them that you weren't on hand last night, when I needed you.'

'What was the emergency, Angela?' Callie says sweetly. 'I left phone numbers where I could be contacted. How odd no-one did.'

Angela doesn't answer this, preferring to list everything she has found wrong with the tour, the excursions, the other group members, and Callie. She is just beginning on the food at the hotel, when Signor Alberti, fearing her loud voice will disturb the other guests, joins them. 'The food, *signora*? My English is no good, but I hear you say the food. You are perhaps the, uh, how do you say? One who is understanding of, who loves very much, the fine food?'

'Gourmet?' Callie offers, wondering what the devious old devil is up to.

'*Sì, sì, hai ragione*, you're right. Gourmet. You are this, perhaps? I have suspected it.' He teases Angela with his eyes, implying not just a shared intimacy with food, but with other, more subtle things.

'Why yes.' Angela forgets to be angry and begins to be flattered. 'When I stayed at the Cipriani—'

'Ah, *che bellezza*! How wonderful! The chef there, he is the great friend of mine. We mix up – no, we exchange, this is the word – we exchange the recipes. *Spesso.*'

'Often,' Callie says helpfully.

'I know what *spesso* means,' Angela snaps. She turns her bosom full on Signor Alberti. 'Oh really? Why, what a coincidence! I thought your menu had a ring of familiarity.' She places her hand confidentially on his arm, taking care to check that Signora Alberti is nowhere in sight.

The *signore* invites Angela into the kitchen, to meet the chef. When they're gone, Deirdre and Callie slump with both relief and hilarity. 'I don't believe it,' Callie cries, hardly able to talk she's laughing so hard.

'You would if you knew her like I do.'

'I can't believe Signor Alberti. What a crafty old opportunist.'

'He saved your skin, Callie.'

'Don't I know it!'

When they finally control themselves, Callie says more seriously, 'Well, I wish the good *signore* had come to my rescue before Angela phoned Comet Trail.'

'He did try last night, but she was too furious with Dexter to take much notice of him then. Will you be in a lot of trouble?'

Callie shrugs. 'No, not really. Angela could have found me if she'd really wanted to, if there really had been an emergency. And it wasn't that late, just after midnight. Signor Alberti will vouch for me. I've been around a long time; they know I'm a good tour manager.' She looks ruefully at Deirdre. 'Well, I am usually. I can't say as much for this tour.'

Before Deirdre can answer, one of the hotel staff comes to their table to say there is a phone call for Callie. She excuses herself and takes the call in the office.

It's Patsy, sounding strained, her voice forced.

'Callie, can you handle both our groups in Padua today? Not many of mine are going, so it shouldn't be too bad.'

Callie has never, ever known Patsy to miss an excursion in all the years she has worked with her. 'Are you all right?' she asks, concerned. 'Are you ill? What's up?'

There's a long silence, then some muffled noises, as if Patsy is struggling to speak. Alarmed, Callie says, 'I'll be right there.'

She runs from the Hotel Isabella, across the *campo* and down Calle delle Botteghe, and is at Patsy's hotel in two or three minutes. Patsy is in her room, sitting slumped on the bed as Callie opens the unlocked door. 'What's happened?' Patsy is puffy with past tears, her face streaked with the lines of grief.

Callie goes to her and sits with her on the bed. It takes some moments for Patsy to speak, even though she's no longer crying. She opens her mouth and tries to say something, but the only sound that comes out is a slight mewing sound, like a wounded seabird. She closes her mouth, shakes her head and tries again. 'I spoke to Stuart last night. He's leaving me. For another woman.' Her mouth snaps shut after she has spoken the words, her lips pressed together tightly, as if afraid that what she said will be regurgitated, like poison.

Now Callie cannot speak. Indeed, it is as if Patsy's words have poisoned *her*, for her face has turned ashen, her hands are trembling. Patsy says, her voice stiff, 'He met her in January, when I was on that tour in Spain.'

Still Callie says nothing, but Patsy doesn't seem to need a response. The words, stuck in her throat, now come frothing out of her mouth like foam. 'I knew about her; it was nothing secret to start with. He met her through work, through a colleague. There was a leaving party, someone going to a new job. Stuart felt he had to go and she was there. He mentioned her

when I got back from Spain, said she was nice. Liked gardening, so the two of them talked about that all evening. They met again, accidentally. She took him home and showed him her garden. He told me all about it, it was no big deal. Not then, anyway.' She begins biting her lower lip, tense, tiny little bites that will soon draw blood, but she doesn't seem to notice.

Callie says, 'Did you ever suspect? That the friendship was . . . developing?'

A tiny speck of blood appears on Patsy's lip. Callie restrains the impulse to find a tissue and wipe it away as if Patsy were a child. Patsy cries, loudly, 'Friendship? I thought that's what it was. I came home for a week, went away again for three. When I got back, Stuart mentioned her again. That she'd been to our house, to see *his* garden. I was pleased for him, that someone was interested in him, in his garden. Stuart works so hard in it, it's such a joy to him. I never thought—' She's unable to go on.

Callie at last rouses herself, moves her limbs, which feel leaden, unco-ordinated, and takes Patsy in her arms, holding the weeping woman like a baby. There's nothing she can say, but lets Patsy first cry, then talk, alternating between grief, despair and rage, then back to grief. Callie murmurs platitudes, hollow words of comfort. At one point Patsy cries bitterly, 'I wish he hadn't told me in the middle of a tour, in the middle of my work! It's all I have left now, and he is ruining that, too.'

Callie seizes on this. 'It was rotten of him to tell you all this on the phone,' she agrees vigorously. 'He, at least, could have waited until you got home, talked to you face-to-face.'

Patsy has stood up from the bed and is looking out the window of her hotel room. There is no view, only the dilapidated old building opposite, but Patsy has been staring at it intensely for the past few moments, as if the answer were there, written on the peeling

plaster, the eroded old bricks, the fading paintwork. But when Callie makes this last remark, she turns quickly and faces her angrily. 'That would make it all right, would it? That would make it just fine, I suppose, to you. So long as he leaves me honourably, face-to-face like a man, then it's perfectly all right. Fuck twenty years of marriage, all the things we have gone through together and meant to each other in the past, so long as he ends it like a man.'

Callie stammers, 'Look, I didn't mean, I didn't say—'

'I know damn well what you are saying, Callie. Do you think I haven't talked to Giovanni, that I don't know what you and Tommaso are planning on doing? Another fucking broken marriage.'

Callie runs her hand shakily through her uncombed hair. The phone in the room begins to ring, loudly, frantically in the stillness that follows Patsy's outburst, but neither moves to answer it. Callie says slowly, 'I was going to tell you, Patsy. About me and Tommaso. There hasn't been time.'

'You haven't had the guts.' She turns away from Callie to stare out the window again. 'You knew what I'd think about it.'

Callie takes a deep breath. Through the open window comes the buzz of people chattering, a pleasant droning hum like the soft sound of distant bees. A woman's voice calls lightly, '*Ciao, Matteo, ciao!*' There is a ripple of Italian farewells, well wishes, promises to meet again. '*Ciao, Maria,*' a man's voice is heard loudly above the others, and Callie knows that this goodbye at any rate will not be for long, for the man and woman both laugh, sweetly, delightedly. Above the laughter comes the trilling of a bird, the song of a canary perched in his cage in the window of the house opposite.

Callie listens to the bird, to the laughter, to the mellifluous Italian, and thinks, I will remember this

moment, the moment when everything changed. She says carefully, 'You're right, Patsy, I didn't have the guts to tell you. And it wouldn't have made it all right if Stuart had told you in person, waited until you were together. Any more than it will be all right when Tommaso tells Sandra about me.'

Patsy, crumpled and defeated, sits on the bed again. 'I'm sorry, I shouldn't have lashed out like that. What's happening between you and Tommaso has nothing to do with me and Stuart.'

But it is, Callie thinks, yet she says only, 'Do you want to go back home? See him, talk? I'll phone head office, get them to send a replacement for the last few days. Or I can take over, in a pinch. Your lot are leaving a day earlier, I can see them to the airport. I know you're supposed to stay on here after that to meet another group, but head office can find someone else.'

'No.' Patsy's voice is sharp, fearful. 'If you can cope with both groups on your own in Padua today, that would help. I don't want to go back to England; there's nothing to say. Stuart's mind is made up.' Her voice cracks again. 'I need to work, Callie, I need to keep going.'

Callie understands. In the end, it's Patsy's work that has, in a sense, broken up her marriage, for even Patsy has admitted that not many men would tolerate the long days, weeks, she was forced to leave him. Her mistake was in thinking Stuart was different.

The phone rings again, and this time Patsy asks Callie to answer it. It's one of the group members, wondering when they are meeting, why Patsy has not been at breakfast. Callie explains that Patsy is ill, that she will be handling the trip to Padua and will be down shortly to give them details.

'I'll have to go,' Callie says. 'I need to get the two groups together, get them to Piazzale Roma for the coach. Will you be all right? I'll come back straight away when we've returned. Try to get some sleep.'

Patsy nods. She's weary now, so weary she would like to drop like the stones of Venice into the deep lagoon of sleep and never wake up. She closes her eyes and lies back on the bed. Still with her eyes shut, she says, 'I got it all wrong, didn't I. I thought Stuart was a loner, didn't need people much. I was hardly ever there, but I thought it worked well for both of us. I thought we had it sussed out.'

Callie tries to answer, can't think of what to say. She stands for a moment at the door, helplessly, then turns and leaves Patsy alone with her despair.

Later, in Padua, standing in the Scrovegni Chapel surrounded by the paintings of Giotto, Callie tries to capture the peace, the contentment, she usually feels when she's here. It's gone, all of it. There is no serenity, none of the quiet joy that the simple narrative drama of these paintings have always given her. After giving her talk on Giotto, she leaves the two groups to their own private contemplation and turns her back on the chapel. She walks out into the open air, knowing that nothing is as it was.

In Venice, in Campo Santa Margherita, Pogo presides over cappuccino like a gleeful, white-faced, stubbly boy king. He has been out of hospital for several days, and is ebullient over how lightly he has got off this time. Lavender keeps a wary eye on him, warning him that he should be taking it easy.

'Well, say now, sweetie pie, what's easier than this? This is terrific,' Pogo says expansively. He sweeps a scrawny arm to indicate the *campo*, crammed with market stalls, with busy cafés, with children kicking a football and old men and housewives sitting on the red benches under the trees. Next to them, under the red-and-white striped awning, the tables and chairs of the café are full. Two Italian women are discussing a party they went to last night; three men are talking politics;

Dutch tourists at a corner table are studying a map of the city.

Suddenly there's a commotion in the *campo* that overrides the usual afternoon hubbub. A group of about twenty Italians, most of them college students, crowd the square, pulling a proud but embarrassed young man with them. He has a thick shiny laurel wreath draped round his neck.

Archie, who is there with Ellen, says, 'He has just graduated, obtained a degree, or laureate as they call it. The wreath is traditional.' He smiles at Ellen, who takes this nugget of information and adds it to the large pile of little gems she has gleaned from Archie. They're not in Padua with the others because Archie's hip is still painful. Ellen, much to Candice's disgust, chose also to remain behind, so Candice is in the Hotel Isabella sulking. Ellen is delighted that she feels absolutely no responsibility, no guilt, for this. She's urged Candice to go without her; after all, the tour is in its last week now, and it's not as if Candice would have been on her own in Padua. If she wishes to sulk instead of joining the group, that's up to her.

Deirdre, too, has decided not to go, and is sitting with the others in the square. When Angela had returned from inspecting the kitchen with Signor Alberti, full of the compliments he had given her and already planning to meet him again, Deirdre surprised herself by saying, 'I'm not going on the coach trip today.'

'Of course you are, darling. I know the sweetest little restaurant in Padua; we'll lunch there. Now hurry up and get ready.'

'I said I'm not going.'

Angela had raged, then threatened, but Deirdre, shocking herself, had stayed firm, shouting back at Angela as she fled from the hotel, 'Have Dexter take you to lunch!' She'll pay for it later, but for the moment, sitting here with the others, she feels free, liberated and quite proud of herself.

210

The students are in the middle of the square chanting, '*Dottore, dottore*,' and stripping the young man of his clothes, down to his underwear. He's placed on the stone well-head in the square, and water is thrown on him from buckets that have somehow appeared. 'Another custom,' Archie says, amused.

'How very odd,' Ellen comments. 'Do they always do that when someone gets a degree?'

'Only certain ones, I believe.

Deirdre, watching the students cavorting, joking, singing, says, 'I wish I'd got my degree. I dropped out of college to have my baby. I'm absolutely unqualified for anything.'

'How is Kathy, honey?' Lavender asks. 'Did you talk to her last night?'

Ellen says, 'It won't be long now until you're with her again. We'll soon be home.' Only Archie notes the regretful tone of her voice.

'Home?' Deirdre says. 'What's that?' She says it lightly, but her voice has a sudden quiver. The exhilaration she felt at her tiny rebellion against Angela collapses as she thinks of being in Angela's house again. Perhaps I've made a grave mistake, she thinks unhappily. I should have got out from the start, made my own way with my child, however difficult it was. And yet, at the time, it had seemed so preferable to leaving Kathy with childminders all day. At least I was with her. The price of being with my daughter was my mother. A high price indeed.

Archie has ordered more coffee, and the waiter is now bringing it out, with *panettone*, sweet bread with raisins and orange peel. The college students are dragging their wet bedraggled friend, still with the laurel wreath on, round the square, laughing and chanting. Hovering round the edges of the group are the relatives: proud mother and father, aunts and uncles. The mother clutches a bag with the boy's clothes, and Lavender says, 'There, y'all look, it's always the same,

211

whatever the country. Mom tagging along behind, proudly carrying her kid's laundry.'

They all laugh, except for Deirdre, who says, 'I always wanted a mother like that, not to do my washing, but to be, well, a mother, you know?'

Knowing Angela, they all nod, understanding what she's saying. Deirdre, something unleashed in her by the scene in the hotel this morning, and by the light-hearted but somehow moving celebration of the students in the square, cries, 'I can't do it any more, I can't go back. Not to Angela, not to my life there with her. I've had enough.'

She is as distressed by her outburst as the others are, and while they coo and fuss and sympathize with her, she apologizes profusely.

Pogo says, 'Nothing to be sorry for, y'hear?' He looks over her head at Lavender, and they stare at each other for a few moments in a most peculiar manner. Having lived together for so many years, they aren't surprised when they can read each other's thoughts. Simultaneously they turn to Deirdre. 'Come with us,' Pogo says. 'To Naples. For the winter.'

'We need a driver,' Lavender says. 'Pogo was told he wasn't allowed to drive the camper van, not yet, not for a while. He can't lift anything heavy, either. Between the two of us, we'd be useless on our own. And me, well, I'm a real ol' crock, I've had a tricky back for years. I have to be careful even lifting a sack of groceries.'

Pogo is gleaming with excitement. 'We thought we'd have to give up the idea of travelling through Italy and go back home, but if we had someone young with us, someone to drive, maybe lift up a suitcase now and then—'

'But there's Kathy,' Deirdre interrupts. 'I can't because of her. I couldn't leave her.'

Lavender beams, and her smile is like a halo of hope to Deirdre, shining like all the hundreds of haloes she

has seen in paintings all over Venice. 'Honey, now would we ask you to come anywhere without your little girl? Pogo and I, we miss our kids and grandkids like crazy, so having your girl around would be great, just great.'

Everyone looks at Deirdre expectantly. The students have left the square, but the hum of people talking fills the air like music. At the fruit and vegetable market in front of them a woman is buying several paper bagfuls of salad leaves for her family's dinner, and at the fish stall a young boy is poking his finger in a box of squid, unable to resist the jellied texture. The boy's mother leans down, tickles him gently to get him to stop, and the two laugh.

Families, Deirdre thinks. She wants to be part of one, part of a nucleus of people with a reason for existing, even if that reason is nothing more than a sharing of experiences, of trust and affection. She looks at Pogo and Lavender, at their kind old faces, and feels a deep fondness for them that she knows, if nurtured, could turn into love one day. She would like to nurture it: she needs to love someone other than Kathy, for her daughter's sake, if nothing else.

She says, simply, 'I'll come.'

The others round the table – her group now, her extended family – breathe a collective sigh of relief. Then there are wide smiles and everyone talks at once, surprised and pleased with themselves, with each other. They begin planning the details, financial arrangements are discussed. 'We can't pay you much,' Lavender says, 'to be our driver, to help us out. But we can manage something.'

'I've been saving,' Deidre says excitedly. 'Just a bit, for the day when we could get away from Angela. I've got enough for a short time, and for my plane fare back to Venice with Kathy, to meet you. If you could just feed us and give us a space to live, we'd manage.'

They talk about sleeping arrangements. Deirdre has

213

a large sturdy tent, given to her by a friend who has left the country, perfect for herself and Kathy in a warm climate. 'And Pogo and I were thinking,' Lavender says. 'We might find a place we want to stay for a few months, so maybe we can rent a little house somewhere, nothing fancy.'

'It's all working out so perfectly,' Archie says, Ellen nodding her head in agreement. The other three look at Archie and Ellen, and see, underneath their genuine well wishes, an identical look of wistfulness.

Pogo and Lavender look at each other again, and this time it's Pogo who says, 'Anyone else want to come? We could go in convoy, like true gypsies.' He smiles as he says this, but Archie knows he is serious.

Lavender says, 'A winter of sun would do your hip a world of good, Archie. What do you have to look forward to in England? Cold, wet, dark – you need warmth, sun.'

Ellen says, 'Go, Archie, she is right. It would do you good.'

'I'm too old to sleep in a tent, Ellen.'

She smiles. 'I appreciate that. So am I. But you can buy a camper van, you have some money in the bank, a car to sell—'

He says, very softly, 'You could come with me.'

The sounds in the *campo* seem to shift in intensity, become further away. The bells of a distant church begin to toll the hour. Ellen thinks, Yes, I'm ready to go with you, or rather, the person I really am would go in a minute. But I have had to be someone else for years, and it's too late to go back.

Taking Archie's hand she says, 'Thank you for asking. I wish—'

She breaks off, shaking her head. He nods, understanding. He would like to say so many things to her now, but words of this kind are difficult for him. So he says, instead, to Lavender and Pogo, 'I'm not as young as you two.' He smiles at their protests over this

untruth. 'I couldn't keep up the pace. You'll just have to visit me in England on your way home, when you finally decide to return.'

Deirdre listens to them, as the three old friends banter and tease each other, as Ellen, quiet now, smiles in her kindly way. Deirdre thinks of her daughter, how she will warm to Pogo and Lavender, how they will fuss over her, give her the affection Angela never does.

And me, she thinks. Perhaps some of the nurturing will spill over onto me, just a little, just once in a while.

For the first time, she realizes how desperately she has needed it.

12

As Callie herds the two groups round Padua, Patsy, unable to sleep in the hot hotel room, unable to cry any more, stumbles out into the *calle* and from there into the Campo Santo Stefano. Once there, she stands in the middle of the square, bewildered. The sun is hot, fierce, the air is thick, watery. She walks, dragging her sandalled feet as if they were partially paralyzed. Collapsing under the statue of Nicolò Tommaseo, she attracts no attention, for she looks like just another of the dazed tourists who sit limply on church steps or at the foot of stone winged lions in a state of exhaustion.

Patsy is not exhausted, she is in too much of a state of shock for that. But she is purposeless. It is such an unusual state for her that she cannot cope with it. She is at that stage in grief when numbness takes over; she feels her emotions ice over, frozen. All she can think about is the bewildering fact that she has nowhere to go, no-one to turn to. Certainly there is no-one back home. Her sisters and their families she hardly sees, hardly knows. Her one or two old friends, she realizes with a pang, have become people she no longer knows, no longer keeps in touch with. Her work has consumed her, and so made room for nothing else.

She needs work now. She wishes she hadn't let Callie take both groups to Padua; she should be there now, lecturing them on the frescoes in the Scrovegni Chapel. Patsy is fond of the Giottos. The angels and apostles and shepherds and wise men are like dear friends, with friendly, accessible faces. If she were

talking about Giotto now, she wouldn't feel this painful chip of ice in her chest.

She sits there for a long time, oblivious to the activity on the *campo*. She realizes she is in the sun, that sweat is pouring from her face and neck, down her capacious bosom. Yet she doesn't want to go back to her hotel room, cannot bear the thought of being cooped up there alone. Suddenly she thinks of Giovanni, and with a sharp cry that makes others, sitting on the steps under the statue, look at her oddly, she stands up and begins to walk.

She walks across the Accademia bridge, but doesn't turn left to Ca'Valier, for she knows he won't be there, not at this hour. Instead, she turns right and heads towards the Campo San Barnaba, and then down the narrow streets and bridges until she is at Casa Goldoni. It is closed for restoration as she knows, but she's sure Giovanni is there, and rings the doorbell frantically. The proprietor, whom she vaguely knows, lumbers downstairs from the library to open it. 'Please, can I see Giovanni?' she asks in her halting Italian. '*Veramente è urgente.*'

He leaves her in the courtyard and goes up the marble steps. Within minutes Giovanni comes running down, looks at her face, and without a word says something to the proprietor, grabs his umbrella and ushers Patsy out the door.

The sun is still hot, but the air is heavy, oppressive, and a slate haze is colouring the sky. Giovanni hesitates. He would like to get Patsy to Ca'Valier, make her a pot of coffee and sit her in his tranquil garden by the bay tree. There, as they sipped his good strong coffee, Patsy could tell him what calamity has overcome her, for calamity it surely is, judging from her battered face and strange dead eyes.

A rumble of thunder, a sudden darkening of the sky, decides Giovanni against Ca'Valier. It is a fifteen- or twenty-minute walk and there's going to be a storm.

Patsy is standing mutely beside him, waiting for him to lead her somewhere, and this is so unlike Patsy, always so brisk, so efficient, that he knows something is indeed seriously wrong. Taking her arm, he leads her to the Campo San Tomà near by, and, bypassing the outdoor tables and chairs, takes her to a small bar/café he sometimes frequents.

It is dark inside, and darker because of the gathering storm. Giovanni orders two coffees at the counter and then sits with Patsy at a small wooden table hidden in a back corner. A few people are standing at the bar drinking coffee, but the few inside tables are empty. As the waiter brings them their coffee, the storm breaks and rain pelts the awnings outside. It is so heavy it drives into the open doors of the café, accompanied by howls of thunder.

In the midst of this chaos Patsy says, 'My husband has left me. He's found another woman.'

So this is it, Giovanni thinks. A sudden piercing memory wounds him afresh, and he unconsciously presses his side, as if the blow were indeed a physical one. With his own pain comes a wave of sympathy for Patsy, so strong an undertow it threatens to drown him. With sudden insight, he realizes how fond he is of her, how much he values her friendship.

Looking at her bleak, hopeless face, he says carefully, 'Once, I was married. Oh, not legally, not in the eyes of any church, but to us it was as sacred as any marriage, even though the man was bound to someone else, a woman. He left me, too. After many years of living two lives, one secret and intense, the other a lie, though open and sanctioned by family, he finally returned to his wife. I tell you this so that you know I understand what it is you are suffering, even though there is nothing I can say.'

Patsy nods. Outside the lightning illuminates the eerie darkness of the *campo*. The people sitting at the outer edges of the awning outside have moved inward,

and some have come inside. The hub of voices is loud as people try to talk over the noise of the storm.

They drink their coffee in silence, but it is not an awkward one. As the rain lessens in intensity and becomes a manageable drizzle, the silence in which Patsy sits with Giovanni cocoons her like soft lambs-wool over painful sores. Long after their coffee is finished, and the thunder has receded into the distance, Patsy and Giovanni still do not move, do not speak, but sit in mutual understanding.

It is almost an hour later before Patsy stirs, stops staring into the grey *campo* in front of her through the open doors and says, 'Thanks, Giovanni.'

She will survive this, he thinks. She will survive this. She will go on, like he did; she will learn to live and work and smile and even laugh again, even though the laughter does not come quite from the heart as it did before.

'Come to Ca'Valier with me now, I will prepare *gnocchi* for our lunch, you need to eat. If the rain has stopped we will sit in the garden.'

Patsy winces. 'My husband was a passionate gardener. He left me for someone who shared his passion. I never did. I was never home enough to share his love for our garden, or to share anything with him.'

He's relieved she is talking about it now, it will do her good. He says, 'You must have worried, Patsy, that it would end like this. When you were away so often.'

Patsy says, and a slight, sad smile appears at the corners of her mouth, 'Oddly enough, I didn't. It never crossed my mind that I couldn't have it all. The cake, and the eating of it.'

'What will you do now?'

'Go back to work. The sooner the better.'

Giovanni allows himself a small smile as well. 'Not before lunch, I hope.'

'No. I'm not sure I can eat, but I'll come with you to

219

Ca'Valier. Then I'll go back to the hotel and try to sleep. My group are away until late afternoon, in Padua with Callie. I will meet them at dinner, and then I'm taking them to a concert of medieval music at a church in Castello.'

'Are you sure you should?'

'I am absolutely sure.'

As they leave, walking slowly towards the Accademia through the maze of red brick buildings, under Giovanni's umbrella, Patsy feels a slight, almost imperceptible lightening of the heaviness that had been anchoring her to despair since Stuart's phone call. She loves him, but she will make herself learn to live without him. She has, she realizes, been without him most of their married life, either on a tour, or getting over one, or preparing for one. When she gets back to England, she will go to head office and ask to be put on some of the new, longer tours they are beginning: the Canadian one in the autumn, and perhaps the winter one to New Zealand. She has always wanted to see New Zealand.

'Are you all right?' Giovanni asks, meaning is she still dry under the umbrella.

'I'm not sure,' she replies, misunderstanding. 'But if not now, not yet, I will be.'

He holds the umbrella steady, and they walk on silently until they reach Ca'Valier.

Tommaso has reached the *palazzo* first, for it is lunchtime. Callie is in Padua so he won't be able to see her until tonight, after she has eaten dinner at the Hotel Isabella.

Giovanni is not home, and Tommaso assumes he is lunching out. Before Tommaso became involved with Callie the brothers ate their meals together. So much has changed since she appeared, Tommaso thinks. So much will still have to change before I can be with her always.

The phone rings. Tommaso answers it absent-mindedly, '*Pronto?*'

He hears someone at the other end, but it's too muffled and far away to make out any words or sense. A fault in the connection somewhere, he thinks impatiently, and puts down the phone. He hopes it doesn't ring again. It's probably Paulo on his mobile, wanting an extra half-hour for lunch because his girlfriend is in town again.

In England, in a hospital in Somerset, Tommaso's wife, Sandra, her hands shaking, dials again.

Tommaso picks up the phone. But this time there is nothing, not even a distant murmur; the phone is dead. He holds it to his ear for a moment, to see if it will connect.

'Tommaso?' Sandra says desperately. 'Can you hear me? I'm in hospital, it's Tony—'

But Tommaso, not hearing, has hung up again.

Sandra, putting down the phone in England, begins to cry. Her whole body, dressed in old jeans and a pink cotton jumper, grubby now after the hours in hospital, begins to tremble. She stays like this, weeping and shaking, until a kindly nurse spots her and whisks her away to offer both comfort and practicalities.

It is not until twenty minutes later that the phone in Ca'Valier rings a third and final time. Tommaso has been sitting on the balcony drinking coffee and eating a hunk of mozzarella and a tomato, with a slice of olive bread. He is missing Callie, though he saw her only a few hours ago, and will see her again tonight. He still feels slightly on edge when he is away from her, and thinks with pleasure of how she looked when he saw her last, fresh out of his bed. Her spiky brown hair was rumpled, sticking out like the points of a star all over her head, and her large grey eyes had looked dreamy, unfocused, after their lovemaking. He had watched her as she tumbled out of bed, pulling on underclothes, the

red miniskirt she often wore when not on duty and the black, sleeveless, skimpy top. Running her fingers quickly through her hair, she had grinned at him, and the smile had made him take her in his arms, kiss her again and again. She had broken away laughingly, saying that it was late, she had to get back to the hotel, shower, get ready to face her group. He had let her go reluctantly; always difficult, it had been particularly hard to part with her this morning.

Tommaso smiles at the sight of a wedding gondola drift along the Grand Canal below the balcony. The gondoliers – there are two for this special occasion -- are dressed all in white; the bride and groom are smiling, holding hands. The bride spots Tommaso watching them and waves, her lacy sleeves waving like a banner, triumphant, victorious. It is an omen, Tommaso thinks joyfully; it is an omen for me and Callie.

The phone rings. Tommaso reluctantly goes into the drawing room to answer it. This time the connection is clear; he hears his wife's voice. 'Thank God, I've got through to you at last. The nurse in charge of Tony's ward is letting me use the office phone; the pay phone here at the hospital—'

'Tony?' Tommaso interrupts. 'Hospital?' Weakened by those two words, he sits down on the daybed, facing the double doors leading to the balcony terrace. 'What's happened? What's wrong with Antonio?'

'It's all right, he's all right. He fell off a horse; it was such a stupid accident. He's fine, Tommaso. Bruised and with a broken arm, but it's been set already and he's come out of the anaesthetic. He's sleeping now. He'll be out of hospital tomorrow.'

Tommaso can feel the irregular beating of his heart, the pale layer of sweat that fear wrapped him in when he heard the words Tony and hospital. 'I'll come right home,' he says.

'Don't be daft. It's just a broken arm, a clean break,

too; he was lucky. When he comes out tomorrow I'll bring him right to the camp. Mark and I will both be there with him. We finish at the end of the week anyway. Tony will be fine; he'll be made a huge fuss of by all his friends. Mark will be beside himself with envy.'

'I want to see him.'

Sandra has pulled herself together since her weepy collapse earlier when she couldn't get through to Tommaso. She says, reasonably, 'It's pointless to leave your job so near the end, and honestly, Tony will be so busy showing off the plaster on his arm and having it signed, he'd hardly notice you were back, if you came now. Come home when planned and the four of us will have a lovely reunion.'

Tommaso sees the sense in this, and acquiesces, though it goes against the animal instinct that is making him long to run to his injured son *now*, at once, to ensure that the boy is really all right. Sandra, sensing this, says, 'Listen, I'm going back to the camp now, to change my clothes and pick up Mark and bring him here to see Tony when he wakes up. I'll give you the hospital number and you can talk to both the boys.'

Tommaso takes the number. Then he says, 'I'm sorry, Sandra, that you had to cope with this by yourself. The worry, the terror – all this, to face on your own.'

Sandra runs her strong suntanned fingers through her blond curls, now lank and unkempt. She feels quivery again, and knows it to be relief after the ordeal of the past few hours. 'I saw him fall, Tommaso. We were taking a group of lads for a special early morning ride, before breakfast; it was to be one of the highlights of our last week. I still don't know exactly what happened. It was the worst moment of my life, watching him fall.'

'I should have been there,' Tommaso says helplessly.

'I wanted you here. God, how I wanted you. I tried to phone earlier, but you must have been at work.'

'Yes.'

223

'Thank God it was nothing more serious than a broken arm. Tommaso, he could have been killed.'

'Yes.'

'Thank God.' They are both silent for a moment. Sandra shudders silently, thinking of that moment when Tony lay still, unmoving, on the ground. Tommaso, reading her thoughts, seeing the scene vividly in his imagination, remembers where he was in the early hours of the morning and feels the blackness of guilt enclosing him.

Sandra says, 'It will be so good to see you, Tommaso. So good. Take care of yourself, please? Come home safely. I'm so frightened, the world seems full of such dangers all of a sudden.' Her voice in Tommaso's ear is husky with new tears. 'Sorry,' she whispers, when she can speak again. 'Now that he's all right, I feel shaky.'

'It's a reaction to the accident. You need to rest now, try to sleep, relax.'

Sandra nods wordlessly, sniffs back the tears and says again, 'Don't you go doing anything stupid, Tommaso. On the job. No more accidents?'

'No, no more. I'll come back safely, I promise.'

'No more casualties, I couldn't bear it.'

'No more casualties, Sandra. Don't worry.'

They hang up, and Tommaso sits on the coach unmoving after he puts the phone down. An ambulance motorboat is racing noisily down the canal, its blue light flashing, and he thinks, That could be someone else's son, who was not so lucky as my Antonio. Tommaso is aware that the family has had a very narrow escape. He's aware that he has got off easily. But he knows, too, that he will have to pay for this act of grace, and pay dearly.

Giovanni walks onto the balcony to see Tommaso standing at the balustrade, staring at the canal through the incessant drizzle. He has just left Patsy in the kitchen, settling her there while he went upstairs to see if Tommaso was home for lunch. Giovanni takes one

look at his brother's face and sees there what he has just seen in Patsy's.

'Tommaso?' he says tentatively.

Tommaso rouses himself and faces his brother. 'Antonio's in hospital, but he's fine. A broken arm, a clean break, nothing more.'

But his voice, the look on his face, tells Giovanni that there is a great deal more. 'Tommaso . . .' He breaks off, unsure.

Tommaso has got up, is standing at the door to the balcony. A fresh bowl of lilies, which Giovanni had bought before he went out this morning, is on the table, and their scent will always remind Tommaso of this moment. He says, 'I can't leave them, Giovanni. I can't.'

Giovanni goes to his brother and grasps his shoulder. Tommaso reaches out to him, and the two men embrace in an age-old show of support, sympathy, grief and understanding. Then Tommaso breaks away, turns and walks out of the room, down the stairs and out of the door.

Giovanni wants to follow him, but doesn't. He goes down the stairs, into the kitchen and puts water on to boil for the *gnocchi*. We must all eat, he thinks: he, and Patsy, and Tommaso. And Callie, too; Giovanni hopes that she's having a good lunch in Padua, for food is solid, comforting, reassuring.

He mocks himself for thinking these things, for musing on such banalities as lunch when all the people he is fond of, all the people he loves, seem to be falling apart in front of his very eyes. But he knows from his own sad experience that they will pull themselves together, mend, and that the scars will fade, like the reflections on the canal water fade when the light changes.

That doesn't help now, he thinks, remembering. He remembers for several moments; then, shaking his head, he takes the *gnocchi*, tomatoes and butter from

225

the fridge, basil and sage from the pot on the window, olive oil from the shelf, and carefully, meticulously, begins to prepare lunch.

Tommaso walks. He goes out of the house and turns left, away from the Accademia, and crosses the small stone bridge into the Campo San Vio. A green barge boat, collecting the city's rubbish, is under the bridge, but the boat is late and already the plastic carrier bags, boxes and dustbin bags full of garbage have been broken into by cats or dogs. The midday sun has baked the debris of food, paper, empty tins and bottles into a foul, ill-smelling cake, the crumbs of which lie scattered on the side of the canal where they were left. Tommaso passes, oblivious, and walks along the Fondamenta Venier. Here the canal alongside the *fondamenta* is dotted with parked motorboats, the odd gondola or rowboat; the water pocked with drops of rain. Tommaso doesn't notice the rain either. He crosses over another bridge, then another. The lightning and thunder have abated, but the rain is heavier. Tommaso walks on until he is at the elegant wide steps of the Salute, not pausing, as he usually does, to admire its Baroque elegance, nor even to glance across the mouth of the Grand Canal towards San Marco. He looks straight ahead, on to the tip of Dorsoduro, past the Dogana, the old customs house. A great Greek liner is cruising through the open water where the Grand Canal meets the Giudecca, but Tommaso doesn't stop to look. He rounds the bend to go along the Fondamenta Zattere, not knowing where he's going, or why, or where he will end up. Across the churning water of the Giudecca is the outline of the small island of San Giorgio Maggiore, its majestic sixteenth-century church shining impressively through the rain. Tommaso is unmoved.

He walks along the Zattere until finally he has made almost a complete circle. But instead of turning right at

the church of the Gesuiti and walking through Campo Sant'Agnese to Ca'Valier, he heads straight down the wide walkway of the *fondamenta* until he is at his work site. There is no-one there; all his men are at lunch. Tommaso walks to the safety fence, looks over it at the site, at the grout mixer and pump, the air compressor and hoses, and the other implements of his trade. In another few days he will be finished; the job will be done, the tools gone, the safety fence taken away. He will go home and be reunited with his family. After he has seen the boys, commiserated with Antonio over the accident, he and Sandra will be alone together. They will make love; it's a ritual, when he returns from a job. Another fence will go up: thicker, more durable than the flimsy metal mesh one he is standing next to now. Tommaso doesn't like fences, but they are necessary, he knows, to protect the innocent.

He stares at the work site for a long time, taking in every detail, though he knows it all so well. *Work*, he thinks: it will focus me, so that there is no room for dissecting my life, not yet, not until I can face it, not until it can be handled.

A mist is rising from the canal waters now, like puffs of grey cotton. Tommaso turns and heads towards home, or the building of his parents' house that he has called home since being in Venice. So many places he has named 'home', he thinks, so many towns and cities, so many houses, temporary, transient.

As he walks down past San Trovaso, a lone gondola appears out of the mist, from under the low bridge where he and Callie sat on the steps in the sun outside the *enoteca*, drinking prosecco and eating their antipasti all that time ago, a lifetime, but in reality only three weeks. Tommaso tries cynicism, tries to laugh at the cheap symbolism of it: the mist, the black coffin-like gondola, the rain, but finds instead that he cannot even smile, indeed he is shaken by it. He shivers slightly, suddenly hating Venice, hating what she

stands for: a melancholy reminder that everything is finite. He feels he has never before seen the city so clearly as he does now.

Callie, in Padua, is sitting inside a restaurant not far from the market place. She is on her own, staring at the plate of lasagne in front of her. Her table is by a window, steamy with condensation as the damp from the rain outside infiltrates the crowded room. The waiter looks at her surreptitiously, wondering why she isn't eating, whether she is ill. He wishes she would either eat or go, for he could use her table.

Callie does neither. After some time, she looks at her watch, calls the waiter and pays her bill. '*Che cosa c'e?*' he says, pointing at the food.

She seems not to know what he's talking about. He asks again what is the matter, why she hasn't eaten the food, and she says distractedly, '*Niente*, nothing. I am not hungry.' She takes her change and goes out into the rain, leaving the waiter shaking his head over the peculiarities of foreigners.

It is after ten when Callie appears at Ca'Valier. 'Sorry I'm later than I thought I'd be. I went with Patsy and her group to a medieval concert, and only just got away.'

Tommaso says, 'Should we sit outside? The night is beautiful after the storm and the rain.' He says it bitterly, feeling betrayed.

They go onto the balcony, but Callie can barely look at the night. A few stars gleam, newly polished by the day's rain. The lights of the canal reflect like gems on the black still water.

Callie says, 'Where is Giovanni?'

'Actually with Patsy. I believe they were going to meet for a drink after this concert.'

'You've heard, then.' Callie doesn't look at Tommaso, but tries to find some calm in the lit domes

of the distant Salute. She sees only smugness, and finds she is getting angry. 'They were so sure, weren't they,' she cries. 'All those church builders and painters with their glory-to-God spires and bell towers and domes, their complacent madonnas and fat little Jesuses. They were so sure everything would turn out all right in the end.'

Tommaso does not answer. Callie asks again, 'You know about Patsy? Her husband? It's why I went with her tonight. She said not to, but I wanted to give her some support.'

'Yes. Giovanni told me what happened.'

Callie at last turns, and Tommaso is startled at how harsh, how ravaged she looks, even in the dim light of the terrace. 'If you leave Sandra, I shall always see her face superimposed on Patsy's. The pain, the shock, the betrayal.'

Tommaso notes the *if*. He doesn't reply, doesn't, as he would normally do, reassure her that, in the end, all will be for the best. It will not be for the best, whatever happens. Leaving or staying, there will be terrible grief.

Callie hears his silence and cries, 'You know it, too. That you must go back. You have already decided.'

Tommaso still says nothing, but his face is eloquent. Callie moans softly and leans against the railing with her head in her hands. Tommaso cannot go to her; he feels he has no right. He says, 'It's not because of Patsy. It's Sandra, she phoned. Antonio's in the hospital. He's fine, he will be out tomorrow, but . . .' He's unable to go on.

'But you cannot leave her,' Callie finishes, her voice muffled through her fingers.

Tommaso looks out over the water. A *vaporetto* is chugging past, illuminated like a round, fat spaceship in the black sky of the canal. 'No,' he says finally. He will not say, as he could, that Sandra needs him, that the boys need him. He will not try to explain that

self-respect and dignity would be lost to him if he left them now, when none of them have done anything to deserve it. He hopes Callie will understand all this.

She says, 'I came here to tell you the same thing, Tommaso. After what happened to Patsy, I knew that I couldn't . . . that you couldn't . . .' She breaks off as the tears finally begin to spill over. That we couldn't start a life together built on someone else's pain, she wants to say. That you and I, and our future together, was no more than a deception, as illusory as that second Venice that is reflected in the canals on windless, unruffled days.

Tommaso at last goes to her. He would like not to, to walk away from her right now, never see her again, for he knows that each time he does, he will be thinking of what he has lost. As she weeps in his arms, silent tears that do not break the stillness of the night, he holds her so tightly that tomorrow there will be dark bruises not only under her eyes, but up and down the soft flesh of her arms as well.

Somehow the next few days are got through. Patsy refuses all phone calls from Stuart, and throws her heart into the lion's den of her group, letting its members devour her time, her privacy, her emotions, her life. She will not only get extra large tips at the end of this tour, but will receive superlative comments in the evaluation form each group is given to fill out. These go to head office, and Patsy's career, never in doubt anyway, will bloom even brighter. She will get her trip to New Zealand, and more besides: Australia, Thailand, anything is possible. She lets herself think of this, and not of home, of England. She has no home, not any longer. She realizes that this has been true for a long time, and decides that, in the end, it's a path that she herself has chosen. She will learn to live with this, as she must.

*   *   *

Deirdre and Angela are not speaking, but no-one really notices, or cares. Everyone is buying last-minute souvenirs, visiting the Basilica one last time, saying goodbye to the Bridge of Sighs or their favourite *campo*, to their most cherished church or shop or restaurant. Deirdre has told Angela she is taking Kathy and leaving, will not work for her, or indeed live with her, again. Angela threatened, shrieked, cried and sulked, but Deirdre hardly listened. When the scene was over, she'd found Pogo and Lavender and said, 'I have burned my bridge.'

'You mean bridges,' Lavender had said, as she hugged her and welcomed her into the family.

'No. Only one bridge, but it was a formidable one.'

'You won't regret it, honey,' Pogo had said, waiting in turn for *his* hug. 'Your little girl will love Italy.'

Deidre knows this is true. She knows also that when she and Kathy finally return to England – if they *do* return, for a year is a long time, and anything could happen – she will be free to begin a new life for herself and her daughter.

And it's about time, too, she tells herself, as she hunts through the shops, looking for more little trinkets to bring back to Kathy.

While Candice spends most of these last days in her hotel room, counting the hours until she will be safely home in England, Archie revisits his favourite paintings, taking Ellen with him. He saves his favourites, Carpaccio's St George paintings in the Scuola di San Giorgio degli Schiavoni, until last. The *scuola* is empty when they arrive, for it has just opened. Dark, curtained, snug, the room encloses the paintings like a secret, and after they've looked round, they sit for some time on the wooden bench in the back of the dimly lit room.

'Brave St George,' Ellen says. 'Such a fierce dragon he's slaying. These are superb paintings, Archie.

Thank you so much for sharing them with me.'

Archie nods shyly. Once again, with Ellen, there seems so much he cannot find the words to say. 'It was entirely my pleasure,' he finally manages. It feels inadequate. But he doesn't know that Ellen can read the unsaid words in his eyes, in his face.

They sit in silence, side by side, looking one last time at the paintings. Finally Ellen says, 'When I return home, I shall do another Art History course at our local adult education centre. It will remind me of this very special tour.' She looks at him with such fondness, even, he is sure, with love, that it quite takes his breath away.

Archie hesitates, and the moment is nearly lost, but as Ellen stirs, as if to stand up, he stops her by taking her hand. 'And of me, I hope. Perhaps when you remember Venice, read about the paintings we have seen together, you will think a little of me. It would make me very happy to know we have at least allowed ourselves that: to think sometimes of each other.'

She holds his hand tightly. 'I cannot imagine a day, Archie, that I will not think of you, whatever I am doing.'

He takes a deep breath and closes his eyes. There is so much more he would like to say to her, but cannot, not honourably. She is, after all, a married woman.

But there *is* something he will allow, if she will. She does, and he kisses her long and longingly, until the door of the small chapel opens and the room begins to fill with other tourists.

Now it is her turn to take a breath, briefly shut her eyes and compose herself. Then they leave the *scuola* and walk outside, blinking in the sunshine, walking into their reflected lives for a few more days, before the waters churn and the city fades.

13

Callie spends the last night at Ca'Valier. Tommaso, coming home early from work to prepare a meal for her, since she is, for once, missing dinner at the hotel to spend the whole evening with him, meets Giovanni coming out of the courtyard doors of Ca'Valier. Giovanni is carrying a small suitcase and looks decidedly furtive.

'Tommaso, you're early, I thought . . . I left a note for you, on the kitchen table. I'm going to Padua, staying a couple of nights with my colleague there.' Giovanni looks uncomfortable, shuffling his case from hand to hand and finally putting it down on the cool stone of the courtyard.

Tommaso understands. Giovanni hates partings, cannot say goodbye. He won't be around to say *arrivederci* to Callie, leaving tomorrow, nor to Tommaso, departing the following day. 'It's all right,' Tommaso says. 'Of course, you know I will be gone when you return.'

'I left a note,' Giovanni says again.

'Well, I'm afraid your timing was wrong this time,' Tommaso smiles. 'We'll have to say *ciao* properly, in person. Will you visit us in England?' He looks sombrely at his brother and adds, 'Your nephews? Me and Sandra?'

Giovanni nods, and looks to see whether there is bitterness in this statement, but Tommaso's voice is bland. 'I must go,' Giovanni says, hating this. Since that one long-ago parting, he has not been able to say

goodbye to anyone close to him, not even temporarily, without tears. He is close to them now, but not for himself. For Tommaso, for Callie.

'Give her my love,' he says. 'Callie.'

'Truly?' Tommaso seems detached, curious. Giovanni realizes that his brother is rigid with the effort of trying to hold himself together.

'I liked her in the end, Tommaso, I truly did. I was afraid for Sandra, for your boys, but I grew to like Callie very much. I grew much too fond of her, as a matter of fact. It seemed disloyal to Sandra, to my sister-in-law.'

Tommaso notices the past tense, as if Callie were already gone, already no more than a magician's trick, a Venetian conjuror's charm.

'I'll tell her, Giovanni. Now you'd better go, you'll miss your train. But I'm afraid we'll have to say goodbye first. Partings are inescapable sometimes.' This time there is bitterness there, harsh, rank, angry.

The brothers embrace, promise to phone, promise each other Christmas together in England, perhaps Easter in America. '*Ciao*, Giovanni. Keep well.'

'*Ciao*, Tommaso. You keep well, too.' The words are said, but Giovanni doesn't move. He is stricken with memory, stricken with what he knows Tommaso will be going through tomorrow morning, when Callie leaves Ca'Valier for the last time.

'Are you all right?' Tommaso's voice is concerned. Giovanni nods, shaking the moment, the memory, away, willing the past to recede as it thankfully does, most of the time. This is all, in the end, he can offer his brother. 'It will fade,' he says, knowing he sounds pompous, but hoping Tommaso will understand.

Tommaso does. He embraces his brother again, and Giovanni, distressed, covers up his emotion by bending down to pet the cat, Bambi, who has followed him down to the courtyard. Then he quickly walks away, determinedly not looking back. Tommaso and the cat

watch him until he turns the corner towards the landing stage and out of sight.

'In or out?' Tommaso says distractedly to Bambi, holding open the courtyard door. The cat eyes him thoughtfully, then disdainfully flicks his tail, turns his back on the comforts of Ca'Valier and sets off to roam the night.

When Callie arrives, neither she nor Tommaso can even pretend to eat the pasta he has prepared, the salad of tomatoes and basil. They are sitting at the table on the balcony, the food congealing on the plates in front of them. Down on the water of the canal the gondolas are gathering, preparing the slow glide towards the Accademia bridge. Callie stands, leans across the rough marble of the railing and knows she is seeing this for the last time. 'Can we go in?' she says. 'I'm not sure if I can bear to hear "Santa Lucia" one more time.'

Tommaso chooses to misunderstand her. He says lightly, 'That's one perk, anyway. No more "Santa Lucia" sung by a Venetian gondolier ruining your evening meal.'

She makes herself smile at him. I will not spoil our last night together, she thinks. I will not say, I cannot bear to hear the song because I've heard it so often with you. 'Can we go in?' she says again, for the truth is, 'Santa Lucia' will break her heart if she hears it this one last time.

They make love oddly, savagely, as if punishing each other for bringing this grief upon the other. The more Callie is aroused, the more she digs her fingers into Tommaso's flesh, leaving marks that will take days to heal. He grabs the tie of his dressing gown, lying on the chair next to the bed, takes Callie's arms and hands and ties her wrists together over her head as she pummels his back with her fists. 'Don't do this to me, Tommaso,' she cries, and he knows that she doesn't mean their rough lovemaking, nor her tied wrists, nor

the way his tongue is making her come almost against her will – but the fact that he is doing this, then leaving her.

And because he has no choice, because he never wished to love her, then never believed he could leave her, yet now is leaving her, he pulls the soft cotton cord tighter round her wrists. And as he enters her, he begins to gently, then not so gently, bite her already swollen lips, as if punishing her for his own black despair.

They wake with the first birdsong and a pale grey light outside the window. They have slept huddled in each other's arms, and are still entwined when they wake. Neither of them speak nor move as both the birds and the light gather strength.

Finally Tommaso stirs and turns to look at Callie. Her eyelids are swollen, her lips bruised, a slight cut on her bottom lip is flecked with dried blood. He can feel the soreness of his own lips, and the scratches on his back and shoulders. Sweetly, so as not to hurt her tender mouth, he kisses her. When they make love they are gentle with each other, as if it is their first tentative time, as if there will be many other times.

When their lovemaking is finished, they lie quietly, listening to the bells of San Trovaso, to the sounds of the canal, to the singing of the birds. Church bells and the soft splashing of oars in water, of water on stone and brick: the sounds of Venice, Callie thinks; the sounds of love.

They don't speak at all, not even when Callie silently gets up and begins to dress. Tommaso knows it is time for her to go, and wishes, like Giovanni, that they could both be spared this parting.

When they are dressed, they go together to the courtyard. Callie's flight is not until afternoon, but she must be back with her group for breakfast. When they reach the heavy wooden door to the street outside, they stop,

turn to each other and cling silently for several moments.

Callie is the one who pulls away. 'Don't say anything, please, Tommaso, all right? Don't say that you love me, I couldn't bear it. Don't say goodbye, don't say *arrivederci*. Don't *speak*, Tommaso, please? Just let me go.'

He nods and he doesn't speak, but he cannot open the door for her, and it is Callie who pulls open the heavy latch, runs out the door and down the street and, like Giovanni, doesn't look back. Tommaso watches her go, then runs through the courtyard, into his apartment, up the marble stairs and onto the terrace.

Callie doesn't cry as she walks away, turns the corner, runs up the steps of the Accademia bridge. But there she falters, stops at the top and turns towards the canal. And there he is: Tommaso, on the balcony, waiting for her, waiting to say goodbye.

The tears come, of course, and she doesn't try either to stop them or hide them. The canal is a deep seagreen today, flecked with sunlight: the day will be bright, perfect. The water below her is so glassy that it seems as if she could walk across it to Tommaso, but it is illusory, of course, as is so much of Venice. Yet what in the end is real, she thinks: the buildings, or the reflection of the buildings in the water? It will all be one, one day, buildings and water, illusion and reality.

She looks up from the water and again at Tommaso. For a moment they look steadily at each other, then Callie holds up her hand and waves. '*Arrivederci*, Tommaso,' she says, though she knows he cannot hear her.

Tommaso's wave reflects hers: slow, final. '*Ciao*, Calypso,' he says softly. They stand there for a long time, parted by the water, yet together, until finally she breaks away and runs quickly down the other side of the bridge and out of his life.

'Work, Callie,' Patsy says to her as they say goodbye late that morning, in Callie's room at the Hotel Isabella. 'It's the only thing we've got, the likes of you and me. Work, travel – you'll survive.' She pats Callie's shoulder gruffly, disconcerted by the swollen eyes and lips, the tear-streaked face.

Callie, grimly putting shoes, trousers and shirts into a suitcase on the bed, says, 'No, Patsy. For you, that's fine. I don't want any more of Comet Trail Travel, or any other kind of travel, not for a long time, anyway.'

Patsy is shocked. 'You're not quitting?'

Callie hadn't known herself, until that moment. But now she says, with great clarity, 'Yes, I think I am. Oh, I'll finish this summer's tours, since I haven't any more in Venice this season. I'll see you at Lake Garda in September, but that will be it. I'll give notice as soon as I'm back in England.'

'But what will you do?'

Callie stops packing and thinks about that one. Grieve, she is thinking. I must just keep going until I get this group to Heathrow; then I can go to my empty house and grieve. 'Buy some plants,' she says, and her voice trembles. She presses her lips together and continues more firmly, 'And a cat, and maybe even a dog. Then I'll look for a job, one that doesn't entail travelling, except for now and again.'

As she says this, she knows this is exactly what she will do. Plants and animals, and then perhaps a friend or two just down the road. Easy suppers round the kitchen table, growing intimacy with people who wouldn't be flying off out of her life after a three-week stint.

'You'll miss it,' Patsy says.

But Callie knows she won't. Zipping shut her case, she pulls it to the floor and prepares to leave Venice for the last time.

*   *   *

'Oh, what a view, you can see the Doge's Palace clear as crystal across the water,' Minnie shouts over the noise of the large motorboat taking them to Marco Polo airport. 'Look, everybody!'

They all dutifully look, across the shining lagoon, deeply green under the intense blue of the sky. The ducal palace with its perfect Gothic arches is indeed splendid in this golden, luminous light, this perfect Venetian day.

'It doesn't look real, does it?' Ellen says. 'Perhaps it wasn't. Perhaps none of it was real.'

'It was real, every bit of it,' Archie says, and is rewarded for this by the smile she gives him, the complicit secret smile of lovers, though they have been lovers only in spirit. It's enough, he thinks. It's more than enough.

Callie, too, looks back at receding Venice, but only for a moment. Then she turns her back on the fading city and resolutely faces the open sea.

THE END

A SELECTED LIST OF FINE WRITING AVAILABLE FROM BLACK SWAN

THE PRICES SHOWN BELOW WERE CORRECT AT THE TIME OF GOING TO PRESS. HOWEVER TRANSWORLD PUBLISHERS RESERVE THE RIGHT TO SHOW NEW RETAIL PRICES ON COVERS WHICH MAY DIFFER FROM THOSE PREVIOUSLY ADVERTISED IN THE TEXT OR ELSEWHERE.

All Transworld titles are available by post from:

Book Services By Post, P.O. Box 29, Douglas, Isle of Man IM99 1BQ

Credit cards accepted. Please telephone 01624 675137, fax 01624 670923 or Internet http://www.bookpost.co.uk. or e-mail: bookshop@enterprise.net for details

Free postage and packing in the UK. Overseas customers: allow £1 per book (paperbacks) and £3 per book (hardbacks).

For Jacki

A PATCH OF GREEN WATER
A BLACK SWAN BOOK : 0 552 99778 1

First publication in Great Britain

PRINTING HISTORY
Black Swan edition published 1998

Set in 11pt Melior by
County Typesetters, Margate, Kent

Black Swan Books are published by Transworld Publishers Ltd,
61–63 Uxbridge Road, London W5 5SA,
in Australia by Transworld Publishers (Australia) Pty Ltd,
15–25 Helles Avenue, Moorebank, NSW 2170,
and in New Zealand by Transworld Publishers (NZ) Ltd,
3 William Pickering Drive, Albany, Auckland.

Reproduced, printed and bound in Great Britain by
Cox & Wyman Ltd, Reading, Berks.

A PATCH OF
GREEN WATER

Karen Hayes

BLACK SWAN

Also by Karen Hayes

STILL LIFE ON SAND
CLOUD MUSIC

and published by Black Swan

CW00376664

Karen Hayes is the au   novels and a volume   Mornings. Her most rec   Sand and Cloud Music, are also published by Black Swan. She lives in Devon with her husband and children.